continued . . .

DEAD WITH THE WIND

Miranda James

BERKLEY PRIME CRIME, NEW YORK

An imprint of Penguin Random House LLC
375 Hudson Street, New York, New York 10014

DEAD WITH THE WIND

A Berkley Prime Crime Book / published by arrangement with the author

BERKLEY® PRIME CRIME and the PRIME CRIME design are trademarks of
Penguin Random House LLC.
For more information, visit penguin.com.

ISBN: 978-0-425-27305-0

PUBLISHING HISTORY
Berkley Prime Crime mass-market edition / October 2015

PRINTED IN THE UNITED STATES OF AMERICA

10 9 8 7 6 5 4 3 2 1

Cover illustration by Dan Craig.
Cover design by Lesley Worrell.
Interior text design by Kelly Lipovich.

For Teresa Sims Taylor, beloved cousin,
who welcomed me home and made me
feel I am where I need to be.

ACKNOWLEDGMENTS

As always, thanks go immediately to my wonderful editor, Michelle Vega; her assistant, Bethany Blair; and the rest of the amazing team at Berkley Prime Crime for the many great things they do to help these books be a success. Thanks as well to my inimitable agent, Nancy Yost, and her team: Natanya Wheeler, Adrienne Rosado, and Sarah E. Younger. It's amazing to have all these talented women in my corner, and I appreciate them all tremendously.

During a time of great transition, my critique pals in Houston made it possible for me to continue with them, even four hundred and fifty miles away. Thanks to Bob, Julie, Kay F., Kay K., Laura, and welcome back to Amy! I swear one day I'm going to bring you more than a few chapters of a book before I have to turn it in! Special thanks as always to the Hairston-Soparkar clan for opening their home (and most recently, Susie's laptop) to help the group.

To my family at Murder by the Book: Brenda, John, Sally, Jack, and McKenna. Thank you for making a difficult time in my life much easier to bear. It meant more to me than you can ever know. I miss you all!

Acknowledgments

Finally, thanks to the two dear friends who cheer me on in my mad dashes toward the completion of every book, Patricia Orr and Terry Farmer. Your words keep me going even when I think I'll never figure out what happens next.

CHAPTER 1

"I declare," Miss An'gel Ducote said, "this dog is smarter than a lot of people I know. And he's not even a year old yet." She gave Peanut the Labradoodle a fond pat on his head. Peanut responded with a happy bark. His tail thumped against the plush carpet by An'gel's chair.

"Yes, he sees you do something one time, and he doesn't forget it." Miss Dickce Ducote, at eighty the younger sister by four years, beamed at the wriggling dog. "Benjy, you've done wonders with this dog's training the past two months."

Benjy Stephens smiled. "He's not hard to train. Like Miss An'gel says, he's really smart."

Endora, an Abyssinian cat with a ruddy coat, surveyed the dog's antics from her vantage point atop the back of Dickce's chair. Her tail flicked in a languorous motion every few seconds close to Dickce's right ear.

Benjy laughed and pointed at the cat. "Endora doesn't look all that impressed."

Peanut barked and picked up An'gel's empty suitcase by its handle with his teeth and carried it to the closet. He placed it inside, then with his right front paw swung shut the closet door. He turned to face his audience, and An'gel told him what a clever boy he was.

"Come sit, Peanut." An'gel motioned for the Labradoodle to approach her chair, and the dog obeyed instantly. An'gel turned to Benjy. "How is your room? Is it comfortable?"

"Yes, ma'am." Benjy nodded. "These guest cottages are pretty awesome."

"Cousin Mireille had them redone a couple of years ago, she said." Dickce glanced around the living room of the two-bedroom cottage she was sharing with An'gel. While the furniture here was reproduction, it was in the style of the antiques in the main house. "I gather her bed-and-breakfast business does well."

"St. Ignatiusville is a pretty town, I grant you." An'gel shook her head. "But I fail to understand why it's such a popular tourist destination."

"There's a lot of history here in Louisiana," Benjy said. "I was reading the brochure in my room. Just like with Riverhill, I guess."

Riverhill, the Ducote family home, was built in the early 1830s in Athena, Mississippi. Willowbank, ancestral home to the sisters' cousin Mireille Champlain, dated to the late eighteenth century.

"I suppose so," Dickce said. "Willowbank is larger, of course, with its third story and the galleries around the upper floors. There's a smaller version in the Vieux Carré in New Orleans, but Mireille sold it years ago."

An'gel checked her watch. "Now that we've unpacked, I suppose we should go over to the main house and check in with Mireille. No doubt there are things we can help her with."

"Three days before her granddaughter's wedding?" Dickce laughed. "I'm sure she can find something for us to do." She cut a sideways glance at Benjy. "Sure you won't change your mind and come with us? I bet Sondra will put on a show."

Benjy grinned. "If she's as spoiled as you say, I bet she will. Right now, though, I think it would be better if I stayed here with Peanut and Endora. There's no telling what they might get up to. Peanut gets so excited when there's new people to meet."

"True," An'gel said, "and Mireille's front parlor is full of Meissen and Limoges—or at least it used to be." She rose. "Good plan, Benjy. Come along, Sister."

Peanut whined when the door opened, but at a command from Benjy, he quieted and stayed where he was. Endora examined her front right paw and yawned.

The door closed behind them, An'gel and Dickce followed the path around an ornamental pond that separated the bed-and-breakfast cottages from Willowbank itself, about two hundred yards away. A mix of willows and live oaks bordered half the pond to the east, and over to the south, a grand procession of live oaks marked the circular drive that led up to the front door of the plantation house.

The sisters trod carefully around the pond, not eager to encounter anything reptilian, particularly snakes. The October afternoon was warm, but pleasant breezes kept the atmosphere temperate. The many trees cast a lot of shade, and An'gel paused in front of one bordering the drive for a moment and gazed at the house.

Willowbank was a magnificent structure in the Greek Revival style, larger than most of its period. Generations of the Champlain clan had lavished considerable money on its upkeep, and it survived as a reminder of the graciousness of certain aspects of the Southern planter class's lifestyle. Mireille, a Champlain by birth, had married a third cousin who was also a Champlain. She was the last of the name to own the house.

"It's spectacular," An'gel murmured, "but I still prefer Riverhill."

"Of course you do," Dickce answered tartly. "So do I, because Riverhill is in our DNA. Just the way Willowbank and all it stands for is in Mireille's. Lordy, you do get maudlin sometimes."

An'gel graced her sister with a withering glance.

Unwithered, Dickce marched forward. "Come on, Mireille's expecting us." She stepped from the grass onto the gravel that formed the surface of the drive and headed toward the steps up to the veranda.

An'gel followed her, eager to see Mireille and find out about the wedding. She also looked forward to seeing Jacqueline, her goddaughter and mother of the bride. They kept in touch somewhat infrequently through e-mail, but they hadn't seen each other face-to-face in over five years.

A thin black man, wizened by age, opened the door to An'gel's knock. "Good afternoon, Jackson. It's wonderful to see you again." She held out her hand.

Jackson, dressed in black tie and tails, smiled broadly

as he clasped the proffered hand in both of his own. "Miss An'gel, it sure has been way too long. And Miss Dickce, too. Y'all are a happy sight for these old eyes. Welcome back to Willowbank." He waved them inside.

An'gel knew Jackson was well over eighty, but he seemed fit enough despite his age. She also knew he was devoted to Mireille, and Mireille relied heavily on him. They had grown up together at Willowbank, where Jackson started as a stable boy when he was only seven. An'gel figured the house would have to fall in before Jackson would even think about retiring.

"Miss Mireille sure has been looking forward to seeing you," the butler said over his shoulder as he ambled toward the front parlor. "She's near run ragged with all these wedding goings-on, and you know how Miss Sondra does like to fuss."

An'gel and Dickce exchanged glances. They were not surprised the bride-to-be was up to her usual antics.

Jackson paused about three feet from the parlor door, and An'gel could hear a raised voice coming from inside the room. The butler cocked his head to one side. He shook it and frowned. "Miss Sondra cuts up something terrible, and Miss Mireille, well, she don't have the heart to say nothing. Nor Miss Jacqueline either."

"I know how to handle Miss Sondra," An'gel said.

Jackson's lips split in a grin. "I reckon you do, Miss An'gel." He stepped forward and opened the double parlor doors.

An'gel and Dickce followed him inside, and both winced immediately as the bride-to-be's voice assaulted their ears.

"I won't, I won't, I won't, *Grand-mère*, no matter what

5

you say. I'm not wearing that hideous old-fashioned dress down the aisle. Lance would take one look at me and run away screaming. I won't, no matter what, I won't, I won't."

The young woman's voice seemed to rise on almost every syllable, until the final words came out at such a high pitch An'gel had to wonder how long it would take all the dogs in the vicinity to come running.

Sondra Delevan, in calmer circumstances, made men stop in their tracks and women want to push her off the nearest tall building. An'gel had rarely seen such perfect blond beauty. Sondra's lustrous hair, thick and almost to the waist, was the color of spun golden silk. Her lips were full and red, and her eyes a deep blue. Her face appeared perfectly sculpted.

At the moment, however, she resembled a middle-aged harpy in full flight instead of a young woman who would soon turn twenty-one. Her face was a blotchy red, and her eyes were wild. Her chest heaved from the force of her tantrum.

Her grandmother Mireille sat quietly on a sofa near the fireplace. "My grandmother and my mother wore that dress on their wedding days. I wore it, and so did your mother. I simply thought tradition might mean something to you." She sighed heavily. "You might have mentioned this earlier since we've had the dress altered to fit you. Three days before your wedding is hardly the time to go looking for a suitable dress. Surely you understand how difficult that's going to be."

An'gel needed only one swift glance at her cousin to detect the strained expression, the weary set of her shoulders, and a general air of exhaustion. Though Mireille was eight years younger than An'gel, at the moment she appeared a decade older.

"I'm not going to wear dead women's clothes on my wedding day, no matter what you say. I don't care what I said before. I've changed my mind." Sondra stamped her foot hard on the ancient Aubusson carpet. "Makes my skin crawl just to think about it. I won't, I won't, I won't." She kept repeating those two words over and over.

An'gel had had enough. Mireille might put up with this ridiculous behavior, but she wasn't going to.

She spotted a vase filled with cut flowers on a table near her. She moved over, pulled out the flowers, and placed them on the table. A check inside the vase assured her there was enough water for her purpose. She took a couple of steps closer to the still-ranting Sondra and dumped the water over the girl's head.

CHAPTER 2

"Don't even open your mouth." An'gel stood in front of Sondra and stared hard into her eyes. "You march right upstairs and clean yourself up, and you come back downstairs with a good attitude. Your grandmother has had enough of this, and I'm not going to let you treat her this way."

Sondra glared right back at her. She opened her mouth, but An'gel didn't give her a chance to speak.

"What did I tell you? Get yourself upstairs *this minute*, Sondra, or I might turn you over my knee and wallop your behind." An'gel held up her right hand in a menacing gesture.

Sondra darted an outraged glance at her grandmother, but Mireille looked away. Evidently deciding that discretion was the better part of valor, Sondra ducked around An'gel and ran out of the room. Moments later An'gel heard footsteps pounding up the wooden stairs.

"Surely that was a bit excessive, An'gel." Mireille's tone was mild, but An'gel could tell her cousin was not pleased.

"Your granddaughter's behavior wasn't, I suppose?" An'gel tried to keep the edge of sarcasm from her tone but didn't completely succeed. She walked over to the sofa and sat by Mireille. She picked up her cousin's left hand and patted it. "Even a stranger could see that you're exhausted, and there's no excuse for putting up with that kind of behavior."

Mireille leaned back and closed her eyes. Her voice came out barely above a whisper. "I know, and you're right, my nerves are at the breaking point. We've indulged that child all her life, and you see what she's become." She rubbed her forehead with her free hand. "And now we have to find her another dress."

Dickce made herself comfortable in a chair across from the other women. "Mireille, honey, An'gel and I are here to help, and we'll take as much of the strain off you as we can. We'll even take Sondra shopping for another dress, though it will probably be a complete waste of time."

Mireille's eyelids fluttered open, and a dab of color reappeared in her cheeks. She pulled her hand from An'gel's grasp and sat up. "Bless you both for that." She smiled. "Perhaps Sondra will behave better, now that she's found someone who will stand up to her. Jacqueline and I can't. Never could."

"Jacqueline couldn't what?" A new voice entered the conversation.

An'gel glanced toward the doorway to see her goddaughter approaching. Jacqueline Mims was a blurred, shopworn copy of her only child. An'gel winced inwardly at the change in the woman since they had last met. Jacqueline had let her hair go gray, though there were still a few streaks of faded blond. She looked a couple of decades older than her forty-five years. An'gel wondered if Sondra was the reason for her mother's haggard appearance, or was there trouble in her second marriage? Jacqueline had not confided any problems in their most recent exchange of e-mails.

An'gel rose as Jacqueline stopped in front of her, and clasped her goddaughter's outstretched hands. "Hello, my dear, I'm so happy to see you." An'gel saw no point in ducking the issue. "I was saying you could never stand up to your daughter."

Jacqueline gave a faint smile. "*Tante* An'gel, diplomatic as ever." She kissed the older woman's cheek, then released her hands.

Dickce smothered a laugh as Jacqueline turned to her. "There's a reason no president ever asked An'gel to serve as ambassador."

"*Tante* Dickce, I'm so glad you could come." She gave Dickce a kiss on the cheek as well, then took the chair next to her. "I'm glad you're both here. *Maman* and I have our hands full with Sondra." She sighed and closed her eyes.

"You just tell us what needs doing, and we'll pitch right in," An'gel said.

"For one thing, you can promise not to dump any more vases of water on Sondra's head." Mireille frowned. "I know you meant well, An'gel, but that was going too far."

"Did you really?" Jacqueline gazed at An'gel. At the older woman's nod, she burst into laughter. An'gel thought it had a slightly hysterical tinge to it.

"Jacqueline, *tais-toi*," Mireille said crossly. "It wasn't funny. Sondra will be even more difficult now."

Jacqueline quieted at her mother's command. "Sorry, *Maman*, but it *is* funny. I wish I had the nerve to do that the next time the little wench has a tantrum."

"I regret that you were offended by what I did," An'gel told her cousin, "but I'd do it again. You've let that child run your lives for far too long. It's time someone got the upper hand with her."

"Exactly what I've been saying for years, but of course no one pays attention to the hired help." A short, stocky woman with improbably red hair pushed a tea cart into the room and wheeled it in front of Mireille. "That girl needed her behind paddled at least once a day, but no one would make the effort. She'd've turned out a lot nicer if someone had had the backbone to do it."

"Hello, Estelle," An'gel said into the uneasy silence that followed the woman's pronouncements. She had often thought Mireille's housekeeper was more than a little rude, but Mireille had done nothing to curb the woman's tongue.

"Miss An'gel, Miss Dickce, nice to see you. Maybe the two of you can stiffen up a few spines while you're here. The good Lord knows we need it, but of course the hired help gets ignored when they suggest anything." The housekeeper acknowledged them with curt nods. She pointed to the tea tray. "It won't be my fault if the tea gets cold. I don't have time to stand around pouring tea when you can pour it just as well yourselves. I have way too much on my plate as it is." With that she turned and hurried from the room without a backward glance.

Estelle had been claiming to be overburdened as long as An'gel had known her. She had often thought that if Estelle had put more effort into her work and less effort into complaining about it, she might actually get things done.

Mireille shook her head as she leaned forward to pour out the tea. "Estelle means well, but nothing I can do will ever get her to rein in that tongue of hers."

An'gel exchanged a wry glance with her sister. She and Dickce knew that Mireille abhorred confrontation of any kind and would never make an effort to get the upper hand. She always let things go, no matter how much trouble she was making for herself in the long run.

"She's always been difficult." Jacqueline leant forward to accept a cup from her mother. "But ever since *Maman* made her a partner in the bed-and-breakfast, she's become nearly impossible to deal with. She has opinions on *every*-thing, and they're all negative." She sipped her tea.

An'gel decided a change of subject was overdue. "Dickce and I don't know anything about the groom, though his name sounded somewhat familiar. Has Sondra known him long?"

Mireille stared into her tea as she answered. "Lance? She's known him practically all her life, since they were in kindergarten."

"They've been sweethearts since their junior year in high school." Jacqueline helped herself to a lemon square from the tea tray.

"Have we ever met the boy?" An'gel glanced at her sister.

Dickce nodded. "I believe I remember him. A pretty little boy with blond curls that Sondra used to drag around all over the place."

"Yes, now I remember him," An'gel said. The boy had been even prettier than Sondra, as she recalled, and excessively biddable.

Jacqueline chuckled. "Yes, that was Lance. They have always adored each other. I've never heard them have a cross word between them. At least not since they were little children."

An'gel's eyebrows arched over this statement. *Perhaps not in* your *hearing*, she thought. Once again she shared a glance with her sister. Dickce evidently didn't believe this claim of angelic behavior on Sondra's part any more than An'gel did.

"So obviously you've known the family a long time," Dickce said. "I can't remember who his people are."

"The Perigords used to own a large plantation up the river from here. They have been in St. Ignatiusville almost as long as the Champlains." Mireille had a sip of her tea. "They have not prospered in the past couple of generations, but they're still important members of the community."

The Perigords must be thrilled at the coming wedding, An'gel thought, especially if they needed money. Sondra's father had left the bulk of his considerable fortune in trust for his daughter until she married or turned twenty-five, whichever came first. Young Mr. Perigord could very well be a fortune hunter, even though he and Sondra had known each other since childhood.

"Do you like the young man?" An'gel directed her question to the mother of the bride.

Jacqueline shrugged. "He has nice manners, and he's astonishingly gorgeous to look at."

"But?" Dickce said in a leading tone.

Estelle Winfield appeared suddenly beside her, startling Dickce into almost dropping her cup.

"But he has the brainpower the good Lord gave a fence post. Beautiful like no man on this earth has a right to be. He and Sondra'd better have lots of mirrors in their house; otherwise, they'll knock each other out trying to stand in front of one." Estelle glared at Mireille. "Is that enough tea, or do you want more?"

Mireille waved a hand. "We have plenty, thank you, Estelle. I will ring when I'm ready for you to clear the tea things away."

The housekeeper snorted—in irritation, An'gel presumed—and scurried out of the room.

"Is that a fair assessment of the young man?" An'gel couldn't quite bring herself to say the groom's name. Why on earth would parents name a child *Lance*? It sounded like a name out of a particularly torrid romance novel.

"Estelle may not be tactful, but she is generally honest." Jacqueline grimaced. "Lance is a dear, sweet boy, but I've often wondered how he gets dressed by himself every day. I suspect his mother has to inspect him before he leaves the house to make sure he's not wearing his underpants on the outside."

Dickce giggled at that, and An'gel shot her a sharp glance, even though she was amused by her goddaughter's tart comments.

"Sondra is not the smartest child, I have to admit," Mireille said, "but she is at least more intelligent than Lance."

An'gel did her best to keep her tone neutral as she inquired, "You're happy with Sondra's choice of husband?" She thought the marriage could be a terrible mistake if the groom were as lacking in intelligence as Jacqueline and Estelle claimed.

"Sondra is set on marrying him." Jacqueline shrugged. "And Tippy adores him. He is really good with her."

An'gel and Dickce looked at each other, puzzled. Who was Tippy?

An'gel voiced the question and was rather taken aback to see Mireille's face flush a deep red.

"Tippy is Sondra's daughter." Mireille turned her head away. "Her illegitimate daughter."

CHAPTER 3

Even seated beside her cousin, An'gel barely heard Mireille's last three words. Evidently Mireille was deeply embarrassed to admit that her great-grandchild was born out of wedlock. An'gel was rather taken aback by the news herself, but Mireille's shame over her great-grandchild's illegitimacy probably explained why there had been no birth announcement.

"How old is Tippy?" Dickce asked brightly.

"Three," Jacqueline said. "I'm sorry, *Tante* An'gel, *Tante* Dickce. I know we should have told you before now, but, well . . ." Her voice trailed off as she gestured toward her mother.

An'gel nodded. She understood Mireille's outraged sensibilities—if indeed she felt that strongly about it—but what was done was done. An'gel firmly believed that the sins of the father—or in this case, the mother—should not be visited upon the child. She was about to express these thoughts, but Dickce spoke first.

"I know this is indelicate of me to ask," she said with a brief smile. "But after all, we are family. I suppose Lance is the father, since he and Sondra have been sweethearts for several years?"

Jacqueline shook her head. "No, Lance is not Tippy's father." She paused for a deep breath. "In fact, we don't know who her father is. Sondra refuses to say."

"The groom isn't bothered by this?" An'gel asked, trying to mask her astonishment with a bland tone. "Especially since it must have happened during the time he and Sondra were dating."

"Evidently not," Mireille said a trifle snappishly. "At the time Sondra told us all she was going to have a child, he uttered not one word of complaint or recrimination. At least not in my hearing." She glanced at her daughter.

Jacqueline nodded. "It's just as *Maman* says. Lance doesn't seem at all bothered by the situation. Of course, he may not actually understand just how children are conceived." She giggled.

"It is not in the least amusing." Mireille dropped her teacup on the silver tray with a loud clatter.

An'gel thought for a moment the delicate porcelain might have broken, but the cup seemed intact. Not so her cousin, however. One glance told her Mireille's face was flushed again—whether with anger or embarrassment, or a combination of both, she wasn't sure.

Mireille stood. "I'm sorry, but you must excuse me. I have to talk with Estelle. I will see you again at dinnertime." She walked out of the room, her shoulders slumped.

Jacqueline waited until her mother was clear of the doorway before she spoke. "I'm so sorry about all this. I would have told you before now, but *Maman* is so distressed over the whole situation. She adores Tippy, of course. She's a sweet child, and no one could help but love her, but *Maman* has never forgiven Sondra for causing such a scandal."

Dickce spoke in a mild tone. "Surely, my dear, these days having a child out of wedlock isn't so scandalous. It happens in many families."

Jacqueline's response was tart. "Not in the Champlain family, it doesn't." She threw up her hands. "You both know what *Maman* is like. You've known her longer than I have, for goodness' sake. All my life she's been the epitome of rectitude—and a pillar of the community. But since Tippy was born, she hardly sets foot out of the house or off the grounds, except to go to mass on Sundays. She's convinced that she's the laughingstock of St. Ignatiusville."

"There are probably those in town who do find the situation amusing because of the family's long history in the area," An'gel said. "There are always people who love to see others embarrassed, and I'm sorry that Mireille has been hurt by it."

"She's *noblessing* her *oblige* a little too much, if you ask me." Jacqueline shook her head. "Just because the Champlains settled here first. I've tried talking to her about it, but you know how stubborn she can be. Just like Sondra."

"Just like Sondra *what*?" A petulant voice from the doorway drew An'gel's attention.

Jacqueline turned in her chair to face her daughter. "Don't stand there, darling, come in."

"I don't want any more water dumped on my head." Sondra scowled at them as she took a couple of steps into the room.

"If you behave properly, no one will do that." An'gel decided, after that gruff statement, she perhaps ought to offer an olive branch. "That's a lovely dress you're wearing. The color is perfect for your complexion." She meant what she said. Sondra's dress, a sheath of iridescent blue, set off her creamy skin and golden hair beautifully.

"Thank you." Sondra preened for them. "Lance picked it out for me. He has wonderful taste, doesn't he?"

"My goodness, yes," Dickce said. "He obviously has an eye for color."

"I'm going to wear it for the wedding," Sondra said. "White is so old-fashioned, and I won't have to wear that old dress that Grandmother is so crazy about." She shuddered. "Dead people's clothes. Yuck."

An'gel caught Jacqueline's horrified expression and wondered how her goddaughter would deal with Sondra's odd notion.

Jacqueline took a deep breath. "Well, darling, what you're wearing is beautiful. We'll talk about it later with your grandmother, okay?"

Sondra shot her mother a mutinous glance as she advanced farther into the room until she stood by her mother's chair. When she spoke, she ignored Jacqueline's question.

"Mama, what are you going to wear to dinner tonight? I hope it's not going to be that awful black thing. It makes you look like an old crow."

An'gel noticed her goddaughter wince under Sondra's critical gaze.

"No, darling, I'm not. I thought I might wear the green."
Jacqueline appeared anxious, An'gel thought.

"Well, it's better anyway." Sondra grimaced, then glared
at An'gel and Dickce. "Are you two going to be there?"

The sisters nodded.

"I hope you brought some decent clothes." Sondra eyed
their casual Vera Wang dresses uncertainly. "Lance will be
here, and I know he won't be able to enjoy his food if he sees
ugly clothes."

"We'll do our best to avoid that." Dickce's prim tone didn't
fool her sister. An'gel marveled that Dickce kept a straight
face. Sondra evidently knew little about designer clothing,
or she would have recognized what the sisters wore. *Just as
well we brought along those Worth dresses of Mother's*, she
thought. If Lance can't eat in the presence of true *haute
couture*, he deserved to go hungry.

An'gel glanced at her watch. She nodded at Dickce, and
they rose in unison. "Time for us to get back to our rooms,"
she said. "We both need a little time to rest before dinner."

"Of course." Jacqueline stood to give each of the sisters
a quick peck on the cheek. "If there's anything you need,
just let Estelle know."

"We will, dear," An'gel said. "Now, you do remember
that we are bringing our ward, Benjy Stephens, with us for
dinner?"

"Yes, I remember." Jacqueline smiled. "And as soon as
we have some time, I want to hear all about how the two of
you came to have a *ward*. Your e-mails have been skimpy
on details."

An'gel suppressed the urge to comment that the same

could be said about the news of Tippy's birth. "Of course, dear. We'll see ourselves out."

An'gel and Dickce nodded to Sondra, who moved warily aside as the sisters walked past her. An'gel, as she walked through the doorway into the front hall, heard Sondra ask her mother what a *ward* was. "Is it some man they picked up?"

An'gel didn't linger to hear Jacqueline's response. Really, the child was not only vulgar, she was also rather stupid.

On the veranda, the door shut carefully behind them, An'gel paused with Dickce and enjoyed the beautiful view for a moment.

"I shudder to think what will happen to all of this when Mireille and Jacqueline are gone and Sondra is responsible for it." Dickce sighed. "We'll be long gone by then, so I guess I shouldn't even think about it, but it's hard not to."

An'gel patted her sister's shoulder, and Dickce caught the hand and gave it a quick squeeze.

Dickce's words held a deeper meaning for both of them, because their own beloved Riverhill would have to pass to someone who might not care for it as devotedly as they and the generations of Ducotes before them had. The fate of Riverhill was never far from An'gel's thoughts, though she hoped to have more than a few years left to oversee its care, along with her sister.

The sisters made their way down the steps, across the lawn, and around the edge of the ornamental pond. To An'gel's relief, they reached the block of bed-and-breakfast cottages without spotting anything slithering past their feet.

"Wonder who that can be?" Dickce pointed to a strange

car, a worn-looking sedan, parked beside their Lexus. "I didn't think any other out-of-town guests would arrive until tomorrow or the next day."

An'gel moved closer to inspect the license plate. "Louisiana, so perhaps it's someone local. Where could they be?" She glanced around but didn't see anyone on the grounds near them.

"I didn't think about locking the door," Dickce said. "Did you?"

"Not that I can remember." An'gel frowned as she moved quickly toward their door.

Before she even touched the knob, the door of Benjy's room opened. Instead of Benjy, however, a strange young man stepped out and closed the door behind him.

An'gel's eyes widened in surprise. She had never seen such a beautiful young man in her life. Tall, well-proportioned, with a head of golden ringlets and eyes of a brilliant green, he was a vision of perfection straight from the glossy pages of a magazine.

He smiled sweetly at An'gel. "Have you ever been to New York?"

At first An'gel thought she had misheard him. "New York? Yes, I have been there several times."

"I'm going there right after the wedding. It's my first time, and I can't wait." He beamed at her and wandered past her and Dickce, apparently headed toward Willowbank.

"That has to be Lance," Dickce said in an undertone once the young man was about fifty feet away.

"There can't be two of them in St. Ignatiusville," An'gel said tartly. "Of course it's Lance. Jacqueline certainly wasn't exaggerating about his looks."

"Almost too perfectly beautiful." Dickce snickered. "I suppose the Lord didn't think a man that pretty needed to be weighed down with much of a brain."

"I wonder what he was doing here," An'gel muttered as she moved to knock on Benjy's door.

"Come in," Benjy called. "It's not locked."

When An'gel stepped in the room, she was immediately greeted by Peanut, who acted like she had been gone for two days, instead of an hour. An'gel patted his head and spoke to him before he transferred his attentions to Dickce. The cat, Endora, regarded them languidly from the center of Benjy's bed.

"We ran into your visitor," Dickce said. "We were pretty surprised to see him. Did he want something in particular?"

Benjy laughed. "Yeah, he was looking for the main house. I thought he'd never been here before, but when I pointed out that it was right next door, he just shook his head and said something about taking the wrong driveway." He laughed again. "He definitely seemed a little confused. Do you know who he is?"

"Yes, we do. He's Lance Perigord, the groom," An'gel said in a dour tone.

Benjy hooted with laughter. "You gotta be kidding me. He's really the groom? Does the bride know he's gay?"

CHAPTER 4

Dickce thought she hadn't heard Benjy correctly. "Did you say that Lance is *gay*?"

"Yes, ma'am," Benjy said. He looked back and forth between the sisters. "At least I'm pretty sure he is. But if he's the groom, well, maybe I'm wrong."

"Why do you think he's gay?" An'gel asked.

Benjy appeared uncomfortable and didn't answer.

"Sister, you sound like you're cross-examining. This isn't a trial." Dickce shook her head at An'gel. "It's okay, Benjy, you can tell us."

"He made a pass at me. Or at least I think he did." Benjy blushed, and Peanut barked. Benjy bent to rub the Labradoodle's head.

"Oh, my," An'gel said.

Dickce could tell her sister was rather nonplussed by their ward's bald response. *Honestly, sometimes An'gel is such an old maid*, she thought. Dickce considered herself more aware of such things, while An'gel could be a bit stuffy.

"He obviously has excellent taste." Dickce grinned at Benjy, and he flashed her a grateful smile in return. Dickce thought their nineteen-year-old ward handsome, even with the eyebrow ring he continued to wear. With good food and plenty of exercise, he had filled out, no longer the scrawny youth they had first met a couple of months ago. He had also gained in self-confidence, and Dickce was particularly proud of him for that. He was such a bright boy.

"You said you *think* he made a pass," Dickce said. "Tell us exactly what happened."

"Okay," Benjy said. "But please sit down. I didn't mean to keep you standing there." He gestured toward the armchairs and the sofa in his suite.

Dickce was pleased by his good manners. He had picked up a lot the past two months. She chose one of the armchairs, and Endora left the bed and hopped into her lap. The cat laid a paw on Dickce's arm, and Dickce recognized the signal that Endora needed attention.

An'gel sat on the sofa with Benjy at the other end. Peanut, to Dickce's amusement, jumped in between them and thrust his head toward An'gel's face.

"No, Peanut," Benjy said in a stern tone. "It's rude to stick your nose in a lady's face."

The Labradoodle turned to Benjy for a moment before settling down between Benjy and An'gel, his head in An'gel's lap and his tail across Benjy's.

"Good boy," Benjy said. "Now, about this Lance guy."

"Yes, go on," Dickce said when he paused.

Benjy looked pensive for a moment. "I kinda hate to

say this, because I only talked to him a few minutes." He hesitated. "He's kinda dumb."

"We have heard that from people who know him much better than we do," An'gel said.

Benjy grinned. "Okay, then, I don't feel so bad. Anyway, I was sitting here reading, and Peanut and Endora were sacked out, when somebody knocked on the door. I figured it was one of you back from the big house. But when I opened the door, there stood this guy looking like a model out of a magazine. He stared at me, pretty strange-like. Then he said, *You're not Jackson.*

"Now, I have no idea who Jackson is, so I told him my name and asked him if I could help him." Benjy shook his head. "Then he asked me if I'd ever been to New York, and I told him no. Next he says I look like a model, which was a really weird thing to say, because I don't look anything like a model. I mean, they all look like him, in the magazines. Anyway, then he asked me if I'd like to go to New York with him."

Dickce exchanged a glance with An'gel. Lance sounded like a complete idiot, as far as she was concerned. "What did you say to that?"

Benjy laughed. "I told him I'd like to go to New York sometime, but I didn't think I could go with him. He looked puzzled, at least I think that's what it was, and said he was disappointed because it would be nice to have a cute boyfriend in New York. I really didn't know what to say to that, but it didn't matter, because then he asked me if I knew the way to Willowbank. I told him I did and showed him how to get there. About then was when y'all came back." He rubbed Peanut's head, and the dog's tail thumped in his lap and brushed up against his face until he stopped rubbing.

Dickce glanced at An'gel again, wondering what her sister made of Benjy's story. She returned her gaze to Benjy. "That remark about having a cute boyfriend in New York is definitely odd, especially when I suppose he'll be there with his wife."

"I wonder why he has this fixation on New York." An'gel looked puzzled. "Perhaps that's where he and Sondra are planning to honeymoon."

"It didn't sound to me like he was planning to take her with him," Benjy said. "Do you think maybe he forgot he's getting married?"

Dickce laughed. "Frankly, from what we've been told, it might very well have slipped his mind. He evidently couldn't find his way to Willowbank today, and I'm sure he's been there thousands of times."

"There is definitely something odd going on here," An'gel said. "You might as well know this, Benjy, because I'm sure it will be mentioned soon by others. Sondra will be a wealthy young woman once she's married. Her father left her a huge fortune in trust until she marries or turns twenty-five."

"She's just about to turn twenty-one," Dickce said in response to Benjy's look of inquiry. "It sounds to me like she's impatient to get her hands on her inheritance, and marrying Lance is an easy way to do it."

Benjy regarded her for a moment. "So you're saying this is kinda like a marriage of convenience? Isn't that what they used to call it?"

"Still do, as far as I know," An'gel said. "So here we have

a situation where the bride wants her inheritance but perhaps doesn't want to have a husband who would try to control her or her money."

"So she marries her dumb gay friend and promises him he can go to New York," Dickce said. "Maybe he wants to be a model."

"He sure looks like one," Benjy said. "I'm surprised someone hasn't discovered him before now."

"He probably hasn't been anywhere that an agency could discover him," An'gel said. "His family apparently doesn't have much money."

"You'd think, with a son who looks like he does, they might have made an effort to get him noticed by somebody," Dickce said. Endora nudged her again, because Dickce had stopped the attention. She rubbed the cat's head in response. "He could be a supermodel, for all we know. They make huge amounts of money."

"Do you think her mom knows he may be gay?" Benjy asked.

Dickce shrugged. "I wouldn't be surprised if Jacqueline has figured it out. She's probably so grateful to have Sondra off her hands, she doesn't care."

"True," An'gel said. "But Mireille is another matter. I suspect she has no idea her prospective grandson-in-law might be gay."

"Even if she did, do you really think she would speak up?" Dickce said. "You know how she is, she'd rather stick her head in the sand than cause a fuss."

"I'd like to think there are some situations where she'd show a bit of backbone," An'gel replied tartly. "But sadly it wouldn't surprise me if she didn't."

"You'll have to guard your tongue at dinner tonight." Dickce aimed a pointed glance at her sister. "The last thing the situation needs is for you to start expressing your forthright opinion."

An'gel scowled. "Credit me with *some* tact and discretion, Sister. I'm not going to make an issue of this in public." She paused. "However, I might talk to Jacqueline about it in private."

"Have you ever considered the fact that this really is none of our business? Yes, they are family, but we don't live here, and we're certainly not part of their daily lives. I think you'd best keep your advice to yourself for once."

Dickce waited for her sister to throw a hissy fit. An'gel didn't like to be told she shouldn't do something.

An'gel did not erupt, much to Dickce's surprise and relief. Instead, she simply replied, "Perhaps you're right. I think I'll wait and see if Jacqueline asks for my advice."

"That's a good plan." Dickce cast a glance at Benjy and was amused to catch him smothering a grin.

An'gel rose after gently dislodging Peanut's head and front paws from her lap. "I am going to rest for a while before we have to get ready for dinner. You should, too, Sister. I expect we're in for quite a long and tedious evening."

Dickce tried to lift Endora from her lap to set her on the floor, but the cat resisted. Endora was obviously in one of her clingy moods, probably because of the strange surroundings, and Dickce was secretly flattered. Endora occasionally sought attention from An'gel, but the cat generally preferred Benjy or Dickce.

"You can come take a nap with me," Dickce said to the

cat, and Endora relaxed her claws. She allowed Dickce to lift her into her arms and carry her out of the room.

"I'm going to take Peanut out for a walk," Benjy called after the sisters. "I have my cell phone if you need me."

Dickce replied, "That sounds good. Wear him out a bit so he'll be quiet while we're at dinner."

An'gel opened the door to their cottage, and Dickce entered, Endora happily riding in her arms. The cat remained in position until Dickce reached her bedroom. Then Endora leapt from her arms onto the bed and started her ritual circling on one of the pillows. While Dickce disrobed and slipped on a cotton nightgown, Endora curled up on the pillow, tucked in her head, and went to sleep.

Amused, Dickce slid into the bed, under the top layer of cover, and lay on her side facing the cat. She watched the gentle breathing of the feline and soon her own eyelids closed. She drifted into sleep thinking drowsily about dinner, hoping it wouldn't be dreary and rife with tension.

A loud bang jerked her awake. She sat up in bed, and Endora jumped to the floor and scooted under the bed.

What on earth? Hastily she donned a robe and slipped on her shoes. She met An'gel in the living room of the cottage, similarly attired. "What was that?" she asked.

"Sounded like a car crash," An'gel said as she strode to the door. Dickce followed.

They stepped out into the late afternoon sunlight and squinted into it, looking for the source of the noise.

"There." Dickce pointed toward the driveway down the rise from Willowbank where a small car evidently had struck one of the live oaks head on. "Oh, dear Lord, I hope no one's hurt." She pulled the cottage door shut and scurried along with her sister toward the accident.

By the time they got there, Benjy and Peanut were already on the scene. Benjy wrenched open the driver's side door of the red BMW convertible and assisted Sondra out of it. To Dickce's relief, the girl didn't appear injured, but she was trembling.

"Sondra, dear, are you okay?" Dickce held out a hand toward the girl.

"Do I *look* like I'm okay?" Sondra waved away Dickce's hand.

Dickce recoiled from the venomous tone. After a moment she realized Sondra appeared more furious than hurt.

"Just look at my car." Sondra stomped her foot on the ground. "It's ruined, and I just got it yesterday. Stupid brakes. You'd think they would work on a brand-new car." She kicked one of the tires. That caused her shoe to pop off her foot. Dickce stared at the six-inch stilettos and wondered if the shoes were at fault.

Sondra bent to retrieve the shoe and then stepped out of its mate. High heels in hand, she glared in turn at the car and at the sisters and Benjy. "I know what you're thinking." She brandished the shoes. "I drive in these all the time. It wasn't my fault."

Dickce exchanged an uneasy glance with An'gel. If Sondra wasn't lying about being used to driving in high heels, what had caused her brakes to fail?

CHAPTER 5

An'gel stepped closer to examine the damage while she considered the implications of the failed brakes. Despite Sondra's claim that she was used to driving in high heels, An'gel still thought driver error could have caused the accident.

Sondra had hit the live oak with the right front side of the car, smashing the headlight and crumpling the fender. An'gel marveled that the girl hadn't been hurt, but then she saw that the airbag had deployed.

"Get that thing away from me. I don't want hair all over me."

An'gel turned to see Sondra flapping her hands at Peanut. The Labradoodle was sniffing around her but shied away from the unfriendly hands.

"Calm down," Benjy said sharply. "Peanut doesn't shed.

Your stupid dress is safe." He pulled the dog away from Sondra.

An'gel had learned from Benjy that, depending on genetics, Labradoodles might not shed. Happily for her, Peanut was in that category.

"That's what you say." Sondra tossed her head. "I'd better not find a single dog hair on my dress, or you'll have to pay to have it cleaned." She paused for a breath and stared hard at Benjy. "Just who the heck are you anyway? You're trespassing on private property, you know."

"I'm not trespassing." Benjy stared right back at Sondra. "I'm a guest, along with Miss An'gel and Miss Dickce."

Sondra grimaced. "Oh, you're their *ward*."

An'gel marveled at how the girl managed to inject that one word with such venom.

"Yes, he is our ward, and your grandmother invited him." An'gel spoke tersely. She was relieved that the girl appeared unharmed, but An'gel was annoyed with her behavior. "Tell us how the accident happened."

Sondra responded to the tone of authority, though sullenly. "I was on my way into town, and I was coming down the driveway."

"Way too fast," Benjy said in an undertone, but An'gel heard him.

Sondra appeared not to have heard as she continued, "I saw these two"—she indicated Benjy and Peanut with a dismissive gesture—"and I thought they were trespassers. When I hit the brakes so I could stop and tell them to get off our property, nothing happened." She shrugged. "I guess I panicked and drove into the tree. That was the only way to stop the car."

An'gel exchanged another uneasy glance with Dickce. This was definitely odd. She was thankful, however, that Sondra had been close to home when the accident happened. Had she been on the highway and driving faster when she needed to stop, she could have been badly injured, if not killed.

"Let's get you up to the house," Dickce said briskly, taking Sondra's arm. "We need to make sure you weren't hurt. You may feel all right now, but later on you might not."

To An'gel's surprise, Sondra let Dickce lead her toward Willowbank. An'gel remained behind a moment with Benjy and Peanut.

When the others were out of earshot, Benjy said, "Don't you think it's weird about the brakes? A brand-new car like that, shouldn't happen. But maybe she's just a lousy driver."

An'gel said, her tone grim, "I'm going to talk to Sondra's mother. Sondra might be a bad driver. I certainly wouldn't drive in heels like that." She paused for a breath. "That car needs to be examined by an expert, however. If Sondra wasn't at fault, I'm worried someone tampered with the brakes, hoping for a bad accident."

"That's sick." Benjy shook his head. "Why would someone want to hurt her?" Peanut woofed, and An'gel thought how interesting it was that the dog always seemed to understand when Benjy was feeling tense or upset about something.

"Exactly what I want to know, although I'm hoping it was simply bad driving." An'gel paused for a moment, deciding what to do. "I need to talk to Jacqueline. I'm going back to the cottage to change first, though."

Peanut whimpered and tugged against his leash. Benjy laughed. "This guy's got plenty of energy he needs to burn off. I'll let him run around a bit, so we'll be outside for a while."

An'gel nodded then turned to head back to her cottage. Before she had gone a hundred feet, however, she heard Jacqueline call her name. Her goddaughter was running down the driveway toward her.

An'gel stopped and waited for Jacqueline to reach her. Jacqueline stared at the car for a moment while she breathed deeply. She closed her eyes, crossed herself, and mumbled a few words.

An'gel took her arm and led her closer to the vehicle.

"Oh, *Maman*, thank goodness," Jacqueline said. An'gel thought that was odd, but she forbore to question it.

After a moment Jacqueline seemed to gather herself. "Thank you, *Tante* An'gel," she said. "I'm okay now. Sondra drove the car home from the dealership yesterday, and everything was fine. How could this have happened?"

An'gel decided to be blunt. "Sondra was driving in very high heels. I think she might simply have lost control of the car. Benjy said she was driving too fast down the driveway."

Jacqueline shook her head. "I know Sondra drives fast, but she's been driving in heels since she got her license. I don't think it was entirely her fault."

Benjy and Peanut approached them, the dog straining at his leash to get to Jacqueline. Peanut loved meeting new people, and he wagged his tail as he sniffed at Jacqueline's outstretched hand.

While her goddaughter greeted the dog, An'gel said, "I hate to say this, but if it wasn't Sondra's fault, I think it had to be deliberate. Someone tampered with the brakes. Maybe I have too suspicious a mind, but I'm worried that Sondra is being targeted."

Jacqueline appeared startled, and she drew her hand

back abruptly from stroking Peanut's silken head. "That's ridiculous. Why would someone try to harm my daughter?" Then she blanched and whispered, "*Maman*."

"What about your mother?" An'gel said.

Jacqueline shook her head. "Nothing really, just that *Maman* will be upset over this." She scratched her nose several times.

An'gel's eyes narrowed as she regarded her goddaughter. The nose scratching was a dead giveaway. Jacqueline was lying to her, but why?

An'gel decided not to challenge her because Jacqueline was obviously upset. She focused on a practical matter instead. "I think you should have the car examined just to be sure."

Jacqueline stared at her for a moment. "I suppose you're right," she said. "I'll call the dealership. The car will have to be towed in for repairs anyway." Without taking her leave of them, she turned and hurried back toward Willowbank.

"I hope it turns out to be just an accident," Benjy said.

"I do, too," An'gel replied. *Though I'm afraid it won't*, she added in her mind. "Well, I'd better go get dressed." She was suddenly conscious of standing there in her gown and robe.

"Yes, ma'am," Benjy said. "We'll be here until the tow truck gets here."

Back in the cottage, all thought of a nap gone now, An'gel began to dress for dinner. While she completed her toilette, she thought about Sondra's misadventure with the car.

If Sondra were a target for either severe injury or murder, An'gel reckoned, the motive had to be money. The girl could be exasperating beyond measure, but An'gel doubted anyone would kill her out of sheer irritation.

No, money lay at the root of it, she was convinced. Sondra, upon her marriage, would be an extremely wealthy young woman. An'gel didn't know the exact figure, but she reckoned it must be well over fifty million, if not twice that. Sondra's father, Terence Delevan, had been a shrewd businessman who inherited a decent amount of money and turned it into a massive one.

The question was, who got the money if Sondra died? An'gel had heard the terms of the will at some point, but now she struggled to recall them. That Sondra would inherit upon marriage or her twenty-fifth birthday, whichever came first, An'gel knew. She thought the money would then go to Sondra's offspring when Sondra died. In this case, the child Tippy, whom An'gel had yet to meet.

If Tippy inherited before she became an adult, who controlled the money? Surely Terence Delevan had considered that possibility and stipulated the terms in the will. Perhaps Sondra's husband?

An'gel grimaced at the thought of Lance Perigord in charge of the Delevan fortune. If there were no restrictions on his handling of the money, Lance would probably be penniless in less than a year, and Tippy would be left with nothing.

No, An'gel decided as she peered into the bathroom mirror to finish with her makeup, Terence had surely made provisions. He had been too good at making money to risk letting it be squandered quickly after his death. The likeliest answer was that Sondra's executors would be entrusted with Tippy's inheritance. Sondra's stepfather, Horace Mims Junior, and Terence's closest friend, Richmond Thurston, were the chief trustees, as An'gel recalled.

A tap on her leg brought her out of her reverie. She glanced down to see Endora sitting at her feet. Endora meowed, and An'gel extended her hand to rub the cat's head. Endora pushed against the hand and started to purr. An'gel rubbed a few moments longer, then informed Endora that she had other things to do. She felt foolish when she caught herself talking to the cat, or to Peanut for that matter, but she supposed most people with house pets must do the same.

Endora rubbed against her leg while An'gel peered into the mirror again to satisfy herself that her makeup was as impeccable as she could make it. "It's a good thing I don't have my stockings on yet," An'gel muttered.

"Sister, where are you?" Dickce's voice rang out in the living room. "Are you decent?"

"Yes, come in." An'gel turned to await her sister's entrance. Endora, hearing Dickce, trotted out to greet her. When Dickce came in the bedroom, the cat rode in her arms.

"How is Sondra?" An'gel asked.

"A little shaken up, once the reaction set in. Still able to fuss and carry on and give everyone a headache, though." Dickce perched on the edge of the bed and eyed her sister critically. "I thought Mireille might have a conniption fit on the spot when she heard what happened. Jacqueline had to give her a shot of brandy to buck her up."

"For all that shrinking violet bit she displays on occasion, Mireille has always been strong as a horse." An'gel frowned. "I hope she isn't having health problems she hasn't shared with us."

"A few sips of brandy put her right," Dickce said. "Fortunately Estelle was busy elsewhere, or she would have had all of us on the edge of a nervous breakdown."

"Mireille has enough stress at the moment without strange events like this adding to it," An'gel said. "I'm afraid, Sister. I've got a feeling that something nasty is going on under the surface here."

"I agree," Dickce said. "I have a bad feeling about those brakes and why they failed."

They stared at each other for a moment. An'gel couldn't help remembering the events of a couple of months ago, when an old school friend turned up uninvited on their doorstep. Tragedy arrived with her, and An'gel didn't care to go through anything like that again. She might not have a choice, she realized. She and Dickce would simply have to remain vigilant and do their best to guard against any further looming disasters.

CHAPTER 6

Dickce glanced around the twelve-foot-long Louis XV walnut dining table and did a quick count. Nine people. *Isn't that supposed to be unlucky, an odd number at the table?* she wondered. *No, it was thirteen at dinner, like in the Agatha Christie book, that was unlucky.* She had a sip of her sweet iced tea and glanced at Benjy, seated to her left. He seemed a bit overwhelmed by the assembled company, and she didn't blame him. With the exception of Mireille and Jacqueline, no one had made much of an effort to speak to him or make him feel welcome. The atmosphere in the room felt oppressive, and Dickce had little urge to talk herself.

From across the table, Lance kept gazing vacantly at Benjy and not paying much attention to Sondra on his right. Sondra, directly across from Dickce, appeared not to notice the older woman's presence. Instead, Sondra, too, gazed at Benjy, but not vacantly. *Predatorily*, Dickce decided, and then wondered if that was an actual word. *Poor Benjy.*

At the head of the table, as befit her position as mistress of Willowbank, Mireille looked splendid in lilac silk. Dickce had always admired the pearl necklace and earrings Mireille wore. They had belonged to Mireille's great-great-grandmother and were worth a fortune. Dickce didn't think it was her imagination that Horace Mims, seated on Mireille's right, kept gazing hungrily at the jewels. They would someday belong to Jacqueline, his wife, but Dickce had the oddest feeling Horace would like to have them in his fat, clammy hands right now.

To Mireille's left sat Richmond Thurston, an old friend of Terence Delevan's and a prominent attorney in St. Ignatiusville. He had been best man at Terence and Jacqueline's wedding, and he was also Sondra's godfather. Dickce thought him a fine figure of a man—tall, stately, with an imposing presence. His dark hair sprinkled liberally with gray, he had a beak of a nose that gave his face character. Unlike poor Horace, Dickce thought, who looked more like the Michelin Man or the Pillsbury Doughboy. What Jacqueline saw in him—other than his money—Dickce hadn't a clue. Where Richmond Thurston was urbane and sophisticated, Horace Mims was provincial and crass. Dickce and An'gel had often wondered why Jacqueline hadn't married Thurston. He wasn't as rich as Horace, but he was far more attractive.

No accounting for taste, Dickce thought. She tuned back into the conversation—more like a monologue, she realized, as Horace appeared to be winding down a tedious story about some deal he had made and how he'd made *mincemeat* out of the other man.

"Guy was ready to lick my boots and thank me for the privilege by the time I got through with him," Horace said with a nasty grin.

"You're a hard man, Horace." Thurston smiled. "Can't tell you how happy I am we're not in the same business."

"Horace is such a hard worker," Jacqueline said. "He's always working on some new deal or other."

Dickce thought she detected a note of complaint in Jacqueline's voice. Perhaps Horace spent more time on his business than he did on his marriage. Dickce wouldn't be surprised if that was the case.

"That sure is the truth, darling." Horace beamed across the table at his wife. "Takes every bit of money I earn selling cars to make sure you got everything you need. When you got a beautiful wife, you want to make sure and show her off to everybody."

Jacqueline blushed and reached with a not quite steady hand for her wineglass. "Thank you, Horace. You've very sweet to say such things. But we should be talking about Sondra and what a beautiful bride she will be."

"About time," Sondra muttered.

Dickce glanced at the girl sharply, then at Jacqueline. She didn't think Jacqueline had heard her daughter's rude remark.

Lance continued to appear oblivious to the scene around him as he gazed across the table at Benjy. Benjy seemed fascinated with his food and was not paying attention to

Lance. Dickce gave his arm a surreptitious pat, and he flashed her a grateful smile.

"Yes, Sondra will be the most beautiful bride St. Ignatiusville has ever seen—at least since her mother walked down the aisle with Terence Delevan twenty-three years ago." Thurston bent forward slightly to look down the table at Sondra.

"The wedding will be lovely," Mireille said. "I'm so pleased that Sondra has agreed to wear her great-great-grandmother's dress and pearls for the ceremony. It has been a tradition for several generations of Champlain women, and it means so much to me that my lovely grand-daughter will be a part of it on her wedding day."

Dickce leaned forward slightly to see An'gel's expression. Her sister was as surprised as she was over Sondra's capitulation. Dickce wondered how on earth Mireille had prevailed in this, because Sondra had seemed determined not to wear the antique gown. She was surprised that An'gel didn't ask right then and there.

Estelle bustled in at the end of Mireille's remarks, with Jackson the butler trailing behind, both carrying trays. They started removing the first course, a delicious French onion soup, and worked swiftly and competently.

"As long as you're happy, *Grand-mère*, that's all that matters," Sondra said, her expression mulish.

"There's bad weather coming," Estelle announced suddenly. "It's going to be storming the night before the wedding, and that's a bad omen." She removed An'gel's soup service and set it on the tray. "It's bad luck for brides in St. Ignatiusville, and I am going to be praying that nothing terrible happens."

"Estelle, I'd rather you didn't talk about such superstitious nonsense." Mireille sounded outraged, and Dickce was a bit surprised. She had never heard her cousin speak in that tone to the housekeeper.

"Ain't superstition," Estelle said as she set the tray on the table and glared at her employer. "You know as well as I do what happened to Melusine Devereux on the night before her wedding. Sondra never should have picked the same date as Melusine did. I told y'all it was courting disaster." She shook her head. "And now there's a storm coming, just like when Melusine was fixing to get married."

"Estelle, that's enough." Mireille stood, her face contorted with anger. "If you utter one more word about that old wives' tale, I swear I will throw you out of this house myself."

Dickce didn't like the thick air of tension that suddenly seemed to fill the room. She thought Estelle was not only rude, but stupid to talk like this in front of her employer's family and guests. If Estelle had worked for her and An'gel, she would have been out the door years ago. Dickce and An'gel never could understand why Mireille had put up with the woman for so long.

Estelle seemed taken aback by Mireille's threat. She picked up the tray with trembling hands and scurried out of the dining room, leaving Jackson to clear the rest of the table. The elderly butler shook his head and continued his work.

Mireille dropped abruptly into her chair. "You must all forgive me, and Estelle, too. I don't know what brought that on. Please, pay no attention to that absurd idea of hers."

Thurston reached over and clasped one of his hostess's hands in his. "It's a silly old story, and there's probably no truth to it. Don't let it upset you, my dear." He laughed.

"Everybody in St. Ignatiusville has probably heard that story, but no one believes it really happened."

"Course not." Horace Mims shook his head. "I been telling you for the past three years, Mama Mireille, you ought to get rid of that old witch. She's a misery, and that's the plain truth. I'll tell her to get out of the house if you want me to."

Mireille smiled faintly as she pulled her hand free from Thurston's grasp. "Thank you both, but I will deal with Estelle in my own way. Now, let's forget about all that nonsense. The next course will be here shortly."

Dickce had never heard the story of Melusine Devereux, at least not that she could recall, and now she burned with curiosity to know what had happened. Something tragic, obviously.

"*Grand-mère*, you have got to promise me you'll get rid of that woman." Sondra pushed back her chair and dropped her linen napkin on the table. "I hate her, she's always saying mean things to me when no one else is around, and I don't want her anywhere near me. If you want me to wear that old moldy dead woman's dress, then you'd better get Estelle out of this house." She stalked out of the room, and no one made a move to go after her.

The remaining eight at table sat in silence for a long moment until Jackson coughed discreetly. "Miss Mireille, I'll be back with the main course momentarily. I'll ask Miz Winwood to stay in the kitchen."

"Thank you, Jackson," Mireille said. "Please tell her I will talk with her later."

The butler nodded and walked out with a heavily laden tray. Mireille offered her guests a shaky smile. "Everyone's nerves are a bit on edge, I'm afraid. There is still so much to do with the wedding so close now."

"Of course, my dear," Thurston said. "We all know what Estelle's like, think nothing of it. Now, tell me, who is going to sing at the wedding? At one point, I think you told me you were hoping that girl Sondra went to high school with would be able to do it."

Conversation turned to this and other details of the wedding, and Dickce was thankful they made it through to the dessert course without any further emotional outbursts. Sondra had not returned, and Dickce was a bit puzzled that no one appeared to be concerned about her absence. Perhaps it happened so frequently it wasn't remarkable.

Lance ate bits of his food and smiled vaguely at Benjy, who remained silent along with Dickce. An'gel joined in the conversation enough for both sisters, and Dickce was content to leave her to it.

She kept hoping someone would bring up the subject of Melusine Devereux before they finished dessert. Her curiosity was getting the better of her, however, and she finally decided she might as well do it herself. An'gel would probably have a fit with her later, but so what.

There was a sudden lull in the flow of conversation while the diners addressed themselves to the delicious white chocolate mousse Jackson served them.

Dickce leaned forward to gaze down the table in her cousin's direction. "Mireille, I know this is truly bad of me, but won't you tell us about this tragic bride? At least I'm assuming it's tragic, the way Estelle was talking."

Mireille set down her dessert spoon and stared at Dickce.

"Would you like me to tell the story?" Thurston asked when Mireille did not respond right away.

Their hostess nodded, her expression one of resignation. "If we must hear it, I'd rather you told it."

Thurston gave a genial smile in Dickce's direction. "Miss Ducote, it's an old story that has been handed down in St. Ignatiusville for well over a century. Nobody knows if it's true, though I suppose we could find out if we really wanted to." He laughed. "But it's probably just an old wives' tale, as I believe someone already said.

"If it happened," Thurston continued, "it was most likely in the decade or two after the War."

Dickce, along with the rest of the company, knew that *the War* meant the Civil War.

"Melusine Devereux was the beautiful daughter and only child of an old plantation family. Their place was abandoned around 1900 or so, and another planter bought the land and had the house torn down. Some say Melusine's ghost still lingers there in the woods."

Dickce shivered, although Thurston laughed at his own words.

"Melusine was betrothed to a handsome young man from New Orleans, and everyone was happy. Until the night before the wedding, that is."

Thurston paused and glanced around the table, perhaps to be sure that everyone was listening. Even Lance, Dickce noticed, had fixed his gaze on the attorney, away from Benjy.

"All day a storm had been brewing, so the story goes, and everyone was jittery. That evening, not long before the storm broke, Melusine went up to her bedroom on the third floor.

The Devereux place was spacious and imposing, so everyone says, and Melusine had a large room with a balcony and French doors that overlooked the front of the house."

Dickce closed her eyes for a moment, and she conjured a mental picture of the scene as Thurston continued the story.

"Melusine decided to try on her wedding dress, evidently claiming that it still needed a few adjustments. The servant who was the best seamstress was with her in her room, along with Melusine's mama. While they worked, the wind began to howl as the storm moved closer. The French doors to the balcony blew open, and a gust of wind sucked up Melusine's veil. She ran toward the balcony to try to save the veil, and another mighty gust sucked her off the balcony and threw her to the ground."

Dickce's eyes popped open. She no longer wanted to envision the scene of such a tragic event.

"Mrs. Devereux roused the household, and Mr. Devereux and one of the servants rushed out into the storm, praying that Melusine was somehow unhurt." Thurston's voice dropped to a husky note. "But it was not to be. Melusine, dressed in her bridal clothes, lay broken and dead on the flagstones below."

CHAPTER 7

Now that she had heard the story of the tragic bride, An'gel was even more incensed that Estelle would talk about it in front of Sondra, Jacqueline, and Mireille. Why Mireille didn't fire the housekeeper on the spot, An'gel couldn't fathom.

She would also have a few choice words for Dickce later on, for bringing up the subject and basically forcing someone to tell the story. At least Sondra wasn't in the room. An'gel had to wonder, however, whether the girl made a regular habit of having a fit and running away from the dinner table.

"That is truly a sad story," An'gel said when the silence began to feel uncomfortable.

"Yes, it is," Jacqueline said, looking sour. "Fortunately it has nothing to do with us or with my daughter's wedding. I can't believe Estelle brought it up like that." She turned to glare at her mother. "*Maman*, I have to say I agree with Sondra. What Estelle did is the last straw. She has to go."

Mireille seemed to shrink in her chair, and An'gel felt sorry for her. Mireille hated confrontation of any kind, and here she was faced with one that she couldn't ignore. From An'gel's point of view, Mireille had no choice now but to fire her housekeeper.

"Now is not the time, nor is this the place, to discuss it further," Mireille finally said, a note of iron in her tone. "I will deal with the situation as I see fit, and I will not be bullied in my own home." She faced her daughter with a defiant expression.

Good for you, An'gel thought. About time Mireille showed some backbone.

The silence after Mireille's declaration became awkward, and An'gel decided it was up to her to put an end to this unpleasant interlude. She pushed back her chair and rose.

"Mireille, my dear, the dinner was excellent, as always. I regret having to break up the party, but I am rather weary after a long day. I hope you won't take it amiss if I excuse myself—along with Dickce and Benjy—and we retire to our cottages." She sent a pointed glance in her sister's direction, and Dickce quickly stood, with a smile for Mireille.

"Yes, as Sister says, we've had a long day, and we belles of a certain age need all the beauty rest we can get." Dickce placed her hand on Benjy's shoulder, and he stood alongside her, nodding.

Thurston rose as well. "I have to say, Miss Dickce, that I can't see where either of you needs any beauty rest." He winked at An'gel. "But I have to be in court first thing tomorrow, so I'd best be taking my leave as well." He bent and picked up Mireille's left hand and bestowed a quick kiss on it. "If there's anything at all I can help you with, *chère madame*, you know you have only to ask."

Mireille looked far more relieved than affronted, An'gel thought, to have the dinner party break up so early. It was barely eight o'clock, she noted from a surreptitious glance at her watch.

"Then I will bid you all a good night." Mireille smiled graciously as she, too, rose from the table.

The next few minutes were spent with the usual business of leave-taking and wishing one another a good night, but finally An'gel, Dickce, and Benjy walked out the front door on their way to peace and quiet in their cottages. Thurston was behind them, still chatting with Jacqueline at the door, as they made their way through the grounds with the aid of flashlights provided by Mireille.

When they were safely out of earshot, An'gel said, "Poor Mireille. She has a tough situation on her hands."

Dickce snorted. "It's her own fault for putting up with that woman all these years. I'm surprised someone hasn't batted Estelle over the head long before now. She's tiresome and difficult."

Benjy extended his arm for An'gel and then for Dickce to grasp as they navigated some exposed tree roots on their path. "Mrs. Champlain seems like a nice lady. I hated to see her looking so uncomfortable because of that weird housekeeper."

"There's no easy solution to the problem." An'gel's tone was grim. "Estelle is sure to have conniptions if Mireille fires her, and Sondra will probably have the lulu of all tantrums if her grandmother doesn't get rid of Estelle."

"They could just put a muzzle on Sondra." Benjy laughed. "I'm surprised no one's clunked *her* over the head, honestly."

"A few good spankings at the right age, or lots of time-outs when she was little, would have done that girl a world of good," Dickce said. "Her daddy spoiled her rotten, and by the time he died, the damage was done. Neither Mireille nor Jacqueline, I hate to say, has ever had enough spine to deal with the girl."

An'gel was relieved when they reached the lights surrounding the cottages and turned off her flashlight with gratitude. Earlier she had simply made a polite remark to put an end to a tense situation, but now that she was close to her bed, she did feel tired. All that emotion was exhausting, even if one was only forced to witness it.

Dickce unlocked their door as An'gel turned to Benjy. "I'm sorry you had to see all that. I hope you weren't too uncomfortable."

Benjy shrugged. "Don't worry about me. I used to see stuff like that all the time."

An'gel knew he was talking about his life with his parents and his stepfather's mother, their old friend Rosabelle Sultan, and felt even guiltier. She patted his shoulder. "This will soon be over, and we can head back to Riverhill and forget about all this drama."

Benjy laughed. "I'm looking forward to getting home. Good night, Miss An'gel, Miss Dickce. I'm going to walk Peanut again in a while, but we'll be settling in for the night soon." He gave each of them a quick peck on the cheek before unlocking his own door and disappearing inside.

An'gel could hear the excited woofing noises from

Peanut next door upon seeing Benjy as she followed Dickce into their cottage.

"What a dear, sweet boy he is," Dickce said. "Thank the Lord he's nothing like Sondra or her loopy fiancé. You should have seen the way Lance was staring at Benjy all during that fiasco of a meal. Sondra, too, come to think of it."

An'gel dropped wearily onto the plush sofa and kicked off her pumps. "We should probably have let Benjy stay at Riverhill with Endora and Peanut. I'm sure they would have been happier."

"What's done is done." Dickce stepped out of her shoes and bent to pick them up. "I don't know about you, but I'm going to get ready for bed. This day has been over-whelming. Good night." She disappeared into her bedroom and shut the door.

An'gel called *good night* after her sister. She remained on the sofa, lacking for the moment the energy to get up and go to her own room. Her thoughts focused on the dinner party and its seething undercurrents. There had seemed an unpleasant undertone to the whole evening. From Horace's occasional vulgarities to Sondra's rude behavior before and during the meal and the ugliness of the scene with Estelle, the whole occasion had been the fiasco Dickce said it was.

They were due back at Willowbank in the morning for breakfast at seven thirty. An'gel wondered whether she, Dickce, and Benjy would be subjected to further drama. Rather bleakly, she laughed. *Probably not a question of "if" but of how much.* With that unpleasant thought, she pushed herself up from the sofa, picked up her shoes, and went to her bedroom.

An'gel slept soundly that night and woke to her travel clock alarm at six thirty. She yawned and pushed aside the covers. The bed was comfortable, and she felt reluctant to leave it. Duty called, however. She couldn't put off getting ready for the day and whatever it entailed.

From the bathroom window she peered outside. The sun wouldn't rise for about half an hour yet, and she hoped the storm that Estelle forecast would not come through until after the wedding. Bad weather would simply make already worn nerves more ragged.

An'gel admonished herself to shake off morbid thoughts. She focused instead on her bath and toilette. By the time she emerged from her bedroom, dressed in a casual, colorful linen print dress and flats, she felt more sanguine. The smell of hot coffee that wafted toward her cheered her even further. She traced the smell to the tiny kitchenette tucked away in a corner of the cottage near the front door. She found Dickce seated at a small banquette, cup in hand.

"Sister, thank you for making the coffee." An'gel poured herself a cup, added a little cream and sugar, stirred, and sipped happily.

Dickce grimaced. "I don't know about you, but I definitely had to have some caffeine before we walk into who-knows-what up at the big house."

"I know exactly what you mean." An'gel took the seat opposite. She peered out the small window above the banquette table. The sun should have been visible by now, but everything still looked murky. "Looks like the weather isn't going to cooperate."

Dickce shivered. "I got chills last night while Richmond

Thurston was telling that story. Imagine a gust of wind being able to suck a woman out of a window like that."

"I'd rather not imagine it," An'gel said. "There was one detail in what Estelle said that I find puzzling. How did she know the date of that poor girl's wedding? Was it really the same as Sondra's? Or was she just making it up to get at Sondra?"

"That is peculiar," Dickce said. "I didn't catch on to that." She shrugged. "I vote for Estelle to be making it up. It's the kind of thing she would do simply to aggravate Sondra *and* Jacqueline."

"Unless she has an unimpeachable source for the truth of that story, I'm sure she did make it up." An'gel nodded firmly to emphasize her point. "If we're lucky, Estelle will be gone when we go up for breakfast."

"Though who's going to cook if she *is* gone, I wonder." Dickce took a sip of coffee. "I don't think Mireille is much of a cook. Perhaps Jacqueline is, though."

"If nothing else, we can have a French country breakfast, like the ones we had in that *pension* in Paris, remember? That lovely, crusty French bread, with butter and jam, and the bowls of milky coffee. I'd never had coffee from a bowl before."

Dickce laughed. "I remember the look on your face when you realized you had to drink out of a bowl. Priceless."

"Yes, well, I got used to it," An'gel muttered. She drained her cup and got up to rinse it out in the sink. "We still have about twenty minutes before we're due for breakfast. I think I'll retrieve our umbrellas from the car, just in case."

"Good idea," Dickce said. "I'll clean up in here while you do that."

An'gel could tell, by the feeling of pressure in her head, that the weather was changing. She stepped outside, and the dark gray sky and slight chill in the air confirmed it. She hurried to the car, the wind rising around her, and dug around in the back of the Lexus for their umbrellas. They had managed to forget any other rain gear, so the umbrellas would have to suffice.

Rain began sprinkling down before An'gel made it back inside. "This day is going to try my patience," she muttered to herself as she shut the door behind her. "It's starting to rain," she called out to her sister.

"Wonderful," Dickce replied as she came out of her bedroom. "And we forgot to bring our raincoats. At least we have the umbrellas."

A knock sounded on their door, and An'gel propped their umbrellas beside a nearby occasional table before she answered.

To her surprise, Jacqueline stood there, damp from the rain.

"Come in, dear," An'gel said. "You'll get soaked." She hurried her goddaughter inside and shut the door.

"Thank you, *Tante* An'gel." Jacqueline shivered. "The temperature is dropping, and I didn't think to bring a jacket or an umbrella with me."

"Come in and sit down," Dickce said. "I'll get you a blanket if you'd like."

Jacqueline shook her head as she sat on the sofa. "No, thank you, I'll be fine." She paused for a deep breath. "I'm sorry to bother you with this, and I can't believe I'm doing it."

"Doing what, dear?" An'gel asked when Jacqueline failed to continue. She sat beside her goddaughter and patted her shoulder. Jacqueline now had a wretched expression, and An'gel grew alarmed. "Tell us what's wrong."

"It's Horace," Jacqueline said, barely above a whisper. She stared down at her hands, clasped tightly in her lap. "He promised me the money would be there, but it isn't, and now I can't pay the florist for Sondra's bridal bouquet and the rest of the flowers."

CHAPTER 8

Over Jacqueline's bowed head, An'gel and Dickce exchanged startled glances. Horace Mims was reputedly worth millions, but he didn't have the money to pay the florist for his stepdaughter's wedding?

"That's certainly unfortunate," An'gel said.

Dickce sat on the other side of Jacqueline and patted her on the back. "What can we do to help?"

"I'm so embarrassed by all this, you cannot believe how much," Jacqueline said, still gazing at her hands. "I don't dare tell *Maman* about Horace's little cash flow problem, as he calls it. It's only temporary, he says, but it couldn't happen at a worse time."

"These things happen in business from time to time," Dickce said, "or so I imagine." She raised her eyebrows in An'gel's direction, and An'gel gave a tiny shrug in return.

"We'll be happy to lend you the money, Jacqueline," An'gel

said in a bracing tone. "I'm sure Horace will get his affairs sorted out quickly. Tell me how much you need, and we'll take care of it."

Jacqueline raised her head, and An'gel was dismayed to see that she had been crying. "Thank you, *Tante* An'gel, *Tante* Dickce, I can't tell you how much this means to me, and to Sondra and *Maman*, of course, although I'll never let either of them know anything about it."

"We'll keep this to ourselves," Dickce promised. "Tell An'gel how much you need, and she'll write you a check."

"Two thousand dollars," Jacqueline said. "I know it's a lot to ask, but if I don't get the money to the florist today, there won't be any flowers for the wedding."

"We certainly can't have that," An'gel said. "I'll get my checkbook, and we'll take care of this right now." She patted Jacqueline's arm before she rose from the sofa.

"Let me get you some tissues," Dickce said. Jacqueline was sniffling, and her face was turning blotchy from crying. Dickce got up and went to the bathroom in search of the tissues.

An'gel came back with checkbook and pen in hand and resumed her seat next to her goddaughter. "Would you like me to make it to you, or to the florist?"

"To the florist would be fine." Jacqueline supplied the name. "Thank you, *Tante* An'gel."

Dickce returned with the tissues and handed them over. Jacqueline smiled her thanks and began dabbing at her eyes. She accepted the check from An'gel with a slightly watery smile.

An'gel glanced at Dickce, as if asking her sister a question. Dickce nodded, and An'gel spoke in a brisk tone to her goddaughter. "I tell you what, my dear. Why don't you let this be one of our wedding gifts? It would be our pleasure."

Jacqueline's face reddened, and she didn't speak for a moment. "You're being far too generous, but I thank you. You'll never know how much."

For a moment An'gel thought her goddaughter was about to burst into tears, but Jacqueline collected herself. She thanked the sisters again as she folded the check and tucked it into the pocket of her pants.

"I'd better get back." Jacqueline rose. "*Maman* will be wondering where I am. You'll be coming up for breakfast soon?"

"Yes," An'gel said, "and if there's anything we can help with this morning, do let us know."

Dickce echoed her sister's words, and Jacqueline thanked them. "I think we have everything under control. Estelle is still here, so it's breakfast as usual."

"Is Mireille going to fire her?" An'gel asked.

Jacqueline shrugged. "Honestly, I don't know. After Estelle's behavior last night and Sondra's ultimatum, I thought she'd be gone this morning. But there she is in the kitchen as if nothing happened. I tried to talk to *Maman* last night about Estelle, but she told me she would take care of everything in her own way and not to pester her about it."

An'gel wasn't surprised. Mireille could be stubborn, and her loyalty to Estelle, though puzzling to everyone else, might turn out to be more important to her than having her granddaughter follow family tradition in wearing the antique wedding gown. An'gel had no doubt Sondra would follow through on her threat not to wear the gown when she saw Estelle still in the house.

"I'm sure Mireille will do what she thinks is best for everyone," An'gel said with a confidence she was far from feeling in her cousin.

"Two more days, and this will all be over." Jacqueline sounded weary, An'gel thought. "I'll see you up at the house in a bit."

Dickce showed her out. She leaned back against the closed door and regarded her sister. "Horace must be having serious problems if he can't come up with two thousand dollars to pay for the florist."

An'gel nodded, her tone grim when she spoke. "Definitely. I'm concerned about Jacqueline. She has money of her own from Terence's estate and should have been able to pay the florist herself. The fact that she had to come to us for money is deeply troubling."

Dickce returned to her place on the sofa near An'gel. "I had forgotten that. I hope Horace hasn't squandered Jacqueline's inheritance."

"I don't remember the terms exactly, but I *thought* Jacqueline had only the income from a trust for her lifetime," An'gel said.

"If that's the case, then she's probably okay," Dickce said, "but I suppose she could be giving money from her trust income to Horace."

"Very possibly." An'gel sighed. "There isn't anything we can do about it, though, other than counsel Jacqueline if she should ask for further help."

"On the other hand, she could be using her income to

help Mireille," Dickce said. "Maurice didn't leave Mireille all that well off; otherwise, she wouldn't have had to go into business with the bed-and-breakfast scheme."

"True," An'gel said. "I hope that's the answer, rather than giving money to Horace." She pushed herself up from the sofa. "It's close enough to breakfast time; we might as well head on up to the house."

Dickce nodded. "I'll go check on Benjy and see if he's ready."

"I'll meet you outside in a moment." An'gel headed to the bathroom to wash her hands and have one last check on her makeup. As she stared into the mirror, she realized she had forgotten to ask Jacqueline about Sondra's car. She was curious to find out what had happened with the brakes. She would ask her goddaughter at the earliest opportunity.

A couple of minutes later she came out of the cottage to find not only Dickce and Benjy awaiting her, but Peanut and Endora as well. Peanut was on the leash, but the cat rode on Benjy's shoulder.

In response to An'gel's expression of surprise, Benjy explained, "Mrs. Champlain told me last night that I could bring the guys to the house with us. She said she loves animals, and she's never seen either a Labradoodle or an Abyssinian before."

"If Mireille okayed it, then it's certainly fine with me." An'gel stared at the animals. "But you two have to be on your best behavior, all right?"

Peanut woofed in response, and An'gel couldn't help but smile. Endora, on the other hand, stared at An'gel like a small Sphinx.

"I'm sure Endora will be a perfect lady," Dickce said. "Won't you, sweetheart?"

Endora turned her head in Dickce's direction and meowed. Dickce shot a triumphant glance at her sister.

An'gel was slightly piqued that Dickce could elicit a response from the cat and she rarely could. Peanut was rapidly becoming her favorite, because he at least appreciated her attention.

"Let's go," An'gel said and headed for Willowbank.

Benjy, with Peanut and Endora, soon overtook the lead, thanks to the Labradoodle's enthusiasm. Twice the dog wanted to hare off after something only he could sense, but each time Benjy called him to heel, and he obeyed quickly. Benjy praised him, and Peanut wagged his tail happily and barked as if to acknowledge the command.

"Such a smart boy," An'gel murmured after the second foiled attempt.

"He sure is," Benjy said over his shoulder in response.

They soon reached the house, and moments later were at the front door. Before they could ring, the door swung open, and Jackson's smiling face greeted them.

"Well, now, who is this?" Jackson extended a hand to Peanut, and the dog sniffed and then licked it. Jackson rubbed the dog's head as Benjy introduced him.

"He sure is a friendly dog," Jackson said. "And what about Miss Precious sitting there on your shoulder. I reckon I never saw a red cat like that before."

"This is Endora," Benjy said. "She's an Abyssinian."

"Do tell." Jackson shook his head. "She come all the way from Africa?"

"A few generations ago," An'gel said with a smile. "Isn't she lovely? She's not particularly friendly, though."

As if to give the lie to An'gel's claim, when Jackson reached out toward the cat, Endora butted her head against his open palm and meowed as if to thank him for the attention. Jackson laughed. An'gel shot the cat a sour look.

"I reckon she's friendly enough," the butler said. After a moment he drew his hand back. "Y'all come on in. We're just getting breakfast set on the sideboard in the dining room." He waved them in and shut the door behind them.

The butler led them into the dining room, where An'gel could see Estelle moving dishes from a serving cart onto the sideboard. The housekeeper did not acknowledge them when she finished. Instead she wheeled the empty cart out of the room as if she hadn't seen them.

An'gel walked over to the sideboard to examine the choices: scrambled eggs, biscuits, sausage and red-eye gravy, three types of jelly, and grits. Almost as an afterthought, An'gel noted, there was a large plate of sliced melon, pineapple, and grapes.

"We certainly won't go hungry," An'gel said.

Peanut, obviously entranced by the smell of food, strained at the leash. "No, boy," Benjy said. "That's people food. You've already had your breakfast."

Peanut looked up at Benjy and whined. Benjy shook his head. "No." With that, the dog settled down, though An'gel thought he looked sulky.

"Good morning," Mireille called out as she entered the dining room. She smiled when she spotted the animals. "Oh, how beautiful they are." She approached Benjy and the animals, and he quickly introduced the cat and the dog to his hostess. Mireille gave them both attention, and An'gel decided grumpily that Endora would be nice to everyone except her.

"What sweet babies they are." Mireille switched her attention from the animals to her cousins. "Please don't wait, go ahead and help yourselves to breakfast. I have something to attend to, but I'll be right back."

A howl of rage echoed through the lower portion of the house, and An'gel and the others started. Peanut barked excitedly, and Benjy worked to calm him.

The source of the noise appeared in the dining room doorway. Sondra stormed in and marched straight up to her grandmother.

"What is that woman still doing here?" Sondra screamed the words. "I told you I wanted her out of this house."

What happened next startled An'gel so badly she almost dropped the plate she had picked up.

In response to Sondra's outburst, Mireille drew back her hand and then slapped her granddaughter resoundingly.

CHAPTER 9

"It's about time you learned who runs this house."
Mireille put her face close to her granddaughter's. "I
say who works and lives here, and no one else."

Sondra started to speak, but her grandmother cut her off.

"The only thing I want to hear from you is an apology."
Mireille's cold tone surprised An'gel even further. She had
never heard her cousin speak in such fashion. "If you can't
apologize and act in a civilized manner, then you can leave
this house yourself. Do you understand me?"

Sondra stepped back, the mark of Mireille's hand showing red in stark contrast to the pale skin of her face. Her
breath came harshly, and she stared wildly at her grandmother. Suddenly she turned and ran, and An'gel heard her
going up the stairs.

Mireille, after a moment, turned to regard them coolly.

"If you'll excuse me, I must do something but I'll be back in a minute." She walked out of the room.

An'gel and Dickce stared at each other. An'gel found her voice first. "Heavens above, I never thought I'd see the day, but the worm finally turned."

"I'll say she did," Dickce replied. "I guess last night's little episode really was the final straw." She walked over to the sideboard and picked up a plate.

An'gel noticed Benjy appeared uncomfortable. She felt suddenly impelled to apologize for her cousin and for bringing him along and subjecting him to these family scenes. She explained this to him, and he gave her an uncertain smile.

"It's not your fault." He shrugged. "If you'd like, I guess I could get a plate and take it back to the cottage. I don't want to be in the way if there's serious family stuff going down."

"As far as we're concerned," Dickce said, "*you* are our family, An'gel's and mine." She gave an impish grin. "You don't have to claim the rest of them, though."

Benjy laughed, and An'gel shot her sister a look of gratitude for lightening the atmosphere.

"I guess we'll stick around, then," he said. "Because I am starving." He looped Peanut's leash around a chair leg and told him to stay. He put Endora in a chair and told her to stay, and to An'gel's pleasure, the cat did as she was told.

The three humans filled their plates, and the sisters poured coffee for themselves while Benjy chose orange juice. They sat together at the far end of the dining table to keep the animals out of the way. Peanut whimpered a couple of times, but Benjy responded with firm *no*'s. Endora curled up placidly in the seat of the chair next to Benjy.

Before they had taken more than a few mouthfuls of their delicious breakfast food, Mireille returned with Jacqueline in tow.

To An'gel's practiced eye, it appeared that there was tension between mother and daughter. Mireille's shoulders had a rigid set, and Jacqueline kept darting furious glances at her mother.

Sondra had no doubt gone to her mother to complain about Mireille's behavior toward her, and An'gel was sure Jacqueline was unhappy over the incident. She hoped they would restrain themselves during breakfast, because she didn't want to sit through another meal fraught with emotion.

That was not to be, she discovered quickly.

"I can't believe you are more loyal to Estelle than you are to your own granddaughter." Jacqueline stood at her mother's back with fists clenched while Mireille calmly filled her plate with food.

"Frankly I don't care what you believe." Mireille used the tongs to pick up a couple of biscuits to add to her choices. She set the tongs down and turned to face her daughter directly. "Sondra will soon be married and out of this house, and I have to think about my needs for once. Sondra couldn't care less about how any of this affects me, and I am tired of pretending that she cares about anything other than herself. She barely pays attention to her own child, Jacqueline, much less to anyone else."

The rest of them might as well be invisible, An'gel

decided. Mireille behaved as if only she and her daughter were in the room. Jacqueline didn't appear to care about having an audience either.

"I know she's selfish, *Maman*," Jacqueline said in a weary tone. "She's been that way since she was a baby. But she does love you, in her own way. She loves me, too, and she adores Tippy."

"You sound like you're trying to convince yourself," Mireille said. "You needn't waste any efforts on me, however. I'm too old at this point to care any longer, and I have finally decided I don't give a damn about what Sondra thinks or wants."

"I suppose you'd like it if Horace and I moved out as well." Jacqueline plopped down in a chair next to her mother's seat at the head of the table. "I just don't understand you. How could you suddenly be so cruel, so unfeeling?"

An'gel watched the scene unfold in horrified fascination. She wondered whether she should interrupt but quickly decided she would do better to keep her mouth shut, at least for the moment. She checked and saw that Dickce and Benjy were staring at their plates and that Endora had climbed into Benjy's lap. No doubt the cat was unsettled by the rampant tension in the room. She didn't blame Endora for seeking comfort. She wouldn't have minded some herself, because it pained her greatly to see her cousin's family unraveling in so nasty a fashion.

"There is no need for you and Horace to move out." Mireille ate a bite of her eggs. "If you want to move out, however, I can't stop you."

"*Maman*, how can you be so hurtful?" Jacqueline burst

69

into tears. After a moment she jumped up from her chair and ran out of the room.

Mireille put down her fork and sighed. "I'm sorry you all had to witness that."

Benjy pushed back his chair. "Mrs. Champlain, ladies, Peanut and Endora need to go outside, if y'all don't mind. We'll be back in a little while."

An'gel nodded, and Dickce said, "Of course."

Mireille nodded, and when Benjy and the animals were out of the room, she gazed at the sisters with a sad smile.

"Do you think I'm being horrible and hurtful?"

An'gel got up from her place and took the chair Jacqueline had vacated. Dickce moved to sit on the other side of their cousin.

"My dear, I honestly don't know what to think." An'gel patted Mireille's hand, then squeezed it. "I know you've had a lot to bear over the years, and it's no wonder you're weary of it."

"You sure have," Dickce said. "We hate to see you and your family in such a terrible state. Is there anything we can do?"

"Thank you both," Mireille said. "Your support means a lot. I can't quite believe myself that I have finally spoken up to say 'enough is enough.'" She sighed heavily. "I guess I don't want to spend whatever time I have left dealing with all this drama. Sometimes it's like living in the middle of a soap opera, and I'm weary from trying to keep things calm and stable around here."

An'gel felt a mild chill at the words *whatever time I have left*. Was that simply an expression, or did it have a deeper meaning in Mireille's case?

She decided she might as well ask. If she didn't, Dickce would. Her sister was too nosy sometimes.

"Mireille, are there any health problems you haven't told us about?" she asked.

Mireille gave a faint smile. "My heart isn't in the best shape, I'm afraid. My doctor says I'm good for a few more years, though."

"Oh, my dear," Dickce said, and An'gel could see her sister's eyes welling with tears. She had to blink back a few herself. She didn't want to distress her cousin by breaking down, however.

"Then you certainly deserve to rid yourself of whatever stress you can." An'gel spoke in what she hoped was a firm, reassuring tone. "Is Jacqueline aware of this?"

"No," Mireille said. "I'd rather you didn't tell her. She's going to have enough to deal with, because I refuse to deal with my granddaughter anymore."

"I should think not," Dickce said.

"I'm so happy you're here." Mireille glanced at each of them in turn. "I don't feel quite so alone now."

An'gel's eyes stung. She felt such pity for her cousin, to have this kind of stress in her life. She should be able to enjoy her last years in calm and quiet. An'gel would happily have taken Sondra over her knees right then and given her a sound spanking for causing her grandmother so much grief.

They were startled by a loud cry from outside the dining room.

"Sondra, no! What are you doing?" Jacqueline was yelling.

An'gel and Dickce rushed into the hall, and Mireille was

a few steps behind them. An'gel stared in shock at Sondra, on the second-floor landing, as the girl threw scraps of white cloth over the rails to the first floor.

With a dull ache in her heart, An'gel realized that the source of the scraps was Mireille's grandmother's lovely wedding gown. Sondra had cut or ripped it to shreds.

She heard Mireille gasp and cry out "No!" As she turned, Mireille fainted and hit the floor.

CHAPTER 10

Jacqueline took one look at her mother on the floor near the stairs and started yelling for the housekeeper. "Estelle, hurry! Call 911! *Maman* has fainted." She and Dickce knelt beside the stricken woman to render aid.

Estelle scurried in from the back of the house where the kitchen lay, cell phone in hand. She was talking to someone and urging speed.

An'gel, once she felt certain everything that could be done for her cousin at the moment was being done, charged up the stairs as quickly as she could to confront the source of Mireille's great distress.

Huffing slightly as she reached the second-floor landing, An'gel paused a moment to catch her breath. A few feet away Sondra leant against the railing, staring down at the scene below. From what An'gel could see, there was not a sign of remorse or concern on the girl's face. At that moment An'gel felt a rage come over her, and it was all she could do not to go and pick the girl up and throw her over the railing, just as Sondra had tossed the remnants of the antique bridal gown. An'gel mastered the impulse, however, and took several steps toward Sondra.

"Do you have any idea what you've done?"

Sondra ignored her, and An'gel's temper flared even higher. She grabbed the girl's shoulder and shook her, hard.

"Don't you dare ignore me, young woman. You look at me when I talk to you."

Sondra stared at An'gel, sullen and hate-filled. An'gel didn't flinch, however, and put all the loathing she felt for this sad excuse for a human being into her gaze and into her tone when she spoke.

"Your grandmother could be lying down there dying at this moment. Is that what you wanted?"

"It's all *her* fault anyway." Sondra spit the words out. Her tone grew shriller the longer she spoke. "Everybody's always trying to make me do things I don't want to do. *She* cares more about that awful woman than she ever cared about *me*. She even tried to make me wear that disgusting dress when I told her I didn't want to. She doesn't want me to get married at all. She made Uncle Rich try to talk me out of it; I know she did. Telling me I shouldn't get married. I hate her; I hate every single one of them. None of them care about me or what I want."

An'gel took a step back from the girl as she raved on, suddenly afraid and all too aware of the difference in their ages. Sondra was decades younger and far stronger than she, and the girl was in such a state there was no telling whom she might attack.

With great relief An'gel heard the sound of a siren rapidly approaching. If she could manage to keep Sondra at bay until the EMTs arrived, she would be fine. The girl still looked like she wanted to claw An'gel's eyes out.

Sondra turned away and ran up the stairs to the third floor, where her bedroom lay. Seconds later An'gel heard a door open and then slam shut. She trembled and grasped the banister rail for support.

The front door burst open and the EMTs came in. They went to work on Mireille immediately while Jacqueline and Estelle both tried to explain what had happened. A tall, sun-bronzed young man dealt with them patiently as An'gel made her way slowly down the stairs. Dickce met her, and they moved well out of the way but within sight of all the activity.

"How is she?" An'gel asked.

Dickce shook her head. "Not good. I think she had a heart attack. I also think she hit her head pretty hard when she fell."

An'gel closed her eyes and prayed for her cousin. She felt Dickce grasp her hand. When she finished her prayer, An'gel opened her eyes to find her sister regarding her with evident concern. "What about you? You're pale and shaky," Dickce said. "I wasn't paying attention to what went on up there with Sondra, but I did hear her yelling at you."

An'gel felt all at once that she had to sit down and told Dickce so. Dickce led her into the front parlor, where they both seated themselves on the sofa. Quickly An'gel told her sister the gist of her conversation with Sondra.

"The girl is a psychopath," Dickce said. "Or is it sociopath? Either way, she's dangerous." She shuddered.

An'gel couldn't disagree. The way that Sondra had behaved, the way she had looked at An'gel, didn't seem human.

"Would you like me to get you some brandy?" Dickce asked. "I wouldn't mind a little shot myself, to be honest."

An'gel nodded. "Sounds good to me."

Dickce got up and went over to the liquor supply, housed discreetly in an antique cabinet in the corner. She came back soon with two small shot glasses of brandy, and the sisters downed them quickly.

An'gel felt the familiar warmth begin to spread, and she thanked Dickce. A good "stiffener," as one of their English friends called it, was exactly what she needed.

Jacqueline hurried into the room then, and An'gel noticed that she had been crying.

"How is your mother?" An'gel asked.

"They think she might have had a heart attack," Jacqueline said, her face drawn and ashen. "They're taking her to the hospital. I'm going right behind them. I was wondering if one of you would mind coming with me?"

Dickce rose from the sofa. "I'll go with you, dear. An'gel should stay here, I think. She had a bit of a shock."

"I'm sorry if Sondra upset you," Jacqueline said. "She's not in her right mind. I don't know what possessed her to do such a thing."

An'gel could have enlightened her goddaughter on the subject of Sondra but felt it would be kinder not to. There was something seriously wrong with the girl, but Jacqueline had enough on her plate at the moment.

"You go on to the hospital and don't worry about anything here," An'gel said. "I'm sure Estelle and I can take care of things."

Jacqueline nodded. "I know you can." She started to turn away. "Oh, dear, I forgot. Rich Thurston is due here any minute. He was planning to talk to Sondra, but now certainly isn't a good time. Please explain to him and ask him not to talk to her just now."

"All right," An'gel said.

Jacqueline barely paused for the response. She hurried out, and Dickce followed her a little more slowly.

"Be careful," she said. "Stay away from Sondra unless there's someone else with you." With that, she disappeared through the doorway.

Moments later An'gel heard the front door open and close, and then silence. The ambulance had already departed with Mireille, and the siren had faded away in the distance. An'gel sat there, allowing time to collect herself before she had to go in search of Estelle. She was surprised the housekeeper hadn't insisted on going to the hospital with Jacqueline, but perhaps Jacqueline hadn't given her a choice.

A mighty crash of thunder startled An'gel, and she glanced toward the windows that faced the front lawn. The day had grown even darker, and An'gel heard the rain splatter hard against the house. She uttered another quick prayer for the safety of everyone on the wet roads. She was getting up to go in search of Estelle when she heard the doorbell ring.

There was no sign of the housekeeper when An'gel walked into the hall. She went to the door and opened it to find Richmond Thurston, Mireille's lawyer, on the verandah.

"Do come in, Mr. Thurston." An'gel waved him in.

"Thank you, Miss Ducote." Thurston propped his dripping umbrella by the door on the verandah and stepped inside. "Terrible storm out there right now. I just about made it to the porch when the heavens opened up."

"Yes, it certainly is a downpour." An'gel started when the thunder crashed again. Her nerves were enough on edge already without the added stress of a violent storm.

"I trust you're keeping well, despite the weather." Thurston smiled, and An'gel felt the pull of the man's charm. He had a way of looking at one that made the person feel like she had the lawyer's complete attention.

"As well as can be expected, under the circumstances," An'gel said. "Won't you come into the parlor, Mr. Thurston? I'm afraid I have something to tell you, something upsetting."

"Of course, dear lady," he said as he followed her. "What is wrong?"

An'gel waited until they were seated in the parlor before she told him about Mireille. His face darkened as she explained the reason for her cousin's sudden collapse.

"I swear I'd like to horsewhip that girl," he said with such fervor that An'gel had no trouble believing he would actually do it, given the opportunity. "I've never in my life known anyone so completely self-absorbed."

Before An'gel could reply, the lawyer stood. "Where is she? I'm going to talk to her."

An'gel thought about protesting but realized that would likely prove futile. "In her bedroom most likely. What are you going to say to her?"

"The first thing I'm going to tell her," the lawyer said, "is that the wedding will have to be postponed. She can't get married while her grandmother is in the hospital." He expelled an angry breath. "Girl has no business getting married anyway, at least not to a congenital idiot like Lance Perigord. The boy's as queer as the proverbial three-dollar bill, for one thing. He should be stopped, for his own protection, if nothing else. Sondra will destroy anyone she marries."

The lawyer didn't wait for a response from An'gel. He strode out of the room, his face again red with anger. An'gel worried for a moment that he might strike Sondra, but then decided she didn't have the energy to involve herself any further. At the moment she felt every one of her eighty-four years, and she leaned wearily back on the sofa.

Her thoughts quickly turned to Mireille. In light of what Mireille had told them earlier, not long before the frightening incident that sent her to the hospital, An'gel fretted that her cousin would not survive. With her heart already in bad shape, the bad shock Mireille had sustained might be more than her heart could bear. An'gel said another quiet prayer for Mireille's recovery.

She wondered how long it would be before Dickce or Jacqueline called to give an update on Mireille's condition. She realized then that she didn't have her cell phone with her.

Where had she left her handbag? She thought hard for a moment. In the dining room, she decided. She got up and went across the hall to the dining room. She found her handbag on the floor beside the chair where she had eaten. She noticed that someone, either Estelle or Jackson, had cleared everything away.

An'gel pulled her phone from the bag and checked to see whether she had missed a call.

No calls. She debated whether to call Benjy to apprise him of the morning's events but decided not to burden him with the news. There would be time enough later to fill him in. Besides, there was nothing he could do. Nothing she could do either, other than wait.

Replacing the phone in her handbag, An'gel headed to the back of the house to the kitchen. As she neared it, she heard voices through the half-open door. When she walked in, she caught the tail end of a remark from Estelle, who was speaking to the butler.

". . . rat poison in her food."

CHAPTER 11

"Estelle, what are you talking about? Rat poison in whose food?"

The housekeeper flushed as she turned to face An'gel. Her tone was defiant when she replied. "Sondra's food, that's who. I figure we'd all be better off if someone put rat poison in her food. That's what I was telling Jackson when you came in."

The elderly butler nodded. "Yes, Miss An'gel, that's what it was. Just talk. Estelle was telling me what happened to Miss Mireille and what Miss Sondra done to cause it."

"As long as it stays talk, then we're fine." An'gel spoke sternly. "I know we're all furious with Sondra, but let's not get carried away."

Estelle didn't respond, but Jackson nodded and said, "Yes'm." He cleared his throat. "Have you heard anything from the hospital yet?"

"No, not yet," An'gel replied. "I came in here hoping for some coffee or some hot tea, if it's not too much trouble."

Estelle muttered something An'gel couldn't hear, but the butler looked startled. The housekeeper brushed past him, headed for the stove. She picked up a kettle, took it to the sink, rinsed it, then filled it with water. "Tea'll be ready in a minute."

"Miss An'gel, why don't you go back to the parlor, and I'll bring your tea soon as it's ready." Jackson moved forward as if to escort An'gel from the room.

"That's fine, thank you. Before I forget, Mr. Thurston is here. He is upstairs with Sondra at the moment." An'gel turned to leave but paused for one more remark. "If either of you hears from Jacqueline, please let me know. I'll do the same if my sister calls me."

Estelle nodded in her direction, and Jackson assured her he would bring her any news immediately. An'gel departed the kitchen and made her way back to the front parlor.

Thunder rattled the windows every so often, and An'gel worried that the storm seemed to be hanging over them. At this rate, she thought, the roads might start flooding.

Seated once again on the sofa in the front parlor, she pulled out her phone. She decided she would call Benjy to assure herself that he and the animals were safe. To her annoyance, she had no reception on her phone, thanks to the weather. Disgusted, she dropped her phone back in her purse. She eyed the telephone extension on a nearby table, but she hated talking on a landline during a storm. She was concerned about Benjy, Peanut, and Endora, but she didn't want to risk either Benjy or herself getting electrocuted.

An'gel felt restless. As long as the storm raged, they

might not get any word from the hospital, and she fretted over Mireille's condition. She was also curious about the conversation taking place upstairs between Thurston and Sondra. Perhaps she ought to go up and check after all.

Before she could suit action to thought, Jackson entered the parlor bearing a tray with her tea. He set the tray on the coffee table in front of the sofa.

"Thank you, Jackson," An'gel said. "I'll pour for myself."

"Yes'm." Jackson hesitated for a moment. "Miss An'gel, do you think Miss Mireille's going to be all right? I just can't imagine this house without her."

An'gel felt a lump in her throat. "I sure hope so, but only the good Lord knows. I've been praying that she'll come back to us and be fine."

"Me, too," the butler said. "I've known Miss Mireille since she was a little bitty girl, and me just a boy myself." He sighed. "I'm going to pray hard as I can she'll be healed."

"That's the best possible thing we can do right now," An'gel said.

Jackson nodded, and An'gel watched him depart, his shoulders slumped. She felt a fresh wave of anger toward Sondra for all the harm and distress she had caused. Then she realized that she had to calm herself or her blood pressure would remain sky-high, and that wouldn't do. She poured herself a cup of tea, added a little cream and sugar, and stirred.

The warm liquid was a welcome balm for her frazzled nerves. As she sipped her tea, she listened for the sound of footsteps on the stairs. She was curious to hear Thurston's report on his conversation with Sondra. If he would share it with her, she thought. He might not want to talk about it.

An'gel didn't have to wait long. A few minutes later Thurston strolled into the parlor. He appeared remarkably calm, An'gel thought, in contrast to his state when he left her to confront Sondra.

"I'm having tea," An'gel said. "Would you care to have some? I can ring Jackson and ask for a second cup if you'd like."

Thurston shook his head. "Thank you, no. Right now I'd rather have a bottle of bourbon, but it's too early in the day for that." He glanced at the windows. "Even though it looks like blackest night outside right now." He chose an armchair near the sofa and leaned back, rubbing his forehead.

"How is Sondra?" An'gel asked. She figured that was general enough an inquiry for Thurston to answer briefly or in detail, depending on how much he wanted to share with her.

Thurston laughed, and the sound was grim to An'gel's ears.

"I think I managed to get through that piece of granite that serves as a brain. I told her the wedding would have to be postponed indefinitely."

"How did she take that?"

"Not well," Thurston replied. "She kept insisting that she was going ahead with the wedding, no matter what, but I told her that Father McKitterick wouldn't officiate under the circumstances."

"I doubt that went over well," An'gel said. She poured a second cup of tea.

"No," the lawyer said. "It didn't, but I kept at her. I finally got through to her, though."

"How?" An'gel asked.

Thurston grinned. "The one thing Sondra is really terrified of is public ridicule. She wants everyone to be impressed with how beautiful she is, and she can't stand being laughed at. I promised her that I would personally tell every single person in St. Ignatiusville what she had done to her grandmother, and I assured her that if she went out in public, everyone would point at her and laugh. People love Miss Mireille in this town, and they'll turn against Sondra completely if any word gets out about this."

An'gel was horrified. "Surely you'd never share this with the whole town. Mireille would be utterly humiliated."

"Of course I wouldn't." Thurston waved a hand in a dismissive gesture. "But Sondra thinks I will. She's so self-centered, she'll never figure that out, however. She is unable to understand anything from a point of view other than her own."

"You're right about that," An'gel said. "I don't suppose she expressed any concern for her grandmother."

"Nothing will touch that petrified heart of hers," the lawyer replied. "She'll never take responsibility for what happened, I can promise you that." He stood and walked over to the liquor cabinet. "Forget about what time it is, I need a drink." He found a glass and a bottle of bourbon and poured himself a sizable portion. He brought the glass back and resumed his seat. He lifted the glass in An'gel's direction and said, "Here's to Miss Mireille's complete recovery."

An'gel said, "Hear, hear," and raised her teacup.

Thurston drained his glass and set it on a side table nearby. He glanced toward the windows. "Looks like the rain is slacking off. It's not as dark out there as it has been." He got up and walked over to look outside.

"Thank heavens," An'gel muttered. The atmosphere in the house felt oppressive, and she would be happy if the weather cleared up enough to allow her to leave.

A chirping sound emanated from her handbag. She delved inside and pulled out her cell phone. She and Dickce had recently upgraded their phones from the old flip versions to phones that could take pictures and send text messages. She hadn't tried the messaging function yet, but it appeared that someone had just sent her one. Dickce, she figured. She touched the screen and the message app opened.

"Mireille in ICU. Jacqueline says she's stable, holding her own. Doctor not sure about chances of recovery."

An'gel sighed and peered at the small screen. She touched the text box, and a keyboard appeared. With one finger she tapped a response. *"Thanks. Will be praying for her."* She hit the Send button, feeling slightly proud of herself for having sent her first text.

Another message appeared. *"Will call later."*

An'gel typed in her response. *"Okay."*

No further message popped up, and An'gel put the phone back in her purse.

Thurston resumed his seat. "News?"

"Yes," An'gel said. She gave him the update on Mireille's condition.

Thurston's face darkened. "It doesn't sound good."

"Unfortunately, no," An'gel replied. "I feel so helpless, as I'm sure you do."

"I feel like going back upstairs and wringing that girl's neck for what she did," the lawyer said.

"You might have to get in line," An'gel said wryly.

Thurston grinned. "Not that it would do Miss Mireille

one iota of good, but it sure would make me feel better."
He stood. "I think the storm's let up enough that I can
probably get back to my office without being washed away.
If you'll excuse me, Miss Ducote, I'll be going."

"Do be careful out there." An'gel got up and followed
him out of the parlor.

As they moved into the hall, the front door crashed open,
and a tall, muscular young man strode in, obviously worked
up over something. He shed a raincoat and let it drop to the
floor where he stood. Then he apparently caught sight of
An'gel and Thurston and pulled up short.

"Where is Sondra?" he demanded. "I'll kill her before I
let her marry that jackass Lance."

CHAPTER 12

Even standing several feet from the open door, An'gel felt the moisture blowing in.

Thurston spoke before she could admonish the stranger to close it, however. "Trey, there's water blowing in. Shut the door."

Trey stared blankly at the lawyer for a moment before Thurston's words evidently sank in. He scowled but complied with the lawyer's command.

"Well, where is she?" he demanded when he turned back, staring hard at Thurston.

"Upstairs in her room," the lawyer replied.

Trey bolted up the staircase. Moments later An'gel heard him bellow Sondra's name.

"Should you follow him, do you think?" An'gel asked. The strange young man's violent words concerned her.

Thurston shrugged. "He's more hot air than action most of the time. I doubt he'll do anything other than get into a screaming match with Sondra."

"Who is he?" An'gel asked, feeling slightly relieved by the lawyer's response. "He looks vaguely familiar."

"Horace Mims the Third," Thurston replied. "Otherwise known as Trey. He's been mooning over Sondra for years, but as far as I know, she's thought of him only as a brother."

"The last time I saw him," An'gel said, "he was much shorter and weedy looking. No wonder I didn't recognize him."

Thurston laughed. "He's a gym rat. Spends three hours a day there, last I heard tell."

"He must be about twenty-three. If I remember correctly, he's a couple of years older than Sondra."

"Sounds about right," Thurston replied. "Now, if you'll excuse me, Miss Ducote, I'd best be going. I'll drop by the hospital on my way to the office, see if I can find out anything more about Miss Mireille."

An'gel repeated her earlier admonition to be careful and bade the lawyer good-bye. Once the door closed behind him, she wandered over to the stairs. Should she go up and check on Sondra and Trey? Make sure the girl came to no harm?

The prospect of climbing to the third floor did not entice her, and she decided to let the situation alone. After all, Thurston knew Trey and she didn't. If the lawyer thought Trey wouldn't harm Sondra, despite the violence of the boy's declaration, then there was no need for her to stick her nose in.

With a guilty start An'gel remembered Jackson and Estelle. She had promised to share any news of Mireille with them right away. She cast one more look up the stairs before she headed for the kitchen.

When she walked in, Estelle was on the phone talking to someone about the wedding. "No, I don't know when it will be, but we surely can't have it while Mireille's in the hospital." She caught sight of An'gel and told the person on the other end of the conversation she would call back.

"Have you heard something?" Estelle demanded.

"Yes, I have," An'gel said. "Where is Jackson?"

"Probably asleep in the pantry," Estelle said. "He has a chair in there where he goes and nods off whenever there's a quiet moment. He's too old for the job, but of course Mireille won't make him retire." She folded her arms across her chest. "Well?"

An'gel shared the information from Dickce's text message, and Estelle nodded. "At least she's not dead yet, the heavens be praised." The housekeeper sniffed loudly. "I've started calling people to tell them the wedding's been postponed. Figured I should get the word out right away."

"Do you need help with that?" An'gel asked. She was a little surprised that Estelle apparently wasn't worried about using the telephone in the midst of a storm. An'gel would be happy to assist with the notifications, but not until the storm passed completely.

"No, I'm fine," Estelle said. "There's not much else I can do right now." She turned away, and An'gel felt like she had been dismissed.

"I'm sure you'll let Jackson know about Mireille," An'gel

said. Once Estelle nodded, An'gel decided to go back to the front parlor.

Once more seated on the sofa, An'gel decided she would practice her texting skills by sending Benjy a message. She wanted to be sure that he, Endora, and Peanut were doing all right.

Less than a minute after An'gel sent her inquiry, Benjy responded with *"Doing fine. R U OK?"* An'gel stared at the screen a moment, slightly puzzled, but then she realized Benjy was using an abbreviated form to communicate. She texted back that she was fine also and that she would be back at the cottages once the storm had passed. Benjy acknowledged that with *"OK."*

An'gel put her phone down and stared rather blankly around the room. After a moment she got up and went to the front windows to look out. The sun was trying to emerge, she could see, and the rain was much lighter. She hadn't heard any thunder for a while now, she realized. Perhaps she could borrow an umbrella and make her way back to the cottages. She considered that but then decided that the ground would be slippery and she didn't want to risk falling.

She was startled by noise coming from the direction of the stairs and went to the door of the parlor to see what was going on. She was in time to see Trey Mims running down the last few treads. He appeared not to have seen her as he strode to the front door, which he slammed shut behind him as he stepped onto the verandah.

Such a noisy young man, An'gel thought, shaking her head. She wondered if he was in such a hurry all the time. Her thoughts turned to Sondra, and she wondered whether she should go up and check on the girl. She listened for a moment and was relieved to hear a door close loudly upstairs. Deciding that Sondra was probably fine, An'gel hovered in the doorway, still feeling restless. She also felt tired, she realized.

Since there wasn't anything else she could think to do, An'gel figured she might as well lie down and rest for a while. She turned off the lights in the front parlor, kicked off her shoes, and made herself comfortable on the sofa.

She lay there and stared at the ceiling, listening to the now-gentle pattering of the rain against the house. She willed herself to relax, to let the stress of the morning slip away, and soon she was drifting off . . .

Dimly An'gel was aware of a voice nearby, a voice that sounded upset. She struggled to identify it and in doing so came out of her slumbering state.

Horace Mims was talking, and An'gel, still drowsy, didn't move from her supine position.

". . . told you already it's just a minor cash-flow issue." Horace paused. "Don't be giving me that crap, Bubba, you know I'm good for it." Another pause, longer this time. Then an expletive, and An'gel winced. "If I have to, Bubba, I'll come right down there and beat some sense into your head."

After that the voice trailed away, and moments later An'gel sat up, cautiously, wondering where Horace had gone. She peered through the dimness in the parlor toward the door into the hallway. To her surprise, Horace stood there, apparently looking up the stairs, with a bright smile on his face.

"Hello, darlin'," he said. "What've you been up to?"

"Hewwo, Gwanpa Howace," a high-pitched child's voice responded. "I've been pwaying in my woom."

That had to be Tippy. Curious to see the child at last, An'gel slipped on her shoes and tiptoed to the door. She didn't want Horace to see her, because then he would realize she had most likely heard his end of the recent phone conversation.

When An'gel peered around the door frame, she saw Horace's back to her, and that pleased her. She glanced past him to stare at the elfin child who stood on the fourth tread from the bottom, gazing solemnly at her step-grandfather. An'gel had expected Sondra's daughter to have coloring similar to her mother's, but the child had pale brown hair, the sides held back by butterfly barrettes, and a slightly olive-skinned complexion. She was also taller than An'gel had reckoned, more the size of a first grader rather than that of a child who wasn't quite four. Tippy wore sandals and a plain cotton dress, and her features vaguely resembled her mother's. Overall, however, the child was ordinary-looking, with none of Sondra's startling beauty.

"Is your mommy up in her room?" Horace asked.

Tippy nodded. "She's been in dere an awf'wy wong time, too. Unca Twey was up dere, and dey was yewwing at each udder. Unca Twey can yeww pwetty woud, just wike Mommy."

Horace snorted, and Tippy giggled. Horace must have made a face at the child, An'gel guessed.

"I hope you didn't pay too much attention to all that yelling," he said. "Grown-ups shouldn't be making all that noise when you're trying to play."

Tippy nodded. "Yewwing is wude, Gwanny Miway says.

I went in my cwoset and pwayed so I didn't hear dem so much."

"That's good, darlin'. I'll have to talk to Uncle Trey and your mommy about making all that noise when you're around." He held out his arms. "Now, who around here would like to ride on my shoulders while we go in the kitchen and see if Miss Estelle has any treats?"

Tippy squealed and clapped her hands together. "Me, Gwanpa. I want to wide on your showders. And I want a tweat, too." She hopped down the remaining treads, and Horace scooped her up, then flipped her around and set her on his shoulders, one leg on either side of his head. He bounced her lightly, and Tippy laughed.

An'gel watched them disappear down the hall and then turned on the lights in the parlor. She went back to the sofa and sat, pondering what she had learning from eavesdropping.

First, she knew that Horace did have financial problems. There was no other construction she could put on Horace's conversation with "Bubba" that made much sense. How serious those problems were remained to be discovered. Horace's money woes weren't really her business, she realized, but she worried about the implications for her goddaughter, of whom she was extremely fond.

Second, she had learned that Sondra and Trey, as stepsiblings, had an apparently rocky relationship. From the exchange between Horace and Tippy, she gathered that they yelled at each other often. An'gel smiled. As Tippy would say, they "yewwed" at each other. The child's lisp was adorable, she thought.

Trey's relationship with Sondra piqued her curiosity.

According to Richmond Thurston, Sondra had only ever treated Trey as a brother. Trey, on the other hand, had been "mooning" after Sondra for quite some time.

Considering the threat Trey had made, An'gel wondered just how far the young man would go to keep Sondra from marrying Lance.

CHAPTER 13

The storm cleared out around eleven, and Dickce and Jacqueline returned to Willowbank shortly after noon. Mireille was still stable, they reported, and Jacqueline intended to go back to the hospital and spend the rest of the day and the night there. When An'gel suggested she have something to eat before she drove back to Baton Rouge, Jacqueline shook her head.

"I'm not hungry right now, *Tante* An'gel. I want to get back to *Maman* as quickly as I can."

An'gel gave her a quick hug. "If there's anything we can do, let us know, my dear. Would you like me to come back with you?"

"No, I'll be fine," Jacqueline said. "There really isn't much any of us can do except wait and pray. I can only go in to see her at four and eight." She shrugged. "I just want to be there in case . . ." Her voice trailed off, and for a moment she looked as if she would burst into tears.

"We will be praying for her," Dickce said, giving Jacqueline's arm a quick squeeze. "We'll look after things here."

"Estelle has been letting people know that the wedding is postponed," An'gel said. "We'll deal with anything that comes up."

Jacqueline clapped a hand to her mouth in a gesture of dismay. "I completely forgot about the wedding. Have you talked to Sondra?"

"No, I haven't, but Richmond Thurston did. Not long after, your stepson came in, and he went up to talk to her, too." An'gel didn't want to worry her goddaughter by telling her about Trey's behavior. If she had to, she would deal with Sondra later herself, or surely Horace could. Jacqueline's place at the moment was with her mother.

"I wish Trey would leave Sondra alone," Jacqueline said after a heavy sigh. "He's convinced he's in love with her, but Sondra has never given him any encouragement. I guess I'll have to ask Horace to talk to him again."

"Don't worry about that now, honey," Dickce said. "You go on and leave things to us."

Jacqueline flashed them a grateful smile. "You're right. I need to get back to the hospital. Thank you." She turned and trotted up the stairs.

As Jacqueline moved out of sight, An'gel took her sister's arm and led her into the parlor. "Tell me about Mireille," she said when they were seated on the sofa.

Dickce shook her head. "Sister, it just about broke my

heart to watch her lying there in that bed. She looks so frail right now. It's hard to see how she's going to recover from this."

An'gel felt a chill creeping over her. What should have been a joyous occasion for a family gathering had now turned into a potential tragedy instead. Her heart ached for her cousin and the turmoil in the family. All due to the utter self-absorption of one person and her vindictive actions when she was thwarted.

"I know." Dickce squeezed An'gel's hand. "That child has so much to answer for."

An'gel's tone was brisk as she responded. "Best not dwell on that, or else I'll march up those stairs and yank every single hair out of her head."

"And I'd help," Dickce said. "I hate to say this, Sister, but I'm starving. We never did finish breakfast, and I need something to eat. Have you had any lunch?"

An'gel nodded. "I finished not long before you and Jacqueline got back. Estelle made bacon-and-cheese quiches and a salad."

"That sounds fine to me." Dickce rose. "Guess I'll go to the kitchen and ask for some."

"Go right ahead," An'gel said. "Benjy came up for his lunch a little while ago, but he took it back with him to his cottage. Peanut and Endora have been jittery with the storm, and he didn't want to leave them alone too long."

"He's such a sweet, caring boy," Dickce said. "Will you be in here? I guess I'll eat in the kitchen, if it's okay with Estelle. Seems silly to eat in the dining room."

"That's what I did." An'gel stood. "I'm going to make a run into town and buy a few things for our dinner. With everything that's going on, I'd just as soon fix something in our cottage tonight. There's supposed to be another line of storms moving in later this afternoon or early evening."

"All right, then," Dickce said. "I'll see you back at our cottage." She headed for the kitchen.

An'gel picked up her purse, checked to make sure she had her keys and her wallet, and then let herself out the front door to make her way carefully through the wet grounds to where the Lexus was parked.

She returned an hour later with several bags, and Benjy came out to assist her with them. She thanked him, then said, "I overheard a woman at the grocery store talking about the weather. Apparently the next wave of thunderstorms that's headed our way will be more violent than what we've had already."

"Yes, ma'am," Benjy said. "I checked the forecast on the Internet a little while ago, and it was saying the same thing." He took all but one of the bags from her, and she let them into the cottage.

"How are Peanut and Endora doing?" An'gel asked as they walked into the tiny kitchen area off the small living room.

"They were pretty restless earlier." Benjy set the bags on the counter and began unpacking them. "They're still a little on edge, I guess because they can sense there's more to come. Funny how animals can tell things like that."

"I feel a bit edgy myself," An'gel confessed. She opened the compact refrigerator and put the eggs, milk, and cheese inside.

"I'm sorry about your cousin," Benjy said. "I know you're worried about her."

"Yes, it's a bad situation," An'gel said. "All we can do now is pray."

In his quietly efficient way, Benjy had finished putting things away. He rolled up the plastic bags and stowed them in a drawer. "If there isn't anything else I can do right now, I guess I'll go back next door and read. I don't like to leave the kids alone too long."

"You go right ahead," An'gel said. "And if you want something to snack on, help yourself." She knew Benjy was often hungry between meals, and she had bought extra fruit and a few snack items for him.

Benjy grinned. "Thanks. I'll take a couple of things with me." He chose an apple, a banana, and a package of cheese and crackers. "See you later."

After the door closed behind him, An'gel went to Dickce's bedroom and quietly opened the door. Her sister lay on her side on her bed, evidently asleep, so An'gel pulled the door shut and moved away. She might as well nap herself, she decided, because she knew she wouldn't be able to sleep with a violent storm going on around them. Best take advantage of the lull in the weather and get some rest.

An'gel quickly disrobed and slipped on her nightgown, then lay down on the bed. She prayed for several minutes for her cousin, and then dropped off to sleep not long after.

She jerked awake several hours later, thanks to the crash of thunder. Moments later, lightning flashed, and she counted the seconds until the next boom. Four seconds. The storm was about four miles away.

She dressed quickly and left the bedroom. She found Dickce in the living room, sitting in a chair with its back to the inside wall.

"I was going to wake you up in a minute if the storm didn't," Dickce said. She, like An'gel, hated thunderstorms. Their mother had been terrified of weather like this and would hide herself and her daughters in a first-floor closet at Riverhill whenever storms threatened. The sisters had conquered the worst of their fears of bad weather, but their mother's legacy lingered.

An'gel retrieved a chair from the kitchen area and brought it to sit beside Dickce. For a few minutes, An'gel shared with Dickce the events of the morning at Willowbank, while Dickce was at the hospital in Baton Rouge. Once the storm was overhead, however, neither of them spoke. For the longest time, it seemed to stall right above them. They huddled together, their breathing ragged, until after an eternity the storm began to move away.

An'gel got up, intent on fetching a bottle of water for each of them from the fridge, but a knock on the door halted her. She opened the door to find Benjy, with Endora on his shoulder and Peanut at his side, standing there. Peanut looked frightened, and Endora had her head against the side of Benjy's face.

An'gel motioned them in and shut the door behind them. "Is everything okay?" she asked.

Peanut loped over to Dickce, woofing happily, but Endora remained on Benjy's shoulder.

"We're okay," Benjy said with a faint smile. "But the guys were really spooked by the weather. Peanut spent the whole time under the bed with Endora." He chuckled. "A couple of times I was tempted to join them."

"Poor babies," Dickce said as she rubbed the Labradoodle's head. "I don't blame them. It was a pretty fierce storm."

"It certainly was," An'gel said.

"The bad thing is," Benjy said, his face darkening, "it's not over. I checked the forecast, and there's another wave of it moving right at us. Should be here within the next hour."

An'gel shuddered. She wasn't sure her nerves, or Dickce's, could take much more of this scary weather.

"From what I could see, there are a lot of limbs down, and the ditches are overflowing," Benjy said. "I guess Willowbank is high enough up it's not in danger of flooding, but we're considerably lower here."

"Do you think we should move up to Willowbank then?" An'gel asked. Benjy's evident uneasiness made her even more nervous.

Benjy nodded. "Yes, ma'am. The radar showed a big system, and it's probably packing a lot of rain and high winds. I think we'd be safer up there."

"All right then." An'gel nodded decisively. "Let's pack up quickly what we need for the night, and put it in the car. We'll drive up there. I don't want to leave the car here and have it washed away."

"I've got my stuff and the guys' food and everything ready," Benjy said. "Just need to load it."

An'gel found her handbag and dug out her keys. She gave them to Benjy. "We'll be out right away."

Twenty minutes later they were all safely inside Willowbank, with the Lexus stowed in the old stables that had been transformed decades ago into a multicar garage. Estelle was grumpy but grudgingly agreed to get a couple of bedrooms ready for them.

"I don't want those animals on the bed, though." She shot a dark look at Benjy. "You make sure they stay on the floor."

"Yes, ma'am," he said.

An'gel, Dickce, along with Benjy and the animals, trooped upstairs after Estelle. She showed the sisters to a bedroom on the second floor, then led Benjy up to the third floor. When she returned to the sisters' room, she carried fresh linens.

"We'll make up the bed," Dickce told her. "I'm sure you have enough to do."

"And we certainly appreciate the hospitality," An'gel said. "We're concerned about the storm that's coming, and we thought Willowbank would be safer than the cottages."

Estelle shrugged. "Don't expect much in the way of dinner. We'll be lucky if the electricity stays on. It was flickering on and off earlier." She walked out of the room.

An'gel and Dickce exchanged glances, then Dickce shrugged. "Even if the lights do go out, I'd rather be here," she said.

"Me, too." An'gel started stripping the bed.

~⁀~

The storm reached Willowbank about an hour later, and the old house shook from the force of it. An'gel and Dickce, along with Benjy, Endora, and Peanut, sought refuge downstairs in a small interior room that served as a den. Once part of a larger space that had been divided in two to allow an extension of the kitchen on the outer side, it was cozy and furnished with overstuffed chairs and two small sofas. The sisters planned to ride out the storm there. They were too nervous to eat anything, but Estelle popped in at one point to tell them food was available in the dining room.

They did not see anyone else, though from Jackson they learned that Horace and Trey were in residence, along with Sondra and Tippy. Richmond Thurston had come back and then had been caught by the storm, and he would be staying the night as well.

Benjy huddled with Peanut and Endora on one sofa while the storm raged, with An'gel and Dickce sitting close together on the other. Conversation was ragged.

The fury of the weather seemed to have chosen Willowbank as its target, or so it seemed to An'gel. The system must have stalled in the area, because the wind and rain lashed the mansion for nearly two hours. Finally, though, the noise began to lessen, the house stopped shivering, and An'gel breathed more easily.

"Thank the Lord, I think it's finally gone," she said.

Dickce nodded weakly. "About time."

"I'm going to check out front," Benjy said. "If the rain really has slacked off, I'm going to let Peanut do his business."

"Good idea," An'gel said. "I'm actually hungry now. Let's go see if there's anything edible in the kitchen, Sister." She got up and motioned for Dickce to join her.

"I'll take Endora with me," Dickce said. "I'm sure she doesn't want to go out and get her paws wet." She took the cat from Benjy, and Endora promptly climbed on Dickce's shoulder.

They all trooped out into the hall. An'gel and Dickce made for the kitchen while Benjy headed to the front door. An'gel and Dickce found the kitchen deserted. An'gel opened the refrigerator door to survey the contents.

"There are some cold cuts here," she said. "A bit of left-over chicken. Guess we can make sandwiches, if there's bread."

Before Dickce could respond, they were both startled by the sudden entrance of Benjy and Peanut. Benjy's face was pale.

"There's a body on the ground in front of the house." His voice quavered. "I think it's Sondra."

CHAPTER 14

Dickce stared at Benjy, uncertain whether she had heard him correctly. "Sondra? Lying out there in the rain?"

Benjy nodded. "Yes, ma'am. It is her. Wearing a blue dress."

Dickce felt a chill run down her spine. Sondra had threatened to wear a blue dress for her bridal gown. Was that the dress she had on?

"Did you check to see if she was alive?" An'gel spoke harshly.

"Yes, ma'am. I checked for a pulse, but there wasn't any." He grimaced. "She's soaking wet. She must have been out there awhile during the storm."

A sudden shriek ripped the air, startling them all. The screaming continued. Endora dug her claws into Dickce's shoulders, then launched herself onto a nearby shelf. Peanut tried to worm his way under the sofa, but it was too low to the floor to allow him. Dickce, An'gel, and Benjy hurried from the room, but Benjy paused long enough to shut the door to keep the animals securely inside. The screaming had begun to diminish in volume, and as they neared the front door, Dickce caught a glimpse of Estelle in the dim light on the verandah, hands over her eyes.

Dickce almost collided with Jackson, hurrying in the same direction, but she managed to swerve just in time. Jackson scuttled over to the wall near the front door and flipped several switches. Light flooded the dark night outside.

Dickce heard loud footsteps on the stairs before she stepped onto the verandah.

"What the hell is going on?" Horace Mims demanded. He pushed past Dickce and the others to stride out the door. He grabbed Estelle and shook her lightly. "What are you screaming about?"

"That." Estelle pointed into the front yard, now brightly lit by floodlights set around the yard and on the front of the house.

"Oh my lord," Horace muttered.

Trey pushed past his father and ran down the steps. He lost his balance and went stumbling onto his hands and knees on the wet lawn.

Dickce stared at the body, a huddled mass, that lay about twenty feet from the verandah, near the center of the yard. She closed her eyes for a moment and prayed that Sondra really wasn't dead, that Benjy had been mistaken.

When she opened her eyes, she saw that Trey was on his feet again, moving more cautiously now. Within seconds he reached the body, and everyone heard his frantic orders to Sondra to wake up and get up off the ground.

There was no response.

By now Horace had reached his son, and he put a hand on the young man's shoulder. Dickce moved to the railing to hear what was being said.

"I don't think there's anything you can do for her now, son," Horace said.

Estelle turned to Dickce and An'gel, who had joined her sister at the railing.

"I tried to warn everyone, but nobody would listen to me." Her expression alarmed Dickce. The woman looked almost triumphant.

"What do you mean?" An'gel demanded.

Estelle flung out her arm and pointed. "That out there. Sondra. Lying there dead, just like Melusine Devereux all those years ago. The mighty storm last night took Sondra up and threw her to the ground, the way it did Melusine. Sondra went out on the balcony to see the storm, and the wind took her."

"That's ridiculous," Dickce snapped, and An'gel echoed her.

Estelle's eyes narrowed. "If you think it's so ridiculous, then why is Sondra lying out there dead in her bridal gown? Just like Melusine Devereux."

Dickce realized that there was little point in trying to reason with the woman, she was so obviously convinced that she was right. Dickce admitted to herself that the circumstances of Sondra's death appeared to be similar to those of Melusine Devereux, but that had to be nothing more than bizarre coincidence.

"I've called 911. The ambulance is on its way, along with the police."

Dickce turned to see Richmond Thurston step onto the

verandah, cell phone in hand. He came to stand beside Dickce and An'gel and stared at Horace and Trey, still beside Sondra's body. Horace was trying to pull his son away from the body, but Trey refused to go.

Dickce was struck by the young man's devotion to Sondra. Perhaps he really had been in love with her. She sighed. Then another thought struck her.

What if his actions now were signs of remorse? According to what An'gel told her, he had made threats yesterday. What if he had argued with Sondra during the storm and thrown her out the window in a rage?

Dickce wanted to pull An'gel aside to talk to her about it, but an interruption put an end to her speculations.

"Whewe is Mommy?" a little voice inquired. "I'm hungwy. I want a dwink of water."

The poor baby, Dickce thought. She mustn't be allowed to see her mother's body out there on the lawn. She moved quickly to intercept Tippy, along with An'gel. Dickce moved in front of the child and bent her face toward Tippy's. "Hi, Tippy. We haven't met yet, but I'm your granny's cousin Dickce, and this is my sister An'gel. Why don't you come with us, and we'll find you something to eat and a glass of water, okay?"

Tippy, still dressed in pajamas and dragging a stuffed bear by the ear, regarded the sisters with a frown.

"Okay," she said after a moment. "I guess that would be okay. Mommy must be busy getting weady for de wedding tomowwow anyway." She turned and headed for the kitchen.

Dickce and An'gel hurried along behind her, exchanging glances as they went.

Dickce breathed a bit more easily once they were in the kitchen. Tippy walked over to the table in the corner and climbed into one of the chairs. She settled the bear in the chair next to her.

"What would you like to eat, Tippy?" An'gel asked.

"I want ceweal," she said. "And a banana and owange juice."

Relieved that the child's choices should be simple ones to fulfill, Dickce started hunting through the cabinets to find cereal and a bowl. An'gel went to the refrigerator and rooted around for milk and orange juice. In short order, they gave Tippy her cereal and orange juice, then Dickce found a banana and peeled it.

"Would you like me to cut it up for you, dear?" she asked.

Tippy nodded. "Yes, pwease." She scooped cereal and milk into her mouth and chewed.

While Dickce cut up the banana, An'gel found a half-full pot of coffee, and she poured cups for herself and Dickce.

Dickce accepted her coffee with a quick smile. She pulled out a chair across from Tippy and sat. An'gel chose a seat at the end of the table, to Dickce's left. They watched the child eat for a moment. Tippy seemed content as she continued to work her way through the bowl of cereal.

Dickce glanced at her watch and realized to her surprise that it was nearly nine o'clock. Why was the child out of bed at this hour? Surely she went to bed earlier than this. Perhaps, Dickce reflected, Estelle's screaming woke her. She certainly didn't appear to be affected by the storm that had passed over.

Dickce noticed that An'gel was fidgeting with her coffee. That meant An'gel was restless, and Dickce knew her sister was anxious to go back to the scene at the front of the house. "Why don't you go check on Benjy?" she suggested. "He might need help."

An'gel stood quickly. "Good idea. You don't mind staying here?"

"Not at all," Dickce said. She loved small children, whereas An'gel felt uneasy around them. She was as curious as An'gel about what was going on out front, but she knew Tippy needed an adult with her and was content to watch her.

An'gel hurried out of the kitchen, and Dickce watched Tippy eat. The child finished her cereal and pushed the bowl away. She reached for the saucer with the pieces of banana and examined them carefully before she chose a piece to pop into her mouth.

"You haven't introduced me to your friend." Dickce nodded at the bear in the chair beside Tippy. "I'd like to say hello to him, but I don't know his name."

"He can't tawk." Tippy stared at her for a moment. "But if you want to say hewwo to him, his name is Wance." She stuck another slice of fruit in her mouth and chewed.

Dickce was in a quandary. Was the bear's name really *Wance*? With the child's lisp, she wasn't sure. Perhaps his name was Lance instead.

"Oh, is he named after your mommy's friend Lance?" Dickce asked.

Tippy giggled. "Yes, Wance is siwwy wike my bear, and that's why I named him Wance." She regarded the bear with affection. "Siwwy bear." She went back to eating her banana slices.

What a dear little thing she is. Dickce's heart ached at the thought of having to explain to the child that her mother was gone and wouldn't ever come back. She knew it was not her place to do it, but unless Jacqueline returned soon, she didn't know who would.

Poor Jacqueline. Dickce ached even more. She couldn't imagine how the loss of a child, even one as difficult as Sondra, would affect a mother. She prayed again that Mireille would recover, but Sondra's death might be too much for Mireille. Then Jacqueline would be doubly bereft.

Dickce mentally shook herself for dwelling on the tragedy. *I need to try to be cheerful for Tippy's sake.* She gave the child a bright smile.

"I like silly bears especially," she said, and Tippy rewarded her with a smile. "Has anyone ever told you the story of a very silly bear named Winnie the Pooh?"

Tippy nodded. "Gweat-gwanny told me about him and Pigwet and Tigger. I wike Pigwet because he's funny. We watched dem on TV, too."

"I bet I know some stories about Winnie and Piglet and Tigger that no one else knows," Dickce said, improvising. "When you finish your banana, how about we go to your room, and I'll tell them to you?"

Tippy nodded. "Yes, pwease. I wuv stowies." She stuffed the two remaining slices in her mouth and chewed rapidly. After she swallowed, she grabbed Lance's ear and got out of her chair.

Dickce insisted on washing Tippy's hands first. The right one was sticky from the banana. Tippy submitted patiently to the washing, and then they left the kitchen. Dickce prayed that she could get the child up the stairs without her seeing any of the activity that by now must be going on outside.

She'd heard the siren of the arriving ambulance not long after she and An'gel entered the kitchen.

To her relief, the front door was closed, and the hall was empty. Tippy scrambled up the stairs ahead of her, poor Lance bouncing on most of them, and Dickce did her best to keep up. Tippy reached the third floor when Dickce had barely made it to the second-floor landing. When she made it up the last flight, she spied Tippy coming out of a door to the right of the stairs.

Tippy had a finger to her lips, and Lance was no longer in evidence. "We has to be quiet," she said in a loud whisper. "Wance is asweep in my woom."

Dickce smiled. "Okay," she whispered back.

Tippy turned and walked slowly into her room. Dickce followed, trying to be quiet, but her shoes squeaked on the polished wooden floorboards. When she stepped into the room after Tippy, she expected to see the bear tucked up in bed.

Instead, to her shock, she found Lance Perigord sound asleep on the floor at the foot of the bed.

CHAPTER 15

An'gel was glad to escape the kitchen. Small children made her nervous, but Dickce didn't seem to mind them at all. An'gel's curiosity wouldn't let her rest until she knew what was happening in the front yard. On the way she said more prayers for Mireille. If her cousin survived to come out of the hospital, she might well collapse again when she learned of her granddaughter's death.

She closed the door behind her when she stepped onto the verandah. There was no point in letting a lot of bugs in the house, and heaven only knew how many had already gotten in. Although, she reflected, the storm might have blown or washed most of them away.

The EMTs were climbing out of the ambulance, and while An'gel watched, a St. Ignatiusville Police squad car came to a halt several feet away from the ambulance. A heavyset man got out of the passenger side, while a tall, much thinner man climbed out from behind the wheel.

Estelle and Jackson stood at the railing, watching the scene unfold. An'gel joined them. Horace, Trey, and Thurston stood in the yard on the gravel path about a dozen feet from where Sondra's body lay. Benjy, she realized, must have gone back to the den to stay with Endora and Peanut.

The EMTs went to work with the body, while the two police officers came up to Horace, Trey, and Thurston. They spoke in low tones, and An'gel was frustrated that she couldn't hear anything.

After a few moments' conversation, Horace jerked his head toward the verandah, then he turned and pointed up at the house. An'gel figured he was pointing out the location of Sondra's room, at the front of the third floor, on the right side if one were facing Willowbank.

An'gel decided to join the men. She walked around the silent Estelle and Jackson and down the steps. As she approached, she heard Horace say, ". . . fascinated by storms. Didn't bother her at all. It would be like her to go out on the balcony to watch."

"Don't reckon on it myself," the heavyset man said. "Pure-dee old dangerous, doing something like that."

"Sondra was fearless," Trey said with a catch in his voice. "I argued with her I don't know how many times not to pull a stupid stunt like that, but she never paid any attention to anything I said." Those last words sounded bitter to An'gel.

"Such a tragic thing," Thurston said. "And on the eve of her wedding." He shook his head dolefully.

The heavyset cop, whose name badge An'gel couldn't

read, nodded. "Yep, just like that Melusine Devereux. Y'all heard tell of that old story?"

Horace nodded. "Just last night, as a matter of fact. The housekeeper was carrying on about it while she was serving dinner. Even said Sondra had chosen the same wedding date as her."

"Well, I'll be," the cop said. "Is that a fact? Downright spooky if you was to ask me."

The taller, younger officer tapped his superior on the arm. "Coroner's just arrived, sir."

The older cop grimaced. "She has, has she? Well, I hope she don't mind getting her dainty little feet muddy, 'cause this is sure messy after all that dang rain. Well, why don't y'all go on up to the house? No point in y'all standing around here while we investigate. I'll let you know what Dr. Kovacs has to say."

Horace, Trey, and Thurston turned away and headed back to the house, but An'gel lingered. She wanted to see the female coroner. She didn't appreciate the officer's attitude toward a professional woman. The officer had his back to An'gel, and she hoped he stayed that way.

A tall, slender, dark-haired woman dressed in a rain slicker and rubber boots came into view and made her way up the path to where the policemen waited.

"Evening, Lieutenant Bugg, Officer Sanford," she said in a clear, confident tone. "What have we got here?"

He would *be named Bugg.* An'gel had to suppress a smile because the man did make her think of a giant beetle somehow.

"Howdy, Dr. Kovacs," Bugg said. "Got a young woman

who was apparently watching the storm up yonder on the third-floor gal'ry. Reckon the wind was so vi'lent it snatched her right off and dropped her down on the ground and killed her."

Dr. Kovacs stared at the policeman with what seemed like polite skepticism to An'gel. She found it rather hard to believe herself. It was simply too bizarre an explanation. The doctor nodded and turned away. She strode over to where the body lay. The EMTs had finished, and one of them waited nearby. After a hurried consultation with him, the coroner approached the body and knelt on the plastic sheet the EMTs had laid beside it.

An'gel kept still, hoping Lieutenant Bugg wouldn't notice her and try to send her back into the house. Unfortunately for her, the younger man, Sanford, spotted her and nudged his superior. Bugg walked over to An'gel.

"Ma'am, there something I can do for you?" he asked. "Nice lady like you shouldn't be standing here looking at something like that." He waved a hand in the direction of Sondra's body. "Why don't you go on back up to the house with the menfolk?"

An'gel did not appreciate the man's patronizing tone. He had at least not called her a *little lady*, as some had done in the past and lived to regret. "I'm simply concerned," she said. "I want to be sure that everything is done properly to find out what happened."

Bugg's face darkened. "I can assure you right here and now, ma'am, we know what we're doing. We don't need nobody standing over us telling us how to do our jobs. So if you don't mind, I think you'd better go back to the house."

He didn't wait for a response. He turned away and walked back over to within about three feet of where the coroner was still examining Sondra's body.

An'gel could cheerfully have snatched off what few hairs the man probably had on that insufferable head of his, but she knew she was in the weaker position in this situation. Her mouth set in a grim line, she marched back up the path and up the steps onto the verandah.

"Let's all go back inside," Richmond Thurston said. He opened the door and motioned for everyone to enter. "Let's let the police and the coroner do their work. Bugg will come and give us an update. I'm sure he'll probably have more questions, too."

"Surely he'll also want to go up to Sondra's bedroom," An'gel said as she stepped into the hallway. She was tempted to go right up herself but knew that she could make things difficult if she did. Still, she was extremely curious about the state of Sondra's bedroom and whether it would yield any information to help explain the girl's bizarre death.

"No doubt he will," Thurston said blandly as he shut the door. He walked with An'gel into the front parlor. "Bugg may look and sound like a hick cop, but he's actually pretty shrewd. If there's anything—odd, shall we say?—about Sondra's death, he'll spot it."

An'gel glanced quickly at the lawyer's face, but his expression was every bit as bland as his tone. Did he suspect foul play? She had to admit to herself that she did. She simply could not believe that Sondra had stood out on the balcony in such a violent storm and been swept off to her death by the wind. If the girl hadn't been dressed in her bridal gown, she might have been less suspicious. A young woman wouldn't expose her wedding dress to the elements like that.

Or would she? An'gel asked herself as she took a seat on the sofa. Had Sondra been so angry that the wedding was being postponed that she had, in a self-destructive fit of temper, put on the gown and deliberately put herself in the storm's path?

No, An'gel decided after a few moments of reflection, Sondra wouldn't have done it. Sondra might, in her self-absorption, do something harmful to another person, but she would never harm herself by such an idiotic gesture.

So caught up with her thoughts as she had been, An'gel failed to notice that only she and Richmond Thurston occupied the front parlor. He sat in a nearby chair, looking at his cell phone.

"Where did everyone else go?" she asked.

The lawyer looked up. "Estelle and Jackson went to the kitchen to make coffee and sandwiches. Horace and Trey went upstairs to check on Tippy."

"I imagine my sister is still with the child," An'gel said. "Surely they aren't going to try to tell her about her mother's death tonight. I should think that could wait until the morning."

"I don't believe they intend to tell her. Horace needs to communicate with Jacqueline first." He grimaced. "Poor Jacqueline. Her mother fighting for her life in the hospital, and her daughter dead in a freak accident."

Loud footsteps and voices raised in anger startled both

An'gel and Thurston before An'gel could reply. She turned her head to see Horace and Trey dragging a struggling Lance Perigord into the room with them.

Trey looked murderous, and Horace was obviously in a rage. An'gel felt sorry for Lance. What could he have done to cause such fury?

"Would you believe what this idiot's just told us?" Horace demanded. "We found him in Tippy's room, of all places. Go on, Lance. Tell them why you were here, hiding in the house."

Lance appeared too frightened to speak. He kept struggling to free himself, but Horace and Trey held on to him. Trey had one of Lance's arms twisted behind his back in an obviously painful position.

"Let the poor man go." An'gel rose from the sofa. "Right this minute. How do you expect him to say anything when you're hurting him like that? Let him go." She put considerable force behind the last three words.

Horace and Trey abruptly released their hold, and Lance stumbled forward, barely missing a table with knickknacks and a vase of artificial flowers. He righted himself and grabbed on to the back of a chair. He glared resentfully at the two men who had dragged him downstairs.

"Now, Lance, they won't do anything else to harm you," An'gel said with a pointed glance at the two men. "You go ahead and tell us why you were hiding in the house. I expect Sondra invited you, didn't she?"

Lance nodded. "Yes, ma'am, she did. I don't see why they had to be so mean to me. I wouldn't be here if Sondra didn't tell me to come over." He rubbed his right shoulder and appeared to have forgotten the point of the conversation.

"Was there a reason she asked you to come here?" An'gel asked.

"My shoulder hurts," Lance said. He focused on An'gel after she spoke his name sharply. "Sondra told me I had to come spend the night here, because we were going to run away and get married in the morning."

CHAPTER 16

An'gel wasn't much surprised by Lance's revelation. She had halfway expected Sondra to elope. Sondra had always wanted to have her way, no matter the cost to anyone else.

Trey let out a stream of foul language, and An'gel wanted to walk over and slap him. There was no excuse for such behavior.

Evidently Horace agreed. "Shut the hell up, boy. Right now."

Trey shut up. He crossed his arms over his chest and glared balefully at his father.

"Oh, sit down, Lance," Horace said wearily. He came over to the sofa and plopped down.

An'gel resumed her seat, curious to see what would happen next.

Lance, still rubbing his shoulder, did what Horace told

him. "I don't see why everybody has to pick on me and order me around. I told Sondra a while ago that once we were married, she couldn't boss me around anymore." He nodded. "I am the man, after all."

Trey hooted with derisive laughter while An'gel gazed at Lance, concerned. Obviously, neither Horace nor Trey had informed Lance of Sondra's death.

Lance flushed red. His hand dropped from his shoulder to join the other in his lap, and he stared down at them.

An'gel glanced at Horace, and he shrugged.

"Lance, I'm afraid there's bad news," An'gel said. "About Sondra."

Lance's head snapped up, and he frowned. "She changed her mind, didn't she?"

"No, she didn't," An'gel said. "I'm afraid Sondra is dead, Lance."

He shook his head. "No, she can't be. Unless *he* killed her." He pointed suddenly at Trey. "He's jealous because Sondra wanted to marry me and told him to go away and leave her alone."

"Why, you—" Trey let out another string of obscenities, but Horace told him to shut up again, and he did.

Horace faced Lance. "I'm sorry, son, but Miss An'gel here is right. Sondra's dead. We reckon she went out on the balcony during the storm, and the wind must have picked her up and dropped her on the ground."

Lance made a face, as if he'd smelled something rotten. "That's crazy. It's like that old story my granny used to tell me about a girl in St. Ignatiusville who died that way. I bet you're making it up because you don't want anybody to know Trey killed her." He stood and picked up the vase he'd nearly knocked to the floor only minutes ago. He threw it toward Trey, but the vase fell about a foot short of its mark. It shattered on the floor near Trey's feet.

Before anyone could intervene, Trey stepped over the debris toward Lance and decked him with a punch. Lance went down and stayed down. Horace jumped up and grabbed his son.

Thurston got up and went over to the fallen young man. He got down on one knee and checked Lance's eyes. "Out cold," he said. "Better get the EMTs in here. He could have a bad concussion. Trey hit him pretty hard." He stood and then strode out of the parlor.

An'gel heard the front door open and close. She stared at Horace, who was still visibly restraining his son from attacking Lance again.

She stood. "Young man, you had better control yourself and that temper of yours. If Lance is seriously hurt, you could find yourself in jail for assault. I will be happy to serve as a witness on his behalf. No matter what he said or did, there was no cause to hit him like that. You could have killed him."

Trey appeared stunned at An'gel's words, while Horace glared at her.

Thurston reappeared then, preceded by a couple of EMTs.

Horace hustled Trey out of the room while the EMTs examined Lance. An'gel kept out of the way but watched with keen interest. She was worried about Lance because Trey, as muscular as he was, had hit Lance hard enough to cause serious damage.

One of the EMTs spoke into his walkie-talkie and asked for a gurney. Finished, he looked up at Thurston. "We're taking him in. Probably a concussion but there could be internal bleeding, considering he was hit as hard as you said. Are you related?"

"No," the lawyer said. "I know his family, however, and I'll get in touch with them and tell them to meet you at the ER."

"Thanks," the EMT said. His coworkers came through the door with a gurney and other equipment, and An'gel watched while they got Lance ready to make the journey to the hospital. She said prayers for Lance as well as for Mireille and Jacqueline.

An'gel felt exhausted. She was a bit shaky as well. Reaction from all the dramatic events had begun to set in. She decided her presence wasn't necessary, and she slipped out of the room and went to the den. She opened the door with care, in case Benjy and the animals were asleep.

She found the room empty, to her disappointment, but she spotted a piece of paper lying on a sofa pillow. She went over, picked it up, and quickly scanned its contents. Benjy had taken Endora and Peanut back to their cottage, going the back way to avoid the activity out front. The animals were hungry and restless and had to relieve themselves. They would remain there unless An'gel wanted them to come back to Willowbank.

An'gel crumpled the note and dropped it into a small, decorative wastebasket beside the sofa. She gazed longingly at the sofa, wanting to lie down and take a nap. She knew, however, she had better get something to eat. She was hungry and feeling a bit weak.

She left the den and went to the kitchen, where she found Jackson and Estelle making sandwiches.

"Miss An'gel, can I get you something?" Jackson asked the moment he spotted her. "I reckon you must be truly peckish by now."

An'gel smiled at the old-fashioned expression. "I truly am peckish," she said. "I'd love a couple of those sandwiches and some hot coffee right about now."

Estelle paid no attention, apparently intent on her task. Jackson smiled and said, "You just come on over to the table over here and set yourself down. We've got chicken or ham."

"I'll take one of each," An'gel said as she walked over to the table and chose a chair. "Thank you so much, Jackson." She would have been happy to help herself, but she knew the old man's feelings would be hurt if he wasn't allowed to take care of her. He must be drooping with exhaustion by now himself.

She said as much to him when he set a plate with the sandwiches and a cup of coffee down in front of her.

"I'm okay, Miss An'gel. I had me a little nap a while ago." He shook his head. "All this bad stuff wears me out, and sometimes I have to sit down and rest my eyes a bit."

"I know what you mean," An'gel said. "I was considering taking a nap in the den a few minutes ago, but I decided I was hungrier than I was sleepy."

Jackson nodded. "Have you heard anything more from Miss Jacqueline about Miss Mireille?"

"No, I haven't," An'gel said. She realized then that she had left her handbag in the den all this time. Jacqueline might have tried to call but An'gel had been nowhere near her phone. She got up. "I left my phone in the den. I'll go get it and see if Jacqueline has called."

"You let me do that, Miss An'gel," Jackson said. "You need to eat. I'll be right back."

An'gel nodded and thanked him. After he left the room, she kept an eye on Estelle and began working on a ham sandwich. The housekeeper seemed lost in a world of her own, An'gel decided. She picked up her cup for a sip of coffee.

Estelle spoke suddenly. "Mireille's dead."

An'gel was so startled she nearly spilled coffee all over herself. She set the cup on the table with an unsteady hand.

"When did you find out?" An'gel asked, her heart heavy with sorrow. She wished the housekeeper hadn't announced it so abruptly. "Jacqueline must have called."

"Nobody called," Estelle said.

Taken aback, An'gel couldn't speak for a moment. Then she found her voice. "If nobody called, how do you know that Mireille has died?"

Estelle shrugged. "I just know, that's all."

An'gel spoke sharply, nettled by the housekeeper's casual tone. "I'm sorry, but I find that hard to believe."

"Doesn't matter to me what you believe," Estelle said indifferently. "I know what I know."

"When did it happen?" *If you know so much*, An'gel wanted to add but decided it was better not to.

"A couple of hours ago, during the worst of the storm." Estelle put down the knife she was using to slice the ham and turned to face An'gel. "If you must know, Mireille and I have been close for years, like sisters. I felt it when her soul left her body."

Estelle spoke with such calm assurance that An'gel experienced twinges of doubt. She had heard people say

127

similar things all her life, and sometimes they turned out to be right about a tragic event. She hoped fervently that this was not one of those times and that Estelle was completely wrong.

The housekeeper turned away as if she neither expected nor needed a response, and that chilled An'gel even more. Estelle went back to carving the ham.

Jackson came back then with An'gel's handbag. She thanked him as she accepted it. She wondered if Estelle had shared her revelation with the butler. She thought Estelle hadn't because Jackson would surely have been agitated.

An'gel rummaged in her bag for the phone. She pulled it out and glanced at the screen. She didn't see the small symbol that alerted her to voice mail messages, nor did she see the symbol for a text message. She dropped the phone back in her bag and set it on the floor beside her. "No calls," she said before she picked up her sandwich and resumed eating.

Jackson smiled. "Then I reckon that's good news." He started arranging sandwiches on a silver serving tray.

An'gel felt better with food and coffee in her stomach, but at the same time she felt uneasy. Try and dismiss them as she might, she found Estelle's words unsettling. Did the woman really have some kind of psychic bond with Mireille?

Horace hurried into the room and startled them all. "Jackson, can you put a couple of those sandwiches in a bag for me, and get me a travel mug with coffee? I'm going to go to the hospital. I can't get Jacqueline to answer her phone, and I've got to see her before she comes home."

"Yes sir, Mr. Horace," Jackson said. "I'll have it ready for you in a couple of minutes."

"Thanks," Horace said. He looked really worried, An'gel decided. Was it truly because Jacqueline wasn't responding to his calls, or was it because of his son's violent behavior? He'd better be praying that Lance wasn't seriously hurt and that Trey hadn't had any hand in Sondra's death.

CHAPTER 17

The back door opened, and Peanut bounded into the kitchen, pulling Benjy behind him. Endora struggled to maintain her perch on Benjy's shoulder, and Benjy winced. Endora must have dug her claws in to keep from falling, An'gel realized.

"Peanut, bad boy. Halt." Benjy held firmly to the leash, and the labradoodle stopped. "Now sit." Peanut sat.

Benjy set down the large canvas tote he held in his free hand. Endora scrambled down from his shoulder and climbed into the bag.

"Just look at that mud you tracked in here." Estelle glared as she pointed to Peanut's tracks on the linoleum. "I don't have time to go mopping the floor at this time of night. What were you thinking, bringing that filthy dog in here with mud all over him?"

"I'll clean it up." An'gel rose from the table and walked

over to Benjy. She patted Peanut's head, and his tail thumped the floor. "Where's the mop?"

Estelle indicated a door behind the table. "In there. Bucket and rags, too. Help yourself." She turned to Jackson. "You'd better get a move on and get those sandwiches to Horace. He'll be in a tearing hurry to get to the hospital."

An'gel thought Estelle might make a comment alluding to Mireille's death, but she didn't. She wiped her hands on a dish cloth and then hurried out of the room. Jackson busied himself preparing Horace's requested meal.

"I'll mop up," Benjy told An'gel. I should have wiped Peanut's feet before we came in the kitchen, but I was in too big a hurry to talk to you.

"Is something wrong at the cottages?" An'gel frowned. "Were they damaged during the storm?"

"Everything seemed okay," Benjy said. "The electricity is off down there, though. Good thing I had a flashlight." He shrugged as he looked around the well-lit kitchen. "Guess they're on a different circuit. I'm glad we're going to stay here tonight."

"Yes, me, too." An'gel didn't relish spending the night in a cottage without electricity either.

Benjy rummaged in the canvas tote and brought out an old towel. Endora grabbed at it with her front paws, evidently not happy at being disturbed. She settled down in the bag after Benjy knelt nearby to clean off the dog's dirty feet.

"I'll be back in a minute, Miss An'gel," Jackson said. "Y'all let me know if there's anything you need." He smiled at Benjy. "I bet you wouldn't mind a couple of these here sandwiches."

"No, sir, I sure wouldn't," Benjy said. "Thank you. As soon as I get the floor cleaned, I'll help myself."

Jackson nodded and headed out of the kitchen with the food and drink Horace had requested earlier.

Alone now in the kitchen with Benjy and the animals, An'gel resumed her seat to finish her sandwich and coffee. While Benjy competently and quickly cleaned Peanut's muddy paw prints from the floor, she told him about the unpleasant scenes he had missed.

Benjy winced when An'gel related the part where Trey decked Lance with a punch. "A friend of mine in California got sucker-punched like that once," he said. "Caused brain damage and everything. Besides getting hit in the face, he fell against a table and banged his head really hard against the edge."

"How terrible," An'gel said. "How much of his normal functions did he recover?"

Benjy put the mop and bucket in the closet and shut the door. "About ninety percent, I'd say. He never was quite the same afterwards. It was really tough to watch him struggle with things, like talking." He shook his head. "Poor guy. I hope Lance does better."

He went to the sink to wash his hands before helping himself to sandwiches and milk. An'gel watched him but her mind was suddenly elsewhere. For a few minutes she had been able to banish Estelle's startling announcement from her thoughts, but now it came back to unsettle her again. She prayed the housekeeper was wrong, simply the victim of an overactive imagination and a pessimistic heart.

Jackson returned from his errand with an announcement. "The police are heading upstairs to Miss Sondra's room. I sure hope they don't make too much noise and wake up Miss Tippy, or Miss Dickce'll never get her to sleep again."

"I think I'll go up and check on Dickce and Tippy," An'gel said. She picked up her phone but left her handbag on the table. "Benjy, once you're done eating, I think you'd better stay downstairs until the police are finished on the third floor."

Benjy nodded. "Better to keep the guys out of the way." Endora was still napping in the tote bag while Peanut stretched out under the table, his head near Benjy's feet.

An'gel realized she probably hadn't fooled her ward with her stated intention of checking on Dickce and Tippy. Benjy knew her well enough by now to know that she would also want to see what was going on in Sondra's bedroom. And since Sondra's bedroom was near the third-floor landing, she would have to pass it to get to Tippy's bedroom at the back of the house.

An'gel climbed slowly, thinking about the manner of Sondra's death. No matter how hard she tried, she couldn't really believe that it was an accident. The whole story of Melusine Devereux was too coincidental, and An'gel wondered vaguely if it had given someone an idea about making a murder look like a freak accident.

As she neared the third floor, An'gel heard the murmur of voices coming from Sondra's bedroom. She stepped onto the landing and moved cautiously closer to the door. When she peered inside, she almost cried out in shock.

The storm had wrought destruction through the doors that opened onto the gallery. The furnishings had been moved about, pictures knocked off the wall, small tables and chairs overturned, and water—there was water on the floor, in the sodden rugs and bedclothes and in Sondra's clothes flung about the room. An'gel felt sick over the damage to the room and to the antiques it contained, then felt ashamed of herself for being more upset about the room and its contents than about its occupant.

"Can we do something for you, ma'am?" the younger, taller cop called out to An'gel from where he stood with his superior just inside the room by the French doors onto the gallery.

"No, only looking," An'gel said. "I can't believe the amount of destruction in this room." She shook her head, still aghast at the damage.

"Well, I reckon this is what happens when you leave the doors open during a vi'lent storm," Bugg said in a pompous tone. "Girl couldn't'a been in her right mind going out there like that and standing on the gal'ry. No wonder the wind swooped her up like that."

"Are you sure that's what happened?" An'gel asked sharply. "Doesn't that seem peculiar to you?"

Bugg smiled as he walked toward An'gel. "Now, ma'am, what else you reckon could'a happened here?" He waved a hand to indicate the state of the room. "Her stepdaddy and his son done told us she liked to stand out there during a storm. She was lucky it didn't happen to her before now."

In the face of this irritating condescension, An'gel felt her temper rise rapidly. "Don't you think it strange that she was standing out there in a storm wearing her wedding dress?" An'gel put heavy emphasis on the last two words.

Bugg looked confused. "Weddin' dress?" He shook his head. "She was wearing a blue dress, as I recall. You trying to tell me she was gonna get married in a blue dress? Never heard tell of such."

"Sondra and her grandmother argued over an antique wedding gown that Mireille wanted her to wear. Sondra didn't want to wear it, however, and said she would wear a blue dress instead." An'gel went on to explain briefly what happened to the antique gown and the consequences of Sondra's destructive act.

"I can't believe that girl would do something like that to Miss Mireille," Bugg said. "Miss Mireille's the sweetest lady in the world."

"My youngest sister went to school with the deceased," Sanford said with a grimace. "Said she—the deceased, that is—could be real spiteful if she didn't get her way. All the girls was scared of her and didn't dare cross her. Don't surprise me a bit she'd do something like that, even to her own grandma."

An'gel didn't need further evidence of Sondra's self-absorption. She wanted the policemen to consider the idea that Sondra hadn't died in a freak accident.

"Back to the point about the wedding dress," she said. "I think it's highly unlikely Sondra would have stood out there during a storm in the dress she intended to wear at her wedding."

"Maybe you got a point," Bugg said. "But if it wasn't no accident, then are you saying somebody pushed her over during the storm?"

An'gel smiled grimly. "I'm not saying that's what actually happened, but I think you ought to consider the possibility."

Sanford shook his head. "No, ma'am, I don't think that can be right."

"What do you mean?" Bugg asked.

"All you gotta do is look at where the body was lying," Sanford said. "It was too far out from the house. If somebody'd pushed her over the railing, or even picked her up and dropped her, she would've landed much closer to the house." He looked smug at his own reasoning. "So the wind must've picked her up and dropped her where she was, away from the house."

An'gel had to admit, if only to herself, Sanford made a good point. The location of Sondra's body did complicate her theory. She had a potential answer, however.

"The wind might not have plucked her off the gallery," An'gel said. "But it could have moved her body after she had fallen. Don't you think that's possible?"

Bugg thought about it a moment, then shrugged. "Maybe. I reckon we'll have to give it some thought. What I want to know, though, is why would someone kill her?"

"That, Officer Bugg, is your job to find out." An'gel smiled tiredly, suddenly exhausted by the effort of talking with the policemen and overwhelmed by the chaos of Sondra's room. "Now, if you'll excuse me, I need to go check on my sister, who is looking after little Tippy." She turned and walked down the hall and pretended not to hear a rude comment from Bugg about *nosy old biddies*.

CHAPTER 18

Her shoulders slumped as she trod the hallway toward the back of the house where Tippy's bedroom lay, An'gel knew she would have to seek out her own bed soon. All the stress of the day and the adrenalin released by multiple incidents had left her dragging. Before she went to her room downstairs, however, she wanted to talk to Dickce.

The door was shut, and An'gel knocked lightly so as not to startle her sister when she entered. Inside the room, she discovered she need not have bothered. Dickce sat, sound asleep, in a rocker near the bed. Tippy lay asleep on her stomach, one arm thrown over Lance the teddy bear.

An'gel hated to wake her peacefully reposed sister but she knew Dickce ought to eat something before bed. She could sit and watch over Tippy while Dickce went downstairs. A little nap in the rocker wouldn't keep her from falling asleep in her bed a little later—not as tired as she was.

Dickce roused easily when An'gel lay a hand on her shoulder. She stared blankly up at An'gel for a moment, then her vision cleared and she whispered, "Have you heard anything from the hospital?"

An'gel shook her head. "Come out into the hall with me for a minute." When she opened the door and looked out, she spotted two heads disappearing down the stairs.

Dickce followed her out, and with the door nearly shut behind them, An'gel told her sister about Estelle's claim that Mireille had died earlier during the storm.

Dickce's eyes widened in disbelief. "That's a load of bull hockey, Sister. Surely you don't believe her?"

"I certainly don't want to," An'gel said sharply, "but you know as well as I do, sometimes these things happen. Remember how Vidalia Williams always knew before anyone else when someone in Athena had passed on?"

"She was on the front porch at Riverhill with a casserole before we even called the doctor for Mama." Dickce shivered. "I'll never forget that. We'll just have to pray that Estelle's simply looking for attention. She likes to shock people."

"I have been praying that," An'gel said. "I have more to tell you, but it can wait till morning. I'm exhausted, and you must be starving by now. Why don't you go downstairs and get something to eat? Estelle and Jackson made a stack of sandwiches. I'll stay here with Tippy for a while."

Dickce patted her stomach. "It does feel a bit empty in there. Thanks." She turned to leave, but then turned back. "I'm going to ask Benjy to change rooms with me. I'll feel better if I'm up here close to Tippy." She grimaced. "I can't sleep in that chair all night, but if I leave both our doors open, I'll hear her if she gets up during the night."

"Or what's left of it," An'gel muttered. "That sounds like a good idea."

Dickce departed, and An'gel went back into Tippy's room. A nightlight glowed softly near the bed, and An'gel thought Tippy did look angelic in her sleep. She wondered how much of her personality Tippy had inherited from her mother. Not much, An'gel hoped. The last thing they needed was a demanding toddler running around the house.

She lowered herself into the rocker and after a moment closed her eyes and began to rock slowly. She remembered her mother rocking her when she was little, and how comforting that was. She had gone to sleep happily in her mother's arms in that old rocker. She had it in her own bedroom now. Soon the rocking slowed, and An'gel drifted into sleep.

❧

When An'gel stepped into Tippy's room and closed the door, Dickce moved quickly to the front of the house. She wanted to peek inside Sondra's bedroom.

She gasped in shock when she witnessed the extent of the devastation. The French doors to the gallery were shut now, and Dickce figured the police must have closed them. She stared at the mess for a few moments longer, then forced herself to move away. Her rumbling stomach reminded her that she needed food.

At the foot of the stairs on the first floor she met Jackson, carrying a mop and bucket, with several towels tucked under one arm.

Upon her inquiry Jackson explained that he was going to Sondra's room to mop up the water. "Got to keep it from ruining the floor," he said.

Dickce nodded, and Jackson stepped past her. She wondered at the police not bothering to close off Sondra's room. They must be satisfied that Sondra's death was an accident. She, like her sister, thought it too bizarre to be believable.

She found Benjy in the kitchen with Endora and Peanut. The cat climbed out of the tote bag to come hop into Dickce's lap, where she turned around several times before finally curling up and closing her eyes. Dickce wasn't fond of cat hair on her good clothes, but she didn't have the heart to dislodge Endora.

Benjy insisted on serving her, nodding at the napping cat. "You don't want to disturb her by getting up. I'll get whatever you want."

While Benjy prepared her food—after washing his hands, she was pleased to note—Dickce told him her plan to switch bedrooms with him. He offered to transfer her things to the third floor, and she thanked him. Even restored somewhat by food, she still didn't feel like going up and down those stairs any more than necessary.

Peanut followed Benjy out of the kitchen, but Endora remained in Dickce's lap. Dickce polished off her sandwich quickly, drained the glass of milk, and then gently dislodged the cat while she put her dishes in the sink. Endora followed her back and forth, and Dickce nearly stepped on her once.

Her cleanup finished, Dickce leaned down and scooped the cat into her arms. "Come on, missy, let's get back upstairs. I suppose you'll want to sleep with me tonight."

Endora purred and rubbed her head against the underside of Dickce's chin. Dickce took that for the feline equivalent of "yes." She carried the cat upstairs, puffing slightly by the time she reached the third-floor landing. She paused for a moment to listen. She heard Jackson working in Sondra's room.

Resisting the temptation to look inside again, Dickce moved down the hallway to the back bedroom opposite Tippy's room. When she turned on the light, she saw her things on the bed. She deposited the cat on the pillow and admonished Endora to stay there. "I won't be long, I promise."

Endora blinked and meowed, then started her routine of turning round and round on the pillow, kneading it into the proper shape before she settled down. Dickce smiled as she pulled the door shut behind her.

In Tippy's room she found An'gel snoring lightly in the rocker. Tippy still slept soundly. Dickce shook An'gel gently awake, and An'gel leaned forward, yawning. She pushed herself up on the arms of the chair and stretched.

The sisters exchanged whispered "good nights" and An'gel headed for her room on the second floor. Dickce stood watching Tippy for a few moments to satisfy herself that the child was still asleep. Then she moved quietly out of the room, leaving the door slightly ajar, and crossed the hall to her room.

She undressed and changed into a nightgown, then made one last visit to the bathroom next door before climbing into bed and turning off the lamp. Endora protested sleepily when Dickce dislodged her in order to pull down the bedspread, then the cat settled once more on the pillow beside Dickce's.

Dickce turned onto her side facing the door, with the

cat behind her. As she spied the open door and heard the cat purring, Dickce realized that there could be a problem if Endora decided to go exploring during the night. She debated briefly taking the cat downstairs to Benjy's room but then decided Endora would probably stay with her. Anyway, she was too tired to traipse up and down the stairs again tonight. Minutes later, she was asleep.

Dickce heard a cat meowing somewhere close by, and the sound woke her. At first she thought she had dreamed it, but then she turned her head to check on Endora. The cat wasn't on the bed.

The cat meowed again, and this time Dickce realized the sound came from out in the hall. She groaned as she thrust the covers aside and got out of bed. She hoped Endora wasn't in Tippy's room, trying to engage the child in play. The last thing she needed right now was to have to settle Tippy down again.

Dickce stepped into the hall and glanced around. Someone had turned most of the floodlights off, but at least one cast a dim light into the hallway. She started to cross the hall to Tippy's room when she heard Endora meow again. This time she also heard a scratching sound.

Dickce gazed toward the front of the house and spotted a small dark shape at the closed door of Sondra's room. Endora was scratching and meowing, wanting entrance. Dickce hurried forward, calling out softly. "Endora, stop that. Bad kitty. Come here to me."

Endora turned to gaze in Dickce's direction but evidently was not to be deterred from her occupation of scratching at the door and meowing.

Dickce reached the cat and picked her up at the same

instant the door swung open. Startled, Dickce took a step back.

Trey Mims, still dressed in his day clothes, glared furiously at Dickce and Endora. "Go away and leave me alone." He shut the door hard.

Dickce frowned at the young man's rudeness and started to turn away. Then she stopped.

What was Trey Mims doing in Sondra's bedroom in the middle of the night?

CHAPTER 19

When An'gel awoke that morning, she was disoriented for a moment by the unfamiliar surroundings. Then her brain cleared, and she remembered where she was. A glance at her watch on the bedside table informed her that it was a few minutes before seven. She got out of bed and padded over to the window to pull back the curtains from the French doors. The sun was up, and it promised to be a fair day. Not a cloud in the sky from what she could see.

An'gel checked the floor of the gallery and noted that it looked dry enough. She opened the doors and stepped outside. The cool, clear air woke her further, and she moved to the waist-high railing.

She glanced down at the front lawn at the spot where Sondra's body had lain, and she sighed. The events of the previous day flooded her memory, and all at once she felt the full weight of her eighty-four years. With a heavy heart she closed her eyes and said another prayer for Mireille.

She left the French doors open while she went to shower in the bathroom next door. The hot water eased the ache in her shoulders, and she felt more ready to face the day by the time she finished dressing and putting on her makeup. The cool air coming in off the gallery refreshed her as well. She was ready by seven thirty. As she walked down the stairs, she wondered what news she would hear.

The dining room was empty, and there were no dishes on the sideboard. An'gel wasn't all that surprised, given the chaos of the day before. She would be perfectly happy to fix her own breakfast if Estelle wasn't up to it.

In the kitchen she found the housekeeper busy at the stove. The aroma of frying bacon tantalized An'gel's taste buds, and she smelled biscuits baking in the oven.

"Good morning, Estelle," An'gel said. "Is there anything I can do to help?"

"Not a blessed thing," Estelle said. "I'm perfectly capable of doing my job, thank you. Got off to a late start this morning, but food'll be ready in about ten minutes." She scowled at the frying pan.

An'gel decided to let the rudeness pass, at least for now. "Are Jacqueline and Horace back from the hospital, do you know?"

"They're back." Estelle flipped several strips of bacon with a spatula. She continued in a tone devoid of emotion. "Got in around two. I expect they won't be down to breakfast, although Jacqueline has to start making the arrangements for Mireille and Sondra."

An'gel felt the last words as if Estelle had struck her in the face. She had hoped the housekeeper was completely wrong about Mireille's death. Now the reality began to set in, and her eyes began to well.

"Excuse me," she muttered as she turned away and fumbled for the tissue she had tucked in her sleeve.

"Told you last night," Estelle said. "I could tell you didn't believe me. Makes no difference, though. I know a lot of things, but nobody ever pays any attention to me." She chuckled, and then the chuckle turned into a deep-throated laugh.

An'gel turned to look at the housekeeper. She was taken aback by the woman's evident mirth. What could possibly be so funny? She hoped Estelle wasn't about to get hysterical, although if she did, An'gel would take pleasure in throwing a glass of water in her face to calm her down.

"What kind of things are you talking about?" An'gel asked in a neutral tone.

Estelle shot her a sly glance. "Just things. Things people don't think I know. Now that Mireille's gone, I have to look after myself, because there sure isn't anybody else going to."

An'gel wanted to press Estelle further, because the housekeeper's boastful tone made her uneasy. An'gel thought Estelle's words sounded like a veiled blackmail threat.

"I'd be careful if I were you." The words came out more sharply than An'gel intended. "All this talk about 'knowing things' could get you into a difficult situation."

Estelle turned to face her. "I don't need any advice from you. Why don't you mind your own business and go to the dining room? Breakfast will be ready soon."

An'gel decided she'd had enough. If the woman wouldn't listen to good advice, there was nothing more she could do. She turned and walked out of the kitchen without bothering to reply. At any other time she would discuss the housekeeper's rudeness with Jacqueline, but An'gel didn't want to add to her goddaughter's burdens. She was mighty curious about the things Estelle claimed to know and wondered how the housekeeper planned to make use of her so-called knowledge.

Perhaps she ought to discuss the matter with Horace. An'gel considered that option as she made her way to the dining room. But what if Horace was the object of Estelle's plans? For once she was unsure what to do, an unusual state for her. She finally decided she would discuss the matter with Dickce before she took any action.

She met Benjy and Peanut at the foot of the stairs.

"Morning, Miss An'gel." Benjy smiled. "I hope you had a good night. Peanut and I sure did. I guess Endora spent the night with Miss Dickce."

"I slept well once I finally got to bed." An'gel patted the dog's head, and Peanut's tail thumped against the floor. "Breakfast will be ready before long."

"Good," Benjy said, "because I'm starving. I'm going to take Peanut out for a few minutes, though, and then give him his breakfast. We won't be long."

An'gel nodded and watched as young man and dog opened the front door and stepped out onto the verandah. She sighed. What it would be like to be that age again. Then she shook her head. No use pining after long-spent youth.

"Good morning, Sister."

An'gel glanced up the stairs to see Dickce and Endora coming down toward her. The cat moved as sedately as Dickce, as if she were escorting the woman. An'gel smiled briefly and returned the greeting.

"Any news?" Dickce asked when she and Endora reached the bottom.

"Afraid so," An'gel said. "Mireille did pass away last night."

Dickce closed her eyes for a moment. An'gel squeezed her sister's arm, and Dickce opened her eyes, blinking back tears. An'gel felt the cat rub against her legs. She looked down, and she would have sworn Endora was looking at her with sympathy.

"Breakfast should be ready in a few minutes," An'gel said. "Let's go into the dining room. I have a few things to tell you."

"I have a few things to tell you, too," Dickce said.

"What about Tippy?" An'gel asked. She had almost forgotten the child.

"Jacqueline is with her," Dickce said. "Sound asleep on the bed with her when I looked in earlier."

An'gel could only hope that Jacqueline found some solace in the company of her grandchild. Jacqueline faced bitter days ahead as she grieved for her mother and her daughter.

The sisters met Jackson coming out of the dining room. He looked at them with sorrow-filled eyes. He tried to speak, but couldn't. An'gel and Dickce each took a hand and held it tightly.

"I just can't believe Miss Mireille's gone." Jackson's voice was rough with grief. "Known her since she was a little bitty girl."

"I know," An'gel said softly. She had to keep it together, or all three of them would be crying any minute now. "She thought the world of you. Be strong now, for her sake. That's all any of us can do."

Jackson attempted a smile. "Thank you, Miss An'gel." He sighed deeply. "There's coffee ready in the dining room now. I'll go see if Miss Estelle's ready to bring out the food."

The sisters gave his hands one last squeeze and released him. An'gel watched him as he walked, shoulders slumped and head down, toward the kitchen.

"I hope Jacqueline and Horace will take good care of him," Dickce said.

"I'm sure they will," An'gel said. "I imagine Mireille provided for him." Her tone turned brisk. "I don't know about you, but I could certainly use some coffee right about now." She headed into the dining room.

Dickce and Endora trailed behind her. The cat began to meow when An'gel poured coffee for herself and her sister.

"She's hungry," Dickce said. "I'd better find Benjy and get her food; otherwise, she'll keep talking and complaining." She glanced fondly at the cat.

"Benjy took Peanut out just before you came down," An'gel said as she took a seat at the table. "They should be back any minute now."

"Did you hear that, Endora?" Dickce looked down at the cat. "Benjy will be here soon, and he'll find your food, okay?"

Endora looked up at Dickce and meowed again, with what An'gel thought sounded like an interrogative tone.

Dickce nodded and said, "Yes, really."

Endora settled down by Dickce's chair.

"I swear she understands what you told her," An'gel said.

"Of course she does," Dickce said. "Endora is very smart."

Benjy's entrance with Peanut diverted An'gel from the tart reply she intended to make. Instead she said to Benjy, "We have a hungry cat on our hands."

Benjy grinned. "I'll take care of that. Come on, Endora, let's go upstairs and get you some breakfast." The cat ran over to him and jumped into his arms. "I fed Peanut already," Benjy said. "I'll be back in a few minutes."

Boy and animals disappeared from the dining room, and the sisters enjoyed their coffee. An'gel wondered how much longer breakfast would be. While they waited, she quickly told Dickce about her conversation with Estelle.

"Strange," Dickce said. She was about to comment further when the object of the conversation wheeled a serving trolley into the room and began to put large covered dishes on the sideboard, along with a stack of plates and silverware.

"Help yourselves," Estelle said. "Napkins are in the drawer." She wheeled the trolley out again.

"She is one of the most graceless persons I have ever known," An'gel said when she thought the housekeeper was out of earshot.

"I don't know how Mireille put up with her for so long," Dickce said as she got up from the table and moved to the sideboard.

An'gel joined her, and they began to help themselves to scrambled eggs, biscuits, and bacon. "So what do you think? Should I talk to Horace about what she said to me?"

"Talk to Horace about what?"

An'gel turned to see Jacqueline, with Tippy in her arms, in the doorway of the dining room.

An'gel thought furiously. She didn't want to tell Jacqueline about Estelle's ominous words. What could she tell her instead?

CHAPTER 20

"A car for Benjy," An'gel said quickly, almost stumbling over the words. "Sister and I have been thinking about getting a second car so Benjy can get back and forth to classes when he starts at Athena College in the spring."

"Yes," Dickce said. "Since Horace knows more about cars than anyone we know, we thought he'd be the best person to ask." She flashed Jacqueline a bright smile.

An'gel silently blessed her sister for the quick support. Jacqueline shrugged, seemingly satisfied with the answer. An'gel looked more closely at her goddaughter. She was not surprised to see how tired and worn Jacqueline appeared. The poor girl didn't seem to have slept much, if at all, since she arrived home from the hospital.

Tippy, on the other hand, seemed rested and raring to go. "Wet me down, Gwanny," she said, wriggling. Jacqueline set her down, and Tippy immediately went to the table and found a chair for the teddy bear. "Wance will sit here. I want some scwambud eggs, Gwanny, and Wance does, too."

"Okay, sweetheart," Jacqueline said in a lackluster tone. "I'll fix a plate for you and one for Lance."

"Why don't you sit and let me do that?" An'gel asked. She wanted to wrap her arms around Jacqueline and hold her close, but she feared that they would both dissolve into help-less tears.

"Thank you," Jacqueline said. She slid into a chair and leaned back. "I'm exhausted, but there's so much to do." She glanced at Tippy and then back at An'gel. "I would like to talk to you in a little while about a few things."

"Yes, of course," An'gel replied as she prepared a plate for Tippy. Jacqueline obviously didn't want to discuss the deaths in front of her granddaughter. An'gel took the plate with eggs, a couple of slices of bacon, and one biscuit to the table and set it in front of Tippy.

"Thank you," Tippy said. "Wance wants his bweak-fast, too."

"Here it is, dear." Dickce set an identical serving in front of the teddy bear.

Tippy beamed up at her. "Wance says 'thank you.'"

"He's welcome," Dickce replied with a smile. She went back to the sideboard for a second helping.

In the meanwhile An'gel had poured small glasses of milk for Tippy and her bear. After depositing those on the table, she fixed a plate for Jacqueline and one for herself. Seated, she covertly watched her goddaughter across the table as Jacqueline toyed with her food, taking an occasional bite, but mostly pushing the eggs around on the plate.

An'gel, usually capable in any situation, felt uncertain

at the moment. There were things she wanted to discuss with Jacqueline but she couldn't until Tippy was out of earshot. She concentrated on her food.

Benjy entered the room moments later alone. At An'gel's look of inquiry, he said, "I thought it would be better if they stayed upstairs while I ate. I'll take them down to the cottage in a little while and see if the lights are back on yet."

"Good plan," An'gel said.

Jacqueline acknowledged Benjy's presence with a wan smile. Tippy stared at the young man as if fascinated.

An'gel realized Benjy was a stranger to the little girl. "Tippy, dear, this is Benjy." She paused. "Benjy, this is Tippy, Jacqueline's granddaughter."

Benjy approached Tippy and held out his hand. "Good morning, Tippy. How are you?"

The child smiled shyly at Benjy as she took his hand. "Wance and I are eating bweakfuss, but then we want to pway. Will you pway with us?"

Benjy looked startled but quickly smiled. "I'd love to play with you and, uh, Wance." He reached over and patted the bear's head.

Tippy giggled and ducked her head. Benjy smiled again as he went to the sideboard to fill a plate. That task done, he came back and sat next to the bear. Tippy watched him covertly while he ate, An'gel was amused to note. The child seemed smitten with Benjy.

That was good. She hoped Benjy wouldn't mind looking after Tippy while she and Dickce talked with Jacqueline. He really was a good-natured and kind young man.

"Where are Horace and Trey this morning?" Dickce asked.

Jacqueline stared blankly at her, and Dickce repeated the question. Jacqueline shrugged. "Horace had business in town, and I think Trey went with him." She lapsed into silence and stared again at her plate.

An'gel finished her breakfast, and when Dickce did also, she rose from the table. "Jacqueline, why don't we go into the parlor?" Her goddaughter obviously wasn't going to eat the rest of her food, and they might as well talk. "Benjy will be happy to stay with Tippy."

Jacqueline glanced at her granddaughter and Benjy and nodded. "Okay." She stood and followed the sisters out of the room.

In the parlor An'gel took a seat on the sofa and patted the space beside her. Jacqueline did as she was bidden, and Dickce sat on the other side of her. Jacqueline leaned back, her eyes closed, and An'gel shared a glance with her sister.

"How are you doing?" An'gel asked. She knew the query was banal under the circumstances, but she had to start somewhere.

Jacqueline shrugged. Her eyes remained shut. "Okay, I guess. Mostly numb."

"We are here to do whatever we can," An'gel said. "This is a terrible time for you, and if we can ease your burdens in any way, please let us."

"We're so sorry," Dickce said. "I know the words are inadequate, but we love you and want to support you."

Jacqueline's eyes opened, and An'gel was struck by her goddaughter's bleak expression.

"Thank you," Jacqueline said. "I keep thinking it's a nightmare, and I'll wake up any minute and Sondra will still be here with me." Tears began to stream down.

An'gel moved closer and slipped an arm around her goddaughter's shoulder. Jacqueline laid her head against An'gel's shoulder and wept. Dickce clasped one of Jacqueline's hands and stroked it.

An'gel did her best to choke back her own tears. Breaking down now would be of no help to Jacqueline. She and Dickce had to remain strong and contain their own sorrow in order to support Jacqueline and Tippy. An'gel wondered if Jacqueline had tried to explain the deaths of her mother and great-grandmother to the child.

Soon Jacqueline's tears ended, and she straightened. An'gel released her and squeezed her shoulder. Jacqueline smiled weakly and fumbled in the pocket of her slacks for a handkerchief. She wiped her eyes and blew her nose delicately.

"How about some hot coffee?" An'gel said. "I think we could all use a little pick-me-up right about now."

"Yes, thank you," Jacqueline replied. "I'll be all right. Caffeine will help."

An'gel rose from the couch. "I'll see if there's enough in the pot in the dining room. If not, I'll go ask Estelle for a fresh one."

Jacqueline rose as well. "I think I'll go wash my face in the powder room. I'll be right back." She hurried from the room.

"The poor child." Dickce frowned. "Sister, do you think it's odd that she hasn't mentioned Mireille? She said she keeps thinking she'll wake up and Sondra will be here. But what about her mother?"

"Yes, I noticed that," An'gel said. "I wouldn't reflect too much on it. She's been hit so hard by all this I doubt she realized what she said. I'll be back soon."

She strode from the room and crossed the hall to the dining room. Benjy and Tippy were gone, probably upstairs so that Benjy could introduce Peanut and Endora to the child. Playing with the dog and cat ought to keep Tippy occupied for a while. She checked the coffeepot, found it cold and nearly empty. Then she noticed that nothing had been cleared from the table. She left the room and walked down the hall to the kitchen.

As she neared a large marble-top table along the wall, An'gel glanced down and spotted a small piece of something white. She stooped to retrieve it. About the size of three quarters, it was a jagged-edge piece of satin. An'gel frowned. A piece of the wedding gown that Sondra had ripped apart.

She heard the door to the powder room open, and she thrust the scrap of fabric into the sleeve of her dress. She didn't want Jacqueline to see it and be distressed at the reminder of the incident that had brought on her mother's collapse.

"No coffee in the dining room," An'gel said as her god-daughter approached her. "I'll check with Estelle and be back soon."

Jacqueline nodded and walked past her, shoulders slumped and head at a dejected angle.

An'gel trod on to the kitchen. She found it deserted, but there was a full pot of coffee in the coffeemaker. She quickly prepared a tray and filled a carafe with coffee. She carried the tray to the front parlor. As she stepped inside the room, she heard the trill of a cell phone.

Jacqueline fumbled in her slacks pocket and extracted a phone. An'gel noticed that her goddaughter's hands trembled as she stared at the screen. After a moment of seeming indecision, Jacqueline answered the call.

An'gel set the tray on the table in front of the sofa and began to pour coffee into the three mugs.

"I see. You're absolutely sure?" Jacqueline said after a moment. "Yes, thank you. Don't do anything until you hear from me." She thanked the caller again and ended the conversation. Her hand trembled even more noticeably as she set her phone down on the table next to the tray.

"What's the matter?" An'gel was alarmed by Jacqueline's expression. Her goddaughter looked ill.

"That was the mechanic about Sondra's car," Jacqueline said, her voice shrill. "He says the brake line was deliberately cut."

CHAPTER 21

An'gel added sugar and milk to one of the mugs while Dickce grasped Jacqueline's hands and held them. An'gel resumed her seat beside Jacqueline and held the mug out. "Drink this, my dear."

Jacqueline loosed her hands from Dickce's and accepted the coffee. She took several sips, and An'gel was glad to see the color slowly returning to her goddaughter's face.

"That's better," An'gel said. She judged by Dickce's expression that her sister found the news about Sondra's brakes every bit as disquieting as she did. The connection between that incident and Sondra's death remained to be seen. An'gel, however, was more convinced than ever that Sondra's death was no freak accident.

"The mechanic was sure that the brake line was deliberately cut?" An'gel asked, even though she had heard Jacqueline ask the same question. She had to be sure.

Jacqueline nodded, her hands clasped tightly around her mug. "I can't believe it. Who would do such a dangerous thing?" She drank more coffee. Her next words stunned An'gel. "*Maman* was supposed to be in the car with her."

Dickce gasped. "Oh my lord, that's horrible."

"Why wasn't she in the car?" An'gel asked. Her stomach felt queasy. What kind of evil was at work in this house?

Jacqueline stared into her mug. "Estelle said she needed *Maman* for something, I can't remember what now, and *Maman* told Sondra to go on without her."

An'gel exchanged a glance with her sister. Had Mireille gone with Sondra, she would have been on the side of the car that struck the tree. Of course, whoever cut the brake lines had no way of knowing Sondra would stop the car in that manner. But it didn't really matter. Both Sondra and Mireille could have been badly injured, or killed, in an accident.

Now they were both dead.

An'gel felt chilled to the bone. She reached for her own coffee. She needed warmth, and she watched her sister drink as well.

An'gel again thought of evil. There was something—someone—sick at work in this house, evidently intent on destroying both Mireille and Sondra. He or she had succeeded, An'gel acknowledged grimly.

The question remained: Why?

She hated to do it when her goddaughter was in such a vulnerable state, but An'gel felt impelled to question Jacqueline.

"My dear," she said gently, "I hate to but I really must ask you something."

Jacqueline stared at her, then nodded. "Go ahead."

"How did Mireille leave everything?" An'gel asked.

"To me," Jacqueline said. "There are legacies for Jackson and Estelle, of course, but the house, its contents, and the bulk of *Maman*'s estate all come to me."

"What about Sondra's estate?" Dickce asked. "Is it all controlled by the terms of Terence's will?"

Jacqueline turned to Dickce with a frown. "Yes, Terence laid everything out. Sondra gained control of her money when she married or turned twenty-five, whichever came first."

An'gel asked the next question as gently as she could. "And if she died before either of those events took place?"

Jacqueline shuddered. "It all comes to me." She burst into tears and dropped the mug, now empty, into her lap. It rolled off and dropped to the floor, making a soft thud on the old carpet.

Dickce bent to retrieve the mug while An'gel attempted to calm her goddaughter.

"I'm sorry, my dear, if all this has upset you even further, but I had to ask." An'gel looked sadly at Jacqueline.

"I didn't have anything to do with it," Jacqueline said suddenly. "I wouldn't harm either my mother or my daughter for money. You have to believe me."

"Of course we believe you," An'gel said, though a faint whisper of doubt assailed her. If Horace needed money really badly, would Jacqueline do something desperate to get it for him?

She tried to shake the doubt away. She had known this woman since she was a baby. Jacqueline would never kill anyone for gain.

"Somebody did attempt to harm them," Dickce said in

a calm tone. "And now they're both gone. We have to know the truth about what happened."

An'gel nodded. "We have to call the police and tell them about the damage to Sondra's car. They need to know."

"Sondra's death wasn't an accident." Jacqueline looked suddenly calm and determined as she turned to An'gel. "She did like watching storms and sometimes she took foolish risks." She smiled faintly. "But my daughter loved her clothes almost more than anything. There is no way she would walk out onto the gallery in the middle of a violent storm wearing the dress she planned to walk down the aisle in."

"Sister and I have been thinking the so-called *freak accident* was nothing but a clumsy attempt to hide a murder," Dickce said.

An'gel nodded, glad that one of them had the nerve to finally said the words aloud to Jacqueline.

"Would you make the call for me?" Jacqueline asked and picked her phone up from the table. "I'll put in the number, but you do the talking. I think I'd throw up if I did it." Once she punched in the number, she passed the phone to An'gel.

The conversation was brief. Officer Bugg was not at the police department, but the dispatcher assured An'gel he would get the word to call as soon as possible. An'gel gave the man her number rather than Jacqueline's. She ended the call and replaced the phone on the table.

"He'll call soon, I'm sure," An'gel said after she explained that Bugg wasn't available at the moment.

Jacqueline rubbed her bare arms with shaky hands. "I'm terrified. What if I'm next on the list?"

An'gel had been hoping that Jacqueline wouldn't hit on this frightening possibility for a while yet. But now that she had, the situation had to be acknowledged.

"Do you have a will?" she asked.

"Yes," her goddaughter whispered. "I had Rich Thurston draw it up a couple of years ago, when Tippy turned two."

"What are the terms?" Dickce asked. "We hate to pry, but we need to know."

"Terence left me a lot of money," Jacqueline said, apparently ignoring Dickce's question. "He didn't expect to die so young, and part of me never got over his death." She drew in a shaky breath. "I didn't realize how wealthy he was until he died. He left most of it to Sondra, of course, but he made sure I was well provided for."

An'gel wanted to ask how much Terence had left her. She had never heard an amount mentioned in connection with Jacqueline's portion, but it had no doubt been substantial. With Sondra's share now hers, Jacqueline was a wealthy woman indeed.

"Your will?" Dickce prompted Jacqueline again.

This time she answered. "It's split into thirds. One third to Horace, another to Sondra, and the last one to Tippy." She shuddered. "Tippy would get Sondra's third if she died before Tippy and me. Horace's third is his to dispose of however he wants."

An'gel felt the cold creep over her skin. She stared over Jacqueline's bowed head at Dickce. She knew they shared the same thought.

Was Tippy now in danger from the killer?

~~~

Upstairs, Benjy shifted from his cramped position on the floor of Tippy's bedroom and tried to ease the strain in his back. He couldn't remember ever having a make-believe tea party with a little girl, but Tippy was enjoying it so much he couldn't begrudge her.

He marveled at how patient both Peanut and Endora were being with the little girl. Peanut looked funny with the bows on his ears, and Endora kept losing her hat, but they didn't shy away from the small hands that wanted to dress them. He was sure they sensed the child meant them no harm and went along with the play. The teddy bear, whose name Benjy finally realized was Lance, rather than Wance, watched over all the activities with a benignly vacant gaze and bedraggled smile.

Tippy chattered to the animals and occasionally to Benjy, and Benjy, realizing that she didn't require a response, let his mind drift. He felt sorry for the kid. He knew what it was like to lose a mother, and he had to make an effort not to let grief overwhelm him. He didn't want to have to explain to Tippy why he was so sad.

Then Benjy wondered whether anyone had told her about the deaths of her mother and great-grandmother. He wished he'd thought to ask before he started babysitting. The last thing he wanted to do was upset the kid by saying something out of turn.

Tippy chattered on, telling Peanut how much he would like the cake she had made and then insisting to Endora that she have another sip of tea. He smiled, and Tippy glanced at him and giggled.

"Peanut and Endora sure are enjoying their tea party," Benjy said. "Thank you again for inviting us."

"I wuv tea pawties," Tippy said. She ducked her head and began cutting invisible slices of cake to dole out to the animals for a third or fourth helping.

Benjy thought the lisp was pretty cute, though it brought back uncomfortable memories. He'd had one when he was her age and hoped she would grow out of it sooner than he had. He remembered the teasing in kindergarten and first grade because he had trouble with *l* and *r* sounds.

He heard the word *mommy* suddenly and focused on what Tippy was saying.

"Mommy doesn't wike the bad man," she told Peanut solemnly. "He doesn't wike her either and yewws at her."

"When did you hear the bad man yelling at your mommy, Tippy?" Benjy knew he had to tread carefully. He thought this could be important, but he didn't want to upset Tippy.

"A wot of times," Tippy said. She poked a spoon at the teddy bear. "Wance, have some cweam."

"Did you hear him last night?" Benjy said.

Tippy squinted, her head slightly to one side. "I think so. I was asweep, and dey woke me up. And den dere was a wot of noise. It was scawy, all the wightning and thunder." She stared solemnly at Benjy. "Wance and I hid under de covers until we feww asweep."

"I like to hide under the covers when there's a bad storm," Benjy told the child mendaciously.

Tippy nodded and went back to feeding the bear invisible cream. He scratched Peanut's ears as he thought about what Tippy had told him. If the child was right, and a man had been yelling at Sondra about the time the storm hit, could that man have something to do with Sondra's death? He knew Miss An'gel and Miss Dickce were concerned that Sondra's death was not the result of a freak accident.

Those thoughts disturbed him, but another, more disturbing one came quickly. What would happen if the man knew Tippy had heard the argument?

CHAPTER 22

An'gel didn't want to alarm Jacqueline any further by voicing her concern over Tippy's welfare. Perhaps they could keep watch over the little one without letting on to Jacqueline they thought Tippy could be in danger. She, Dickce, and Benjy would take turns with the child until Sondra's murderer was identified.

There was another subject she wanted to broach with her goddaughter, however, that could be almost as unsettling. An'gel felt she had little choice with this one.

In a gentle tone she asked, "Is Horace having any financial problems?"

Jacqueline closed her eyes and took a deep breath. Eyes open again, she looked at An'gel. "Yes, he is. He says it's only a temporary cash-flow situation. Nothing really serious. He's been through this before."

"Do you think he's telling you the truth?" Dickce asked, and An'gel wished her sister hadn't been quite so blunt.

"Horace hasn't ever lied to me," Jacqueline said. "I have no reason to doubt him."

An'gel thought her goddaughter's statements lacked assurance. She hoped for Jacqueline's sake Horace was as truthful as she claimed. If he was not, and the financial issue was truly serious, An'gel wondered to what lengths Horace would go to gain the money he needed. Would he kill two women to ensure that his wife inherited everything? A wife he could no doubt persuade to invest her considerable wealth in his business ventures?

An'gel wondered about that. She had never really felt she knew Horace beyond a superficial level. On past visits she and Dickce spent their time with Mireille and Jacqueline, seeing Horace mostly at meals. He was always on the go, attending to business, and on some visits they didn't see him at all. On their last visit to Willowbank, almost five years ago, Horace had been out of the country the entire time.

Moreover, An'gel realized, Jacqueline's letters—and later on, her e-mails—mentioned Horace and his activities only infrequently at best. She had nothing more than Jacqueline's assurance that Horace was truthful. Mireille had always been reticent on the subject of her second son-in-law. An'gel didn't think Mireille considered him a bad choice on Jacqueline's part, but Mireille had adored Terence. An'gel thought her cousin had had only lukewarm feelings for Horace.

For An'gel, Jacqueline's confidence in her husband wasn't enough. How could she question Horace discreetly? She would have to come up with a plan to introduce the subject of finances and business and hope that Horace would reveal himself in some way.

"Do you expect me to believe my husband is the one who cut the brake line on Sondra's car?" Jacqueline demanded in a fretful tone. "That's utterly ridiculous."

"We have to consider every possibility," An'gel said. "Look at it this way. Can you think of any other reason, besides money, that would lead someone to murder Sondra?"

"Not when you put it like that, I guess not," Jacqueline said a bit more calmly. "Sondra annoyed many people because she was so self-centered, but that's no reason to kill anyone."

"You told us earlier," Dickce said, "that Mireille had planned to drive into town with Sondra, but she changed her mind and didn't go. Who all knew that Mireille was going to be in the car with Sondra?"

"Well, Estelle and Jackson knew, of course." Jacqueline frowned. "I knew, and I'm sure Horace did, too. Trey probably did as well."

"Anyone else?" An'gel asked. "What about your lawyer, Mr. Thurston?"

Jacqueline thought about that for a moment. "He probably knew, I think. *Maman* had planned to stop by his office while she was in town, but then she ended up calling to cancel the appointment when she had to stay home." She regarded An'gel intently. "Do you think Rich drove out here and cut the brake lines on Sondra's car without anyone seeing him?"

An'gel grimaced. "I know it sounds odd, dear, but we have to take everyone—and everything—into account. He doesn't seem the type to go creeping through the underbrush and the trees, but you never can tell."

"Sounds pretty ridiculous to me," Jacqueline said. "I've known Rich Thurston all my life, and you never met a more fastidious man." She sniffed. "Can't stand to get his hands dirty on anything, and if he knows even how to find a brake line in a car, I'd be surprised."

An'gel heard the conviction in her goddaughter's voice. She wondered whether Jacqueline would understand the implications of what she just told them. If Thurston didn't cut the brake lines—motive to be determined—that left Horace sitting in the seat of chief suspect, at least as far as An'gel was concerned.

"What about Trey?" Dickce asked. She looked oddly at An'gel. "Does he have money of his own? I suppose he works for Horace."

"He does," Jacqueline said. "He manages one of Horace's dealerships in a nearby parish. I know Horace pays him well, and Trey isn't extravagant." She paused. "He can be pretty hotheaded at times, but he has nothing to gain from these deaths."

An'gel reserved judgment on that. If Horace gained by them, then ultimately his son and only child would as well. She asked, "Do you know the terms of Horace's will? Does he leave everything to Trey?"

"Yes, he does," Jacqueline replied. "Horace knows that I'm already provided for."

"I believe you said that if Horace inherited his third of your estate," Dickce said, "he can dispose of it however he likes."

"Yes." Jacqueline nodded. "It would ultimately go to Trey."

Dickce glanced again at An'gel. "I saw Trey last night. Or rather, in the morning." She explained that Endora had been in her bedroom with her and how she heard the cat meowing and scratching somewhere. "When I picked her up, Sondra's door opened, and there stood Trey. He looked mighty upset."

"What was he doing in Sondra's room at such a time?" An'gel asked. "That seems odd to me."

Jacqueline sighed heavily. "He was head over heels in love with Sondra, but she wasn't interested, despite everything. He was angry with her over her decision to marry Lance. I guess he might have wanted to spend some time with her things. He's devastated by her death, I know." Her face crumpled, and a few tears trickled down her cheeks.

An'gel didn't want to distress her goddaughter further, but two words Jacqueline had said caught her attention. "You said Sondra wasn't interested in Trey, *despite everything*. What did you mean by that?"

Jacqueline rubbed her tears away with one hand. "I guess I might as well tell you. He's Tippy's father." She stood abruptly. "All this is giving me a bad headache. I'm sorry, but I've got to go upstairs and lie down for a little while. I have to go back into town soon to take care of some things."

"Of course, dear," An'gel said vaguely, trying to grasp the truth of the bombshell Jacqueline had handed them. "You need to rest. Dickce, Benjy, and I will take care of Tippy for you."

"Thank you." Jacqueline gave them a brief smile before she strode out of the room.

"Well," Dickce said. "I didn't see that coming."

"I didn't either," An'gel replied. "But I can't say I'm completely surprised." She shook her head. "I can't imagine what Jacqueline and Horace were thinking, to allow such a thing to happen."

"Poor Mireille was horrified, I imagine." Dickce made a moue of distaste. "I know they're stepsiblings, but still."

"I imagine Mireille had a few choice words to say on the subject." An'gel shook her head. "I still can't believe she's gone, and so suddenly. This whole mess is truly heart-rending."

"Yes, it is," Dickce said. They sat quietly for a moment, until the sound of the doorbell interrupted their thoughts.

An'gel waited, expecting to hear the footsteps of either Jackson or Estelle as they went to answer the door. There was only silence, and the bell rang again.

"I'll go." Dickce rose and headed out of the room.

She returned moments later, preceded by the policeman Bugg and trailed by his junior officer, Sanford.

"Mornin', ma'am." Bugg nodded at An'gel. "I don't reckon either Mister or Miz Mims is around anywhere, are they? I got something I need to tell 'em."

"I'm sorry, Officer." An'gel rose to address the man. "I believe Horace is at work, and Jacqueline has just this minute gone upstairs to get some rest. She's completely exhausted, and I don't want to disturb her unless it's of vital importance."

Bugg didn't appear happy at An'gel's news. "That's sure unfortunate, ma'am, 'cause I really need to talk to one of 'em."

"My sister and I are cousins of Mrs. Champlain's," An'gel said. "I am also Jacqueline's godmother. Can't you tell us what it is? I'd rather not have Jacqueline hit with any more bad news at the moment. And that reminds me, we have something to tell you as well."

Bugg nodded. "Yes'm, I got the message that Miz Mims

needed to talk to me. How's about you tell me what you got to say, and then I'll do the same?"

"Very well," An'gel said. "Won't you both sit down first?" She waved a hand to indicate a couple of nearby chairs. Bugg nodded and motioned for Sanford to take a seat as soon as An'gel and Dickce took their places on the sofa.

"Now, ma'am, what is it you got to tell me?" Bugg asked after he sat and squirmed gingerly in the antique armchair to find a comfortable position.

Despite the seriousness of the situation, An'gel had to suppress a smile at Bugg's actions. He was clearly not comfortable in that chair and probably afraid that he might damage it.

"Sondra had an accident with her car yesterday morning," An'gel said. "She was coming down the driveway a bit too fast when her brakes gave out, and she ended up crashing her car into one of the live oaks. Luckily she wasn't hurt and was able to walk away from it."

Bugg nodded. "She sure did like to drive fast. Surprised she didn't have no more accidents than she did. Anything special about this one?"

"Yes," An'gel said. "It was a brand-new car. Evidently she had only brought it home the day before. We all thought it was strange that the brakes on a new car were faulty so quickly."

"It turned out, however," Dickce said, "the brake line was deliberately cut. Jacqueline had the car towed to the dealership, and the mechanic called her a little while ago to give her a report."

Sanford emitted a low whistle, but Bugg appeared not to have heard it. He frowned. "Somebody had it in for her, then."

"That's not all, Officer," An'gel said. "My cousin was supposed to be in the car with her. At the last minute, though, she ended up staying home."

Bugg's eyes narrowed. "I aim to do my best to figger out who was responsible for that. You can count on it."

"Thank you," Dickce said. "We will."

"Now, what about the news you have for Jacqueline and Horace?" An'gel asked. "Please tell us."

"All right," Bugg said. He leaned forward in the chair, hands on his knees. "The parish coroner, Dr. Kovacs—you saw her last night, ma'am."

An'gel nodded.

"Well, she ain't real satisfied with what she saw when she examined the body." Bugg paused for a moment, then said in a dramatic tone, "We're going to be treating this as a suspicious death, not no accident."

CHAPTER 23

If Officer Bugg was expecting reactions of outrage or horror, he was definitely disappointed. An'gel merely looked at him and nodded, as did Dickce.

"Y'all don't look like you're surprised." Bugg stared hard at each sister in turn.

"My sister and I thought the freak accident was a little too bizarre to be real. Now you tell us the coroner has found some kind of evidence that makes her suspicious of it, too." An'gel frowned. "Frankly, Officer, we were expecting news like this."

Bugg didn't seem to know what to make of that, An'gel thought. *He probably thinks we're dim-witted old biddies who don't have the brains the good Lord gave a goose.* An'gel had to suppress a chuckle at that thought.

The officer cleared his throat and glanced at his subordinate. Sanford responded by pulling a notebook and pen out of his pocket. He flipped to a blank page, clicked his pen, and looked expectantly at Bugg.

"Seein' as y'all are here and available," Bugg said, "I reckon I need to ask y'all some questions."

"Certainly, Officer," Dickce said, and An'gel nodded. "We're always happy to help fine lawmen like yourselves." Dickce batted her eyelashes at Bugg, and An'gel was amused to note that the man's cheeks reddened. Really, Dickce was incorrigible.

"Well, um, yes, ma'am," Bugg said. "Now let me see here, maybe you can tell me whether you noticed anything suspicious while you been here."

"The main suspicious thing we saw we've already mentioned," An'gel said. At Bugg's questioning look, she continued, "I'm talking about the accident with Sondra's car. The cut brake lines. I think if you can discover who was responsible for that, you'll find your killer."

"Maybe so, ma'am," Bugg said. "I need you to give an account of your time since you been here. What time you arrived, and all that."

An'gel realized this was all probably necessary, at least from Bugg's point of view, but she really wished he'd get on with things. She suppressed her irritation and gave him a summary of their arrival and activities afterward.

Sanford scribbled furiously in his notebook while An'gel talked. She hoped he knew shorthand because she wasn't going to slow down just so he could write everything longhand. She was itching to get the police out of the room so she and Dickce could talk and share information.

When An'gel finished, Bugg turned to Dickce. "You got anything to add to that?"

"Yes, I do," Dickce said. She proceeded to tell him about the time spent apart from her sister, and how she encountered Trey Mims in Sondra's bedroom early that morning.

Bugg appeared to perk up slightly when he heard Trey's name, but he made no comment. When Dickce's recital was complete, he thanked them both. He stood, and Sanford hastily returned his pen and notebook to his pocket and stood behind his superior.

"If I have any more questions, I reckon y'all will be here for a few days," Bugg said.

"Yes," An'gel replied. "Until the funerals have occurred, at least."

"Good." Bugg nodded. "Now where can I find this young man you call your ward? What's his name?"

"Benjy Stephens," Dickce said. "He's upstairs with Tippy, Sondra's daughter. I'll go up and send him down to you. Someone needs to stay with Tippy, and I don't think you should question him in front of the child."

"Of course not, ma'am," Bugg said indignantly. "I wouldn't do that. You go on and tell him to come down here, if you don't mind."

Dickce smiled serenely as she walked from the room. Moments later An'gel heard her footsteps on the stairs.

Bugg watched An'gel—uneasily, she thought. *Does he think I'll bite?* She was hard pressed not to laugh. *At least he's not going to discount us any longer.*

The policeman cleared his throat. "Ma'am, you don't need to wait with us, if you've got something else you need to be doing."

"I thought I would introduce our ward to you," An'gel said. "Then I will leave you." She had really wanted to stay while Bugg questioned Benjy, but it was obvious that the policeman wanted her out of the room.

Bugg nodded. Not long after, Benjy came into the room at a fast pace, but he slowed down when he saw An'gel. She rose and made the introductions. Benjy nodded in a friendly manner to the policemen, and Bugg suggested he have a seat. An'gel left the room.

In the hallway she hovered for a moment not far from the door. She heard Bugg ask Benjy for his name, age, and relationship to the deceased. Then she decided there was no point in eavesdropping. Benjy would be fine.

Instead she decided to track down Estelle. She wanted to find out whether the housekeeper knew any further details about Mireille's death and what Jacqueline's plans were.

The kitchen was empty, and An'gel frowned. She checked the small butler's pantry off the kitchen, but there was no sign of Jackson. An'gel thought he might be in his small apartment in a nearby outbuilding that Mireille's grandfather had long ago converted into servants' quarters. Estelle lodged there as well. An'gel debated going there but on a hunch she went back to the hallway to the stairs.

On the second floor she turned and walked back toward the front of the house. Mireille's room was on the right facing the front lawn. Sondra's, on the floor above, was to the left. An'gel found the door open a few inches. She hesitated a moment, then pushed the door open and walked into the room.

The doors to the gallery outside were shut and the curtains drawn against the sunlight. The room was dim and smelled faintly of lavender, Mireille's favorite scent for the sachets and potpourri she used. In a rocking chair in the corner near the old-fashioned four-poster, An'gel found Estelle sitting quietly. At first An'gel thought the woman was asleep, but then the housekeeper spoke.

"You need something?" she asked, her tone harsh and impatient. She started the chair rocking. "I don't feel like making anything for anybody right now. You want something, go make it yourself."

An'gel decided to ignore Estelle's rudeness. She knew the woman was upset by Mireille's death.

"I want to talk to you." She walked closer to Estelle and stood by the bed. She sighed and stroked the beautiful Double Wedding Ring quilt that lay across the bed. Mireille's mother had made it as a bride gift fifty years ago.

"What about?" Estelle asked.

An'gel knew the woman would rather be by herself and could sympathize with her, but Estelle couldn't hide herself away completely when there was so much to be done.

"I wondered if Jacqueline had a chance to talk to you about any of the plans for Mireille's service," An'gel said. "My sister and I will be here and will be glad to help any way we can. We can pitch in with the cooking and cleaning, whatever you need."

"Thank you," Estelle said, her tone slightly less rude. "Jacqueline hasn't said anything to me. I tried talking to her when she and Horace got back from the hospital but she told me she didn't feel up to it."

"I know she was worn out," An'gel said. "Maybe I can call the funeral home. Which one is it?"

Estelle snorted. "Won't do you any good. I called them

this morning, and they told me they were waiting to talk to Jacqueline. Nothing's going to happen till she's ready to handle it."

"I see," An'gel said. She felt frustrated. She really wanted to do something to ease Jacqueline's burdens, but until Jacqueline was ready, she couldn't do anything but wait.

"What will you do now?" An'gel asked. "Will you stay on and continue to run the bed-and-breakfast?" She wondered whether Jacqueline would have any interest in it, without Mireille.

"Won't have any choice, will I?" Estelle's tone was bitter. "The daughter of the house will get everything, and I won't get anything. I'll be out of this place the day after we lay Mireille to rest."

"Surely Jacqueline won't make you leave," An'gel said. "You're family, aren't you?"

"Too distant to matter to Jacqueline, only a third cousin once removed," Estelle said. "With Mireille it was different. Family was family to her. Jacqueline never has liked me, and that bitch of a daughter of hers hated me. I hated her right back. She made everyone around her miserable. Never in my life saw a person as stuck on herself as Sondra." She chuckled, and the sound made An'gel uneasy. "Look where it got her. Finally got what she deserved."

In the face of such hatred and spite, An'gel didn't know how to respond. An'gel couldn't blame Jacqueline for wanting Estelle out of the house. Who would want to harbor malice like this if she didn't have to?

An'gel turned and walked out, having decided there was no response she could make. Estelle's mocking laughter followed her, cut off only when An'gel closed the door.

In the hall she moved to stand in front of the window. The light from the sun warmed her, and she realized how cold she was. She glanced uneasily at Mireille's door. She knew that Estelle didn't care for Sondra, and one could hardly blame her for that. But she had never reckoned on the sheer hatred the woman felt for the dead girl.

Had Estelle hated Sondra enough to kill her?

CHAPTER 24

An'gel decided not to linger where she was, in case Estelle came out of Mireille's room. She didn't want the housekeeper to catch her standing out there. She thought about climbing up to the third floor to check on Dickce and Tippy, but before she could make up her mind, Jacqueline's door opened and Horace stepped out.

An'gel stared at him in blank surprise. She thought Horace was at work. She greeted him, and he held up a finger. Then he moved quietly down the hall to the head of the stairs, motioning for An'gel to follow him.

His voice low, Horace said, "Jackie's sleeping, and I didn't want to take a chance on waking her up. She's so wore out from all this mess with her mama and Sondra. I don't want her getting sick from it. She'll push herself too hard and then collapse."

Horace's expression of concern for his wife seemed

genuine, and An'gel warmed to him more than she ever had before.

"Yes, she certainly is," An'gel replied, matching her tone to his. "I'm worried about her. There's so much on her right now. If there's anything Dickce and I can do to help, all you have to do is ask."

Horace started down the stairs with An'gel beside him. "I sure appreciate that, Miss An'gel," he said. "This has all been almost more than I can take in myself, and I can't imagine how hard it is for Jackie."

"Have you spoken to the police recently?" An'gel asked as they reached the bottom of the stairs.

"No, ma'am," Horace said. "I saw a cop car here when I drove up a few minutes ago, but I came in the back way and went right upstairs to check on Jackie."

"You need to hear what Officer Bugg has to say. It's about Sondra's death." An'gel steered him to the front parlor. She heard voices coming from the room. "I believe he is still in here talking to Benjy."

Horace nodded. He strode into the room, and An'gel followed.

"Hey, Elmont." Horace stuck out his hand as he reached Bugg. He and the policeman shook hands. "I hear you got something to tell me."

"That I do, Horace, that I do. Coupla things, actually, and neither one of 'em ain't good news." Bugg looked around Horace's substantial bulk and noticed An'gel. "Ma'am, I'm finished with this young man here, so y'all can go on about your bidness. I'll let you know if there's anything else I need from you."

"Thank you, Officer," An'gel said, frost in her voice.

She did not appreciate Bugg's tone or his choice of words. *Go about my* bidness *indeed.* "Benjy, why don't we go up and check on Dickce and Tippy?"

Benjy nodded as he slipped around the two police officers but he stopped in front of Horace. "Mr. Mims, I know you're busy, but I wanted to ask if you've heard how Lance is doing. I've been babysitting Tippy, and she was asking about him. Seems he usually visits her, and she wondered when he was coming."

Oh my heavens. An'gel had forgotten all about poor Lance and his altercation with Trey last night. She felt terrible for not thinking about the young man's welfare even once since the EMTs took him off to the hospital. She also recalled the furious look Horace had shot her way when she informed Trey she would be a witness for Lance if he decided to bring charges of assault.

"Yes, how is he?" she asked. "I'm ashamed I'd forgotten about him until Benjy mentioned him. Was he badly hurt?" She decided not to mention the circumstances. No point in riling Horace up again if she could avoid it. She wanted to question him later about other matters.

Horace looked grim. "Last I heard he was doing okay. Got a pretty hard head on him, apparently. Minor concussion, a black eye, and a bruised nose. They sent him home early this morning."

An'gel was relieved to hear that Lance's condition wasn't more serious.

"You can tell Tippy that Lance won't be coming to visit anytime soon," Horace said to Benjy. "Even if she cuts up a fuss, I'm not having that idiot back in this house."

Benjy flinched at Horace's tone but said, "Okay, sir." He

moved quickly away from Horace and came to stand beside An'gel.

"That's one of the things I got to talk to you about, Horace," Bugg said. He cut a sideways glance at Benjy and An'gel. When neither of them moved, he sighed and went on, "You know how mamas can be when they have only one chick, and that Miz Perigord is more protective than most." He sniggered. "Reckon she has to be, since that one chick of hers is lucky if he can find his way out of his bedroom in less than three hours." Behind him, Sanford laughed.

Horace made a gesture with his right hand, as if telling Bugg to get on with it. The policeman sobered. "Well, anyways, Horace, Miz Perigord is threatening to press charges against Trey for assault."

Horace uttered a string of obscenities, and An'gel said, "Come along, Benjy." She wasn't going to stay and listen to any more of that kind of vulgar talk. She thought it served Trey right and hoped that Mrs. Perigord followed through on her threat. That young man had to learn to control his temper, and this might teach him a lesson. *Unless he killed Sondra, and then he'll have a much worse lesson to learn.* Her thoughts were bleak as she climbed the stairs with Benjy.

"Miss An'gel," Benjy said, "when we get upstairs, I need to talk to you and Miss Dickce. It's about something I heard Tippy say while she was playing a little while ago."

Benjy sounded concerned, An'gel thought. "Okay. It's time the three of us had a talk and shared whatever information we've been able to pick up."

By the time they reached the third floor, An'gel was wishing—and not for the first time—that Mireille had installed an elevator. One long flight of stairs was bad enough, but two were a bit wearisome.

An'gel and Benjy walked down the hall toward Tippy's room. Dickce stepped out when they were a few feet away and pulled the door halfway closed. She held a finger to her lips, then beckoned them with the same finger to follow her across the hall to the bedroom where she spent the night.

"Where are Peanut and Endora?" Benjy asked in an undertone as he followed the sisters.

Dickce whispered back, "Sound asleep on the bed with Tippy." She grinned. "She wore them and herself out, and I didn't think anyone would mind if they napped with her." She ushered An'gel and Benjy into the room and left her door half open.

Dickce sat on the bed, feet dangling slightly. An'gel took the chair in front of the vanity and Benjy the armchair in the corner.

"I can't believe how much energy a four-year-old has," Dickce said. "I swear I could take a nap myself right about now."

"Better you than me," An'gel said. "Benjy has something to tell us."

"I think I know what it is," Dickce said, "but go ahead, Benjy."

Benjy replied, "While I was watching Tippy earlier, she was talking a mile a minute. I tuned out some of it, but I heard her say something a man yelling at her mother." He related the rest of Tippy's story.

Dickce nodded. "She told me pretty much the same story."

"Did either of you ask her whether she recognized the man?"

Benjy shook his head, but Dickce said, "I did, in a round-about way. But it was no use. The voices were too far away, even though they were loud. And when the storm hit, Tippy was too frightened and got under the covers and hid there till she fell asleep." Dickce frowned. "Poor little thing. She shouldn't have been on her own during a storm like that."

"No, she shouldn't," An'gel said. "Her mother should have been looking after her." She paused. "But of course, Sondra could have been killed soon after Tippy overheard the argument. Thank the Lord the child hid under the covers, or she might have been killed as well."

"The storm was the perfect cover for the killer," Dickce said. "Especially if everyone else was hunkered down somewhere in the house until it passed."

"We really don't know where anyone was, besides our-selves, Tippy, and Sondra," Benjy pointed out. "What would happen if we asked everybody?"

"It would arouse suspicion pretty quickly," An'gel said. "We can't do it directly. We'll have to get them all to tell us some other way."

"The killer will lie," Benjy said.

"True." An'gel nodded. "But he might give himself away somehow. We just have to be cleverer than he is."

"Do you think the killer is a man?" Dickce asked.

"I do," Benjy said. "It had to be somebody pretty strong to lift Sondra up and throw her over the railing into the yard."

"Exactly," An'gel said. "Estelle is wiry, but Sondra was bigger than she is. And Jacqueline was in town at the hos-pital with her mother."

"So that leaves us with Horace, Trey, Richmond Thur-ston, and Jackson," Dickce said.

"*Jackson?*" An'gel said. "That's utterly ridiculous. The poor man can hardly get himself around, much less pick up a woman and throw her over a railing. I say we rule him out."

Dickce's mouth set in a stern line, and An'gel recognized this sign of her sister's stubbornness. "No, think about it. Jackson adored Mireille, and he knew what Sondra had done. If he was truly furious at Sondra, the adrenaline might have been enough to make it possible for him to do it."

"She's got a point," Benjy said. "Although I'd hate to think it of him. He's such a sweet old man."

An'gel sighed. "I suppose you're right. But by the same token, we can't rule out Estelle either. She was devoted to Mireille, and I know she loathed Sondra." She told them about her conversation a little earlier with the housekeeper.

"I vote for her, then," Benjy said. "She creeps me out anyway. Reminds me of that old lady on *The Addams Family.* You know, the grandmother, although the lady on the show wears her hair down, and Estelle doesn't."

An'gel dimly remembered the character to whom Benjy referred, and she had to admit a certain resemblance between the fictional grandma and Estelle.

Dickce giggled. "I see what you mean, Benjy. I hadn't thought about it before, but Estelle could be a character right out of that show."

"Be serious." An'gel frowned. She herself had a rather dark sense of humor on occasion, but this was not one of them.

"What about the man Tippy heard yelling at her mother?" Benjy said. "What about Lance Perigord? Wasn't he in the house last night, too?"

"Why do I keep forgetting that young man?" An'gel shook her head. "Yes, he was here, too. Although I really can't see him harming Sondra. She was his ticket out of St. Ignatiusville."

"He's not exactly a deep thinker," Dickce said in a wry tone. "If Sondra made him angry, he might not stop to think about lashing out at her."

"She falls and hits her head on a sharp corner or something in her room." Benjy nodded. "Then he panics, the storm hits, and he drags her out to the gallery and tosses her over the railing."

An'gel could envision the scene all too easily. She wondered if that was what really happened. Whether it was Lance who was responsible or someone else remained to be determined, but it seemed like a plausible scenario.

The quiet was shattered a moment later by the sound of Peanut barking frantically across the hall.

CHAPTER 25

B enjy shot up from his chair, out the door, and into the hall before either An'gel or Dickce rose from their respective perches. Peanut kept up the barking until the sisters reached the hall. Then the dog fell silent.

The door to Tippy's room stood wide open, and An'gel and Dickce hurried inside. They found Benjy rubbing the dog's head and talking to a small mound under the bed covers.

"It's okay, Tippy, it's gone. Peanut didn't mean to scare you."

The mound moved, and a small face peeked out from beneath the cover. "You pwomise?" Tippy said solemnly.

"I promise," Benjy said. "That old spider won't scare you or Peanut anymore."

Tippy remained still a moment longer, then evidently decided to take Benjy at his word. She crawled out completely from under the covers and slid to the floor beside her bed.

An'gel felt weak in the knees. Her heart was still racing, and she was annoyed with Peanut. A spider, of all things! A moment later she saw the humorous side of it as she pictured the dog and a spider confronting each other, and neither of them being happy about it. She started laughing.

"Why are you waffing?" Tippy demanded.

Dickce poked An'gel in the side to stop her laughing and answered for her. "My sister laughs when she's afraid of something, like spiders. When she laughs, she isn't afraid anymore."

Tippy considered that a moment and then giggled. "I don't wike spiduhs, but I'm not as scared of them as Peanut. He's a siwwy doggie."

"Yes, he can be silly," Benjy said.

"Where is Endora?" An'gel asked. She didn't see the cat anywhere. Then she spotted another small lump under the bedclothes when it started to move. A moment later the Abyssinian wiggled out. She yawned and stretched.

"Endowa was napping," Tippy explained. "She's not siwwy like Peanut. That siwwy ole spiduh didn't bodder her."

"No, I'm sure it didn't," Dickce said. "Endora is a brave cat."

An'gel was mightily relieved that everything was calm again. When she first heard Peanut barking, she feared that someone had come into the room to harm Tippy. The child was all too vulnerable if left on her own for even a brief period. An'gel was thankful that Peanut had been with Tippy.

"My heart is finally back to its normal pace," she muttered to Dickce. "I don't know about you, but I was terrified there for a moment."

"I was, too," Dickce admitted. "We have to protect this child."

Tippy, evidently unaware of their muted conversation, was rooting around under her bed. She emerged shortly with her teddy bear. "Wance musta hid unda de bed. Siwwy bear."

"Yes, he is silly," Benjy said. "I bet he hid under there when Peanut started barking at the spider." He winked at the sisters over Tippy's head.

An'gel figured the bear must have been knocked off the bed by one of the animals.

"I'm hungwy," Tippy announced. "So is Wance."

"I'm hungry myself," Dickce said. "We'll go down and get something to eat in a minute. First, though, why don't we brush your hair and make you look all pretty."

"Okay," Tippy said. "Mommy wikes it when I wook pwetty wike she does."

An'gel and Benjy exchanged stricken looks while Dickce found Tippy's hairbrush and began to work gently on the tangled light brown strands. "Why don't y'all go on down," she said, a slightly noticeable catch in her voice. "We'll be down in a minute."

"Peanut, come," Benjy said. In an aside to An'gel, he explained that the dog probably needed to go outside.

"What about Endora?" An'gel asked when they were in the hallway with the dog.

"Here she is," Benjy said. "Watch this."

An'gel watched while Endora leapt onto the dog's back and then quickly launched herself onto Benjy's shoulder. "You're so clever," Benjy told Endora. The cat thanked him by rubbing her head against his ear.

"She is clever," An'gel said. "Not to mention agile. I didn't realize cats could jump like that."

Endora rode on Benjy's shoulder all the way down to the first floor. "We'll be back in fifteen minutes or so," Benjy told An'gel. "I'm going to let Peanut burn off some energy after that nap he had. Then I'll put them in my cottage until I eat. They'll be fine there for a little while."

"That sounds good to me," An'gel said. "I'll go to the kitchen and see whether Estelle has done anything about lunch."

She turned down the hall, and Benjy went out with the animals. An'gel listened as she neared the kitchen, but she didn't hear any sounds of food preparation. With a sigh she walked through the open door, wondering what on earth she would find to prepare for lunch. She had not spent much time in the kitchen over a stove for years. Dickce was a better cook than she was, but both sisters had been spoiled for years by their housekeeper, Clementine, who was a very fine Southern cook. Just thinking of Clementine made An'gel hungry for one of the housekeeper's amazing desserts. Her particular favorite was Clementine's carrot cake.

Stop thinking about cake. That's not going to get lunch ready for anybody. An'gel checked the refrigerator and found several pounds of ground beef. There was a bundle of asparagus in the crisper, a head of iceberg lettuce, and several tomatoes. Satisfied that she could cope with what she'd found, An'gel went to the sink to wash her hands.

When she pushed the sleeves of her dress up to keep from wetting them, the scrap of fabric she had found earlier fluttered to the floor. An'gel retrieved it and stood staring at it. The white satin brought the memory of that terrible scene, when Sondra stood upstairs, gleefully ripping the antique gown and throwing the swatches of fabric down to the first floor.

An'gel rubbed the scrap between her fingers. It was warm from having been tucked in the sleeve against her arm. It was also soft, but something about it didn't feel quite right. She held it under the fluorescent light over the sink and examined it more carefully. She quickly came to the conclusion that the piece of fabric she held had not come from an antique wedding gown. The weave was not that of old satin. Instead, it looked like a blended material, perhaps silk and rayon, the kind used to make drapes.

Where had it come from? Had Sondra not destroyed the antique gown after all and instead cut up a piece of drapery?

An'gel shook her head as if to clear it. She tucked the scrap back into her sleeve. There were two answers to this particular puzzle, she decided. Either this was a random piece of material that had somehow found its way to the spot where An'gel discovered it, or Sondra had cut up something besides the dress.

The first answer seemed too bizarre a coincidence, like the freakish accident that supposedly claimed Sondra's life. The second answer was just as bizarre, but for a different reason.

An'gel recalled what Jacqueline had told her and Dickce earlier, about Sondra's care for clothing and how she wouldn't have gone out onto the gallery during the storm wearing her blue gown. Had that care extended to the antique dress? Perhaps Sondra had wanted to punish her grandmother by cutting up fabric that only looked like it came from the dress.

There was one way to answer at least part of the question, An'gel realized. Look for the dress.

She was about to head out of the kitchen when she realized she had no time to hunt for the dress right now. Tippy would be downstairs soon asking for something to eat. She had better focus on putting together a meal for the child and for herself, Dickce, and Benjy.

Before she finished seasoning the ground beef, however, preparatory to forming it into patties, Estelle turned up and informed her that she would take care of lunch. "You can go back to whatever you were doing," Estelle said. "I don't need any help."

"Very well," An'gel said. She went to the sink to wash her hands. "Tippy will be down shortly. She's hungry, and we promised her food."

"I'll see to it," Estelle said. "She likes hot dogs and macaroni and cheese. I'll have them ready for her in a few minutes."

An'gel nodded and left the kitchen, relieved that she wouldn't have to cook after all. Instead, she could go in search of the wedding dress. The likeliest place would be Mireille's room, she decided, because her cousin would have wanted it to hand to prepare it for the wedding. Moreover, Mireille probably wouldn't have trusted Sondra to handle it properly in her absence.

As she neared Mireille's door, An'gel heard Dickce and Tippy on the stairs above her. She didn't want to have to explain to her sister what she was doing and ducked quickly inside her cousin's room and shut the door. She would share whatever she discovered later on.

She flipped the light switch but left the curtains closed.

She stood by the door and surveyed the room to determine the likeliest place to look. Her eyes settled on the old chifforobe in the corner. Its doors were open, and An'gel noted the two long drawers at the bottom, under the compartment for hanging clothes.

She doubted her cousin would keep the dress on a hanger because of its age. The drawers were likelier. They were low, and An'gel had to squat to open them. She started with the bottom drawer, grasping the elderly drawer pulls and sliding the drawer gently out.

There it was. An'gel, even though she had halfway expected to find it, was still a bit surprised. She knew it was the wedding dress because she had seen both Mireille and Jacqueline walk down the aisle in it. The fabric looked fragile, and An'gel wondered why Mireille had been so insistent that Sondra wear it. Surely any damage would have been irreparable.

An'gel slid the drawer closed and slowly got to her feet. Her muscles protested, and she leaned against the chifforobe for a moment to rest.

Sondra had not destroyed the antique gown. So what had she destroyed instead?

CHAPTER 26

Other questions followed quickly. Did Jacqueline know the wedding dress was still intact? And who cleaned up the mess Sondra made?

The answer to that last question was Estelle, An'gel reasoned. Sondra wouldn't have, and Jacqueline had gone with her mother to the hospital.

When Estelle picked up the scattered pieces of fabric, had she realized they did not come from the antique gown?

An'gel wanted to talk to Jacqueline first. Given the loss of her mother and her daughter, Jacqueline might not care in the least about the survival of a piece of clothing. Still, An'gel thought it better to tell her now than have her find it on her own and get a potentially unsettling surprise.

After she talked to Jacqueline, she would confront Estelle. This time she would demand some answers, even if Estelle tried to stonewall her with her usual rudeness.

Once lunch was over, An'gel decided. She left Mireille's room, making sure the door was securely closed behind her. She walked downstairs. When she heard voices coming from the front parlor, she turned that way instead of toward the dining room.

Inside she found Horace and Jacqueline. Horace had his cell phone to his ear while Jacqueline watched him from her perch on one of the armchairs.

"That'll be fine," Horace said. "Soon as you can get somebody here." He ended the call and snapped his phone into a holder attached to his belt. "They should be here in about an hour, Roy said."

"That's good," Jacqueline said, "though I wish someone had thought to call them earlier."

"Hello, my dear," An'gel said. She nodded to Horace. "Are you feeling any better?"

"A little," Jacqueline said. She still appeared drawn and tired to An'gel, but perhaps the nap had helped.

"Miss An'gel, I'll have to be heading back to town in a few," Horace said, "and Jackie's got things to do. I got a crew coming to do the cleanup upstairs. Would you mind showing them where to go when they get here?"

"I'll be happy to," An'gel said. "Anything to help."

"Thank you, *Tante* An'gel." Jacqueline smiled briefly. "I'd rather not be here while they're up there." Her voice faltered on the last two words, and for a moment An'gel thought her goddaughter was going to break down. Jacqueline rallied, however, and asked An'gel to have a seat. "Estelle won't have lunch ready for another ten minutes or so."

An'gel chose a seat on the sofa near Jacqueline. She

wished Horace would depart because she was eager to question her goddaughter about the dress.

"I'll grab something in town." Horace moved close to his wife, leaned down, and kissed her cheek. "You take it easy, sweetheart, and I'll see you later." He ducked his head in An'gel's direction. "Miss An'gel." Then he strode from the room, pulling his cell phone loose from its holster as he walked.

Jacqueline stared after him with what An'gel thought was a curious expression. Affection, An'gel decided, but laced with doubt. Did Jacqueline suspect her husband was responsible for Sondra's death?

"I'm glad we have a few minutes alone together," An'gel said, gently claiming her goddaughter's attention. "I have something to tell you, and I'm afraid it's a bit startling."

Jacqueline appeared alarmed. "It's nothing to do with Tippy, I hope."

An'gel shook her head. "No, Tippy is fine. Dickce and Benjy are taking turns looking after her. She'll be safe with them."

Jacqueline sighed. "I can't tell you how grateful I am. There's so much to do, but I can't take her with me. I haven't even explained to her about Sondra." She closed her eyes for a moment. "How do I tell her she'll never see her mother again?"

"Oh, my dear." An'gel got up from the sofa and went to her goddaughter. She bent down and wrapped her arms around Jacqueline, who leaned against her. An'gel rocked her goddaughter gently.

Jacqueline sighed. "Thank you. I'll be okay." She gently

loosed herself from An'gel's grasp, and An'gel resumed her seat.

"If you'd like one of us with you when you tell her, all you have to do is say so," An'gel said.

"I'll think about it," Jacqueline replied. "Now, what is this startling news you have?"

An'gel pulled the scrap of fabric from her sleeve and leaned forward to hand it to Jacqueline, who looked at it blankly.

"What is this?" she said.

"I thought it was a piece of cloth from the antique wedding dress," An'gel said. "I found it in the hall under a table. When I examined it more closely, however, I realized the fabric wasn't old enough, nor is it satin."

"I don't understand," Jacqueline said. "If it didn't come from the dress, what is it?"

"I don't know," An'gel said, "but I aim to find out. Once I realized it wasn't from the dress, I wondered if the dress was still intact. I suspected, you see, that Sondra might have cut something else up. I confess I went snooping in your mother's room, and I found the dress, unharmed, in the bottom drawer of the chifforobe."

To her surprise, Jacqueline laughed. She stopped abruptly, however, and dropped the scrap onto the coffee table.

"Do you know what it came from?" An'gel asked.

Jacqueline nodded. "It must be from the replica *Maman* had made of the gown a few years ago. The last time I saw it, it was hanging in her closet." She shook her head. "I suppose when Sondra went looking for the gown, she must have found the replica instead. Probably didn't realize it was not the original." Her eyes filled suddenly with tears.

An'gel started to get up, but Jacqueline waved her back. "I'm all right. I'm happy the gown wasn't harmed, for *Maman's* sake. She'll—" Jacqueline halted abruptly.

"Yes, I know," An'gel said. "It's hard to realize she's gone."

"I still don't understand why Sondra would do such a thing." Jacqueline picked up the scrap of fabric and stared at it. "It wasn't like her to do something so cruel."

An'gel was taken aback. From her own assessment of Sondra's character, the girl's act of destruction wasn't all that surprising. She decided not to say this to her goddaughter. Instead she settled for a blander statement. "She was terribly angry over Mireille's refusal to deal with Estelle. Perhaps she was so enraged she acted out of character."

Jacqueline shook her head. "She was angry, certainly, but I've seen her that angry numerous times, and she never did anything like this." She brandished the scrap. "I'd almost swear someone put her up to it, but I can't imagine who would."

An'gel could imagine it. The person who killed Sondra might have incited the act for reasons of his own. Then Sondra might have repented of it in the wake of her grandmother's collapse and threatened to confess. There was a twisted mind at work here, whatever the answer.

"If someone talked Sondra into doing it," An'gel said, "it would seem to me that person wanted to hurt Mireille. Perhaps not to the extent of having her collapse, but to upset her if nothing else."

Jacqueline must already have come to that conclusion,

An'gel thought, because she didn't appear at all surprised by the idea.

"I think you may be right." Jacqueline looked troubled as she deposited the fabric once again on the coffee table. She took a deep breath and faced An'gel squarely. "There's something neither *Maman* nor I told you and *Tante* Dickce. We probably should have, but *Maman* didn't want to worry you." She smiled briefly.

An'gel decided to let that statement pass. Mireille should have confided in them, and perhaps all this could have been averted. She didn't want to upset her goddaughter by telling her that. Instead she said, "What didn't you tell us?"

"There were a few other little incidents that upset *Maman*," Jacqueline said. "At first we thought they were just coincidences, but then they got a bit ugly."

"Tell me about these incidents," An'gel said.

Jacqueline leaned back in her chair, her eyes closed. "A set of Dresden figurines that Papa gave her on their tenth wedding anniversary were broken. *Maman* thought either Estelle or Jackson had done it and were too embarrassed to admit it. She didn't want a confrontation, so she said nothing about it to either of them. Especially because Jackson is rather shaky sometimes, and *Maman* didn't want to upset him."

An'gel nodded. Typical of Mireille, she thought, to refuse to confront someone.

"A couple of other small, treasured possessions got broken," Jacqueline said. "*Maman* still refused to say anything, and she wouldn't allow me to. I was surprised, frankly, that nobody owned up to it. Jackson, in particular, because he's always been so honest. Because of that, I decided it had to be Estelle. She can be spiteful sometimes, and she's angry whenever *Maman* doesn't give in to her and do things her way."

"I think I would have said something to Estelle anyway, no matter what your mother wanted," An'gel said. "That kind of behavior can't be allowed to go on unchecked." *Because it may have escalated into something far worse.*

"I argued with *Maman* about it, but she wouldn't listen. She said she would handle it in her own way. The incidents stopped for a few weeks, and then a couple of days before you arrived, the worst one happened." Jacqueline shuddered.

"What was it this time?" An'gel asked.

"One of Papa's gifts to *Maman*," Jacqueline said. "Probably the one she valued above all, a beautiful seventeenth-century French prayer book, still in its original binding. *Maman* found it cut loose from the binding, and the binding destroyed. I swear I thought she might have a heart attack then."

An'gel felt sick to her stomach. "That was wicked. Mireille should have called the police."

"I tried to get her to," Jacqueline said. "Nothing I said could convince her. She kept insisting she would take care of it. I asked her point-blank if she thought Estelle was the culprit, but she just shook her head." She paused. "I knew it couldn't be Jackson, because he's as devout a Catholic as *Maman*. Estelle isn't devout by any means."

"I agree with you about Jackson," An'gel said. "He would

never do something he would consider blasphemous. If it wasn't Estelle, however, then who do *you* think it was?"

Jacqueline looked ready to burst into tears again. "I don't want to think it, but I'm afraid Horace did it. He was trying to talk *Maman* into lending him money, but she refused. He wasn't happy about it."

CHAPTER 27

An'gel's heart went out to her goddaughter because she could see how troubled Jacqueline was and how much it cost her to admit that she suspected her husband of such a vile act.

"Horace has always seemed like such a confident, successful businessman," An'gel said. "Has he been having financial problems recently?" She began to suspect that this was more than a minor cash-flow issue.

"Horace has been very successful," Jacqueline said, a note of pride in her voice, but it quickly turned bitter. "Horace also likes to gamble. Not at the casinos, mind you, or card games. He gambles with the stock market and investments in business ventures." She looked angry now, An'gel thought.

"And lately those haven't been going too well." An'gel knew from her own experience as an investor that things could quickly turn against a person. She and Dickce, however, always exercised caution when considering any kind of new venture.

"He's never had such a string of back luck," Jacqueline said. "It's like he's lost his touch somehow. He's also lost his confidence, and I hate seeing him this way."

"Why did he approach Mireille for a loan?" An'gel asked. "Couldn't you help him from your own income?"

Jacqueline shook her head. "Not without the permission of the trustees, one of whom is Richmond Thurston. The other is a cranky old stuffy banker in St. Ignatiusville who has turned down every request I've ever made. Both trustees have to agree. Rich would probably say yes, but old fussy pants won't."

"I see," An'gel said. "Mireille obviously turned Horace down. Did she give a reason?"

"No, she didn't," Jacqueline said. "*Maman* has always been secretive about her affairs. She seems to be comfortably off, and I know she and Estelle have made good money from the bed-and-breakfast scheme, but other than that, I don't have a clue what her financial situation is. Daddy left her a fair amount of money, but Willowbank is expensive to maintain."

An'gel certainly understood that last bit. She and Dickce spent a considerable sum every year keeping their own antebellum home in tip-top condition.

Jacqueline went on, "I know how important Willowbank is, er, was, to *Maman*, and I love it, too. But at the end of the day, it's a house, and there are times when people are more important than houses. Don't you think so?"

"Yes, my dear, I do," An'gel said gently. "I understand

your mother's feelings for her home, though. When you get to be our age, you often look back into your past, and there you see all the people you love who are no longer with you. People who lived, loved, and perhaps died in the house, and you want to cherish that house because it holds the memories of those loved ones. The house connects you to so much that makes you who you are."

Jacqueline looked a little teary-eyed by the time An'gel finished, and An'gel felt slightly choked up herself. She always thought of her beloved parents whenever she talked about her home. In every room in Riverhill, she heard echoes of the past, of a time when she and Dickce were children and her parents were young and full of love for each other and for their daughters.

She rarely revealed her feelings to this extent to anyone other than her sister, and she was momentarily embarrassed that she had let her guard down, even to a loved one like her goddaughter.

"I understand," Jacqueline said softly. "Thank you for sharing that with me. You've helped me understand *Maman* even better, and I can't blame her for not wanting to put her home at risk for one of Horace's uncertain ventures."

An'gel smiled. She waited a moment, then she asked the question that had to be asked.

"Other than the fact that he needs money pretty desperately," she said, "why do you think Horace could be behind these nasty incidents? Has he ever done anything of this sort before?"

Jacqueline shook her head. "No, and that's the one thing that makes me a bit doubtful. He can be really hard when it comes to business. He's hard on Trey and makes him toe the line, even when Trey tries to get around him on something. But I've never seen him be vicious or vindictive."

An'gel believed her. Jacqueline and Horace had been married for nearly fifteen years, and surely in that time, if Horace were capable of such revolting behavior, Jacqueline would have seen some evidence of it.

"In that case," An'gel said, "I think Horace is probably not the culprit. With him off the list, along with Jackson, whom does that leave us with?"

"Estelle," Jacqueline said promptly. "There's always been something about her that I've never trusted. She's sly, and that is a quality in a person that I simply can't stand."

An'gel found it hard to disagree with her goddaughter. *Sly* was a good word for Estelle. An'gel would also have added *passive-aggressive* because she thought Estelle was manipulative, particularly when it came to Mireille.

"Estelle, certainly," An'gel said. "But we have to consider others as well." She hesitated a moment. "I hate to ask this, but what about Sondra?"

Jacqueline looked offended for a moment, but then appeared to consider the question seriously. She finally said, "I understand why you mention her, but I really don't think she would have done those things. She might have broken the ornaments and not told *Maman*, but she wouldn't have done it deliberately." She smiled briefly. "I know she wouldn't have dared touch the prayer book, because she was superstitious about anything religious like that."

An'gel wasn't totally convinced, but for the moment she simply nodded. With both Sondra and Mireille now dead, there was no way to know the truth.

"What about Trey?" she asked. "He doesn't live here, does he?"

"No," Jacqueline said. "He has a small house in St. Ignatiusville. Horace insisted he move out after he got Sondra pregnant."

"Would he take it on himself to persecute Mireille to help his father?"

"I honestly don't know," Jacqueline said. "He always wants to please Horace and show his father that he can be every bit as astute a businessman as Horace. But I've never seen him be vicious either. He has a temper, I'll admit that, but once he boils over, he usually calms down quickly."

A person with a temperament like that was the opposite of one who would coldly carry out a campaign of vindictive acts against another, An'gel reasoned. She was inclined to believe Jacqueline, and that meant scratching another name off the list.

"All right then," she said. "Who's left, among persons who are regularly in the house?"

"Lance, of course," Jacqueline said. "But I think we can discount him because, well, because he's Lance. He'd never think up anything like that on his own, and he had no reason I can imagine to want to hurt *Maman*. She's always been quite fond of him, and he of her, in his way."

An'gel agreed that Lance wouldn't have thought of harming Mireille through destruction of beloved possessions, but if another person talked him into it somehow? That was a possibility, even if only a small one. "Is he easily manipulated or suggestible?" An'gel asked.

"I suppose he is," Jacqueline said. "But he's at heart a

truly sweet boy. He would know that *Maman* would be hurt by losing things dear to her, and I don't think he would do it on his own or be manipulated into it because of that."

"Anyone else?" An'gel said. "What about your lawyer, Mr. Thurston? Is he in the house frequently?"

"Yes, he is," Jacqueline said. "He's never married and has no family to speak of, and he was Terence's best friend. *Maman* relies on him a lot as an advisor, and he comes to dinner a couple of times a week." She frowned. "I'd hate to think of him doing such a terrible thing to *Maman* because she's so fond of him, almost treats him like a son in some ways. He took Terence's place, I suppose, because *Maman* adored Terence, and the two of them were friends from childhood."

"No one else?" An'gel asked.

"No, no one that's here on a regular basis," Jacqueline said.

An'gel felt frustrated because Jacqueline had reasonable arguments to explain why almost everyone on the list couldn't, or wouldn't, be the person behind the nasty tricks on Mireille.

Almost everyone, she thought. Everyone except Estelle.

She was so lost in thought she didn't hear Benjy enter the room. He startled her when he spoke.

"Excuse me, ladies, but Estelle wanted me to tell everyone lunch is ready."

"Thank you, Benjy." Jacqueline rose. "Do you know where Tippy is?"

"Yes, ma'am. She's with Miss Dickce in the kitchen. I thought I'd eat in the kitchen with her, and then take her upstairs to play or to nap," Benjy said diffidently. "Does she take a nap in the afternoon?"

"Usually," Jacqueline said, "though she can be difficult to settle down sometimes. If you can get her to be still for a few minutes, though, she'll drop right off."

"If you don't mind me having Peanut and Endora in her room, I'm pretty sure I can get her to be still." Benjy grinned. "I'll tell her the animals need a nap."

Jacqueline smiled. "I don't mind at all. I may have to think about getting a dog or a cat for Tippy. We always used to have both in the house, but not since Tippy was born." Her face darkened for a moment. "Someone told Sondra that old wives' tale about a cat sucking away a baby's breath, and after that she didn't want an animal in the house."

Benjy obviously didn't know how to reply to that, so An'gel spoke to save him any embarrassment.

"Peanut and Endora are smart and well behaved," she said. "They won't harm Tippy, both Benjy and I can promise you that."

"I'm not worried," Jacqueline said. "I really appreciate you looking after my granddaughter." She nodded at Benjy. "I think I'll go wash up before we eat, if you'll excuse me." She walked out of the room after An'gel nodded.

"I never heard that," Benjy said. "About a cat sucking away a baby's breath. That's crazy."

An'gel shook her head. "Folklore, I suppose. Who knows how it got started? Probably something to do with witches and their familiars, who were usually black cats."

"Interesting," Benjy said. "I guess maybe people thought witches sent their cats to harm babies."

"Something like that." An'gel rose. "Enough of that morbid subject. I need to freshen up a bit myself. Thanks for all your help."

"My pleasure." Benjy smiled. "I'll head back to the kitchen. I'll need to take Peanut out again later this afternoon, so if you or Miss Dickce could take over for a little while, that would be great."

"One of us will," An'gel said. She intended for it to be Dickce, but she wouldn't tell Benjy that.

They parted ways at the stairs, and An'gel trod up to her room, right off the landing at the back of the house. She went first to the bathroom to wash her hands, then into her room to check her hair and makeup. The vanity stood next to a window that looked out over the backyard toward the servants' quarters, and when she finished her appraisal of her hair and makeup, An'gel stood and surveyed the scene.

The sun was out, and there were no clouds, she was thankful to note. A movement she noticed with her peripheral vision drew her gaze toward the servants' quarters. She thought she saw the back of some person disappearing around the side of the building, into the trees, but she couldn't be sure. She watched a bit longer, but whoever had ducked around the corner didn't come back.

What reason could someone have for going into the woods? She couldn't imagine why Jackson would be rambling around among the trees, and she knew Estelle should be downstairs in the kitchen.

So who was it? And what was he up to?

CHAPTER 28

An'gel wasted no further time in speculation. She headed downstairs to the kitchen to make sure Estelle was there and to find out where Jackson was.

On her way down the hall past the dining room, she caught a glimpse of the butler placing a dish on the sideboard. There was no way he could have made it from the servants' quarters into the house so soon after An'gel spotted someone there.

Moving into the kitchen, she found Estelle busy at the stove, while Benjy and Tippy occupied two spaces at the table. Estelle noticed her and scowled.

"No need for you in here," she said. "Most of the food's in the dining room."

"Fine," An'gel said. "But I want to talk to you later." She exited the kitchen before Estelle could reply. She really did not appreciate the woman's constant rudeness, and that made her all the more determined to have it out with the housekeeper the moment lunch was done.

In the dining room she found Jacqueline and Dickce, along with an unexpected guest, Lance Perigord. He was sporting a black eye and a bruised nose but otherwise seemed his usual inconsequential self. When An'gel came into the room, he was telling his hostess and Dickce about a television show An'gel had never heard of but that Lance swore was totally riveting.

Jackson hovered near the sideboard, and he smiled when he saw An'gel. She immediately went to him and asked him how he was doing. "I've been worried about you," she said.

"Thank you kindly, Miss An'gel," he said. "I'm doing all right. The Lord is giving me strength."

"Good. He does look after us," An'gel said, and indeed the man did look better, she thought. His back was straighter, and his whole demeanor more positive than the last time she had seen him.

"That He does," Jackson said. "That He does. Now why don't you have a seat, Miss An'gel, and let me serve you your lunch?"

"Thank you," she said with a smile. She joined the others at the table, choosing a seat across from Lance. She wanted to observe him as much as possible.

Lance continued to drone on about the television program, and Jacqueline and Dickce nodded occasionally as they ate their food. Jackson put a plate in front of An'gel. Estelle had taken the ground beef and made it into large patties. There was also grilled asparagus, mashed potatoes, and corn that An'gel suspected came from a can. She tasted

the ground beef, and it was cooked to perfection and sea-
soned with salt, pepper, garlic, and another herb she couldn't
quite place.

When Lance finally ran out of things to say about the
television show, An'gel spoke up. "I'm happy to see you,
Lance. I was worried about you after what happened."

Lance stared at her. "After what happened?"

An'gel pointed to her eye and her nose. "The encounter
you had that left you unconscious on the floor."

Lance looked confused.

"She's talking about when you got the black eye and
the sore nose," Jacqueline explained.

"Oh," Lance said. "I'm okay, but my face is a wreck." He
frowned. "My mother says if I'm permanently scarred because of this, she's going to sue Trey for a million dollars."

Jacqueline paled at that, and Dickce and An'gel exchanged
glances.

"How did your mother come up with that amount?"
Dickce asked. "A million dollars is a lot of money."

"Mama says that's how much my face would be worth
if someone in New York discovered it," Lance replied
smugly. "Mama thinks I should be a model." His expression
turned sour. "And I was going to be, because Sondra and I
were going to New York and I was going to be discovered.
But now that's not going to happen." He brightened. "Unless
Mama gets that million dollars from Trey."

"I'm sure your face will heal just fine and there won't be
any permanent damage," Dickce said soothingly. "This time
next week you'll be back to just the way you were before."

"That would be nice," Lance said. "I couldn't stand
being ugly or disfigured." He frowned. "But if I'm not,

then Mama won't get the million dollars and I won't be able to go to New York. It's all so confusing."

If this is all an act, then he should definitely be in New York, but on the Broadway stage. An'gel didn't think, however, that Lance was acting, but she almost wished he was. The boy was painfully stupid.

"Yes, I'm sure it is," Jacqueline said. "But wait and see what happens, okay, and don't worry too much about it. Even if you end up looking like you always did, you may still find some way to New York without getting that million dollars from Trey."

Lance brightened at that. Before he could launch into further inane speech, An'gel said, "I presume you're going back to town after you finish lunch, Jacqueline. Would you like Dickce or me to come with you?"

Jacqueline shook her head. "Oh, no, I appreciate it, but if I need someone, Horace is in town. No, you stay here."

An'gel and Dickce exchanged glances. Jacqueline clearly did not want either of them to go with her, and An'gel couldn't really understand why. It was Jacqueline's choice, however, and she and Dickce would abide by her wishes.

"All right," An'gel said. "I have things I need to take care of anyway, and Dickce will be helping Benjy look after Tippy."

"I like Tippy," Lance said. "She likes to play with me, and she doesn't ask me hard questions."

"I know Tippy would like to see you, Lance," An'gel said. "She was asking about you earlier."

"That's sweet," Lance said. "I hope she'll still recognize me." He touched his bruised nose and winced. "I look so different right now."

"She'll know who you are," Dickce said. An'gel could see her sister struggling not to giggle. "And if for some reason she doesn't, I'll introduce you."

Lance beamed at her. "Thank you. I wouldn't want her to think I'm a stranger. Little girls aren't supposed to play with strangers." Lance paused, his brow furrowed. "I don't think little boys are supposed to either."

"No, they're not." Jacqueline laid aside her fork and pushed back her chair. "Sorry to rush off like this, but I really need to get to town. Lance, you're welcome to stay for dinner tonight if you'd like, although you'd better check with your mother."

"Mama will be happy if I stay here for dinner," Lance said. "She told me I needed to be here to be a constant reminder." He frowned. "Can't remember what I'm supposed to be a reminder of, but Mama thinks I should stay."

Jacqueline drew a deep breath, and her eyes rolled heavenward for a moment. "Then that's okay. I'll see y'all later." She walked out of the dining room, and moments later An'gel heard her running lightly up the stairs.

An'gel figured she knew why Mama Perigord wanted Lance to hang around Willowbank. She was hoping someone would feel guilty enough about Trey's attack on her baby to offer her some cash. An'gel thought Mama Perigord was probably a bit too mercenary, but she did agree that Lance deserved something from Trey after that nasty assault.

Benjy and Tippy walked into the dining room, and Tippy squealed with happiness the moment she spotted Lance.

"Wance!" She ran to him and held out her arms. Lance pushed back his chair and picked her up. He hugged her tight, and Tippy wrapped her arms around his neck. "Oh, Wance, I'm so gwad you is here. Can you come pway with me and Benjy?"

Lance eased his grip on Tippy and let her down. He smiled. "I'd love to play with you, sweetie. And Benjy, too." He smiled at Benjy as well, and Benjy blushed slightly.

An'gel hoped Lance wouldn't make a nuisance of himself where Benjy was concerned, but she trusted Benjy to handle the situation on his own.

"Come on upstairs with us, then, if you're finished with your meal," Benjy said. "While you and Tippy are playing, I'll go get Tippy's two new friends, Peanut and Endora, so they can play, too."

Lance frowned. "I haven't met them, have I? I don't think I know any children named Peanut and Endora."

Tippy giggled as she tugged on Lance's hand. "Siwwy Wance. Peanut is a doggie, and Endowa is a kitty. Come on." She tugged again, and Lance yielded.

"I like dogs and cats," Lance said earnestly to Benjy. "So I'll be happy to meet these friends of yours."

Benjy glanced quickly at An'gel and then at Dickce, and for a moment An'gel thought he was appealing for help. Then she realized he was trying hard not to laugh. She covered her mouth quickly with her napkin and coughed to keep from laughing herself.

Lance and the excited Tippy left the room, and Benjy, shaking his head, followed them.

Dickce looked at An'gel. "I don't know about you, Sister, but I could use a nap. I didn't get enough sleep last night. If you don't mind, I think I'll go lie down for a bit."

"You go right ahead," An'gel said. "I wouldn't mind doing that myself, but first I want to talk to Estelle."

"About what?" Dickce asked as she rose from the table.

"I'll tell you later," An'gel said. "You go on and get some rest, and we'll discuss it when you're up from your nap."

Dickce shrugged. "I'm not going to argue." She yawned. "See you in a while."

An'gel hadn't quite finished her meal. She ate the remainder quickly, her mind on the looming confrontation with Estelle. This time she was determined not to let the woman's rudeness put her off. She would persevere until Estelle answered her questions.

She pushed back her chair and dropped her napkin beside her plate. She realized Estelle might have left the kitchen by now, but An'gel was determined to find her, wherever she might be.

She found only Jackson in the kitchen. "Where is Estelle? I really need to talk to her."

"She's gone to her apartment," Jackson said. "I reckon she was going to lie down."

"This is something that won't wait," An'gel said. "Thank you, Jackson." She marched to the back door, intent on confronting the housekeeper.

The air outside was cool, and An'gel blinked several times as her eyes adjusted to the bright sun. As soon as they had, she struck off across the backyard toward the servants' quarters. The renovated building lay about fifty yards from the rear of Willowbank, and An'gel reached it quickly. There were four apartments, and as An'gel recalled, Estelle occupied the one at the end farthest from the house.

She knocked on the door. "Estelle, I have to talk to you." She waited a moment, then knocked again. "Estelle, open this door."

Seconds later, the door swung open. Estelle glared at her. "What's so all-fired important that you're bothering me now? I need to rest." She held a large, half-empty bottle in her hand. An'gel recognized it as an expensive brand of whiskey. She hadn't figured Estelle for a tippler, but if she was a heavy drinker, that might explain a few things about her disposition.

"I have some questions, and you're going to answer them." An'gel charged forward. Estelle yielded and backed away from the door.

An'gel didn't waste time examining the surroundings. She intended to push Estelle hard to get her answers.

"You cleaned up the mess after Sondra threw all those scraps of fabric down from the second floor, didn't you?"

Was it her imagination, or did Estelle look relieved at the question?

"Yes, I did." Estelle moved past her and walked over to a table that held a glass and a siphon. "I was always cleaning up Sondra's messes."

An'gel paid no attention to the bitterness in the woman's voice. "Did you happen to notice that the scraps you picked up weren't from the antique wedding gown?"

Estelle appeared faintly surprised. She set the bottle down on the table next to the glass. "How did you find that out?"

"I found a scrap you missed," An'gel said. "When I looked at it closely, I realized it wasn't satin. Then I went upstairs and found the gown, intact, in the bottom drawer of Mireille's chifforobe."

"Then what's the problem?" Estelle asked. "The gown is safe, not that it's going to do anybody any good. Mireille will never be able to look at it again." She picked up the whiskey bottle and poured three fingers into the glass on the table.

"I know it was the replica of the gown that Sondra destroyed," An'gel said. "I talked to Jacqueline, and she believes someone put Sondra up to destroying it as a joke on her grandmother."

Estelle's eyes narrowed. "Do you think I'd do something like that? To Mireille, the best friend I ever had?"

An'gel stared hard at her. "You tell me. If you didn't do it, who did?"

"I've got my own ideas about that." Estelle picked up the glass. "You leave it to me. I'll find out who did it and make him pay for what he did to Mireille." She lifted the glass and tossed the entire contents into her mouth. She swallowed and set the glass down. An'gel wanted to grab hold of her and shake her till her teeth fell out, as her mother used to say.

To An'gel's surprise, Estelle started shaking on her own. Then she began clawing at her throat and gasping. She pitched forward onto the floor, writhed for about five seconds, and then was still.

CHAPTER 29

Benjy wished Lance had stayed at home. He didn't mind looking after Tippy. She was a cute kid and pretty well behaved as long as you kept her entertained.

That Lance, however. Benjy shook his head as he made his way down to the cottage to retrieve Peanut and Endora. Lance was a bigger kid in some ways than the four-year-old. Benjy felt sorry for him, though, because the guy was so dumb. He figured it wouldn't be long before Tippy could outsmart Lance. She seemed like a pretty bright kid.

He walked faster. He was anxious to get back to the house and make sure Tippy was okay. He was hoping Lance wouldn't let something slip about Sondra. He'd almost taken Lance aside before he left to tell him not to talk about Sondra, but then he realized it might not do any good. He would just have to hope Sondra's name didn't come up until he was back with them and able to divert Tippy's attention.

Peanut bounded out the moment Benjy opened the door, woofing happily. Benjy squatted to hug the Labradoodle, and Endora jumped on his shoulder.

"Okay, kids," he said as he stood. "Let's do our business, because I have to get back." Peanut barked, and Benjy grinned at the dog. "Don't worry, you're going with me. Come on now, let's get going."

Endora rode on his shoulder as he headed back toward Willowbank. She had a litter box in the cottage, so it was Peanut who really needed to do his business. Benjy thought the expression was funny. He'd picked it up from the sisters, who never said *pee* or *poop* when it came to the animals' bodily functions. Benjy had learned to be careful about using such words around them. He wouldn't offend them for anything, because they had been so good to him.

Peanut hiked his leg against one of the largest trees Benjy had ever seen. Benjy heard voices coming from somewhere nearby. He glanced around but didn't see anyone. Whoever it was must be on the other side of the tree. Peanut finished, and Benjy was about to lead the dog on toward the house.

Then he caught a couple of words and stayed where he was.

". . . big trouble. You gotta get me out of this, or else I'm going to blow my brains out."

Benjy recognized Horace's voice. Man, he sure sounded upset.

Another man spoke, but Benjy wasn't sure who he was.

"I told you, I can't right now. You've got to sit tight a little longer. And stop that stupid talk about killing yourself. Everything's going to be fine, I promise you. I'll have the money, just tell the creditors you're getting a loan."

The more the guy talked, the more familiar his voice sounded. Benjy struggled to place it, and then he remembered. It was that lawyer guy. What was his name?

The men moved away, headed toward the house, or so Benjy judged by the sound of their footsteps. He had a hand on Peanut's head, and the Labradoodle remained quiet. Benjy didn't want to embarrass the men, or himself, by letting them know he'd overheard their conversation. He also wondered whether what they were talking about had anything to do with what was going on with the family.

As soon as he thought the men were out of sight, Benjy emerged from behind the tree with Peanut beside him and Endora still on his shoulder. The first chance he got, he would tell the sisters about what he'd heard.

First, though, he needed to check on Tippy and Lance. Once they were in the house, he raced up the stairs, Endora in his arms now. Peanut ran ahead of him. There was no sign of the men, and Benjy was thankful for that.

The door of Tippy's bedroom was shut, and Peanut stood in front of it, whining. "Shhh," Benjy told him, and the dog quieted. Benjy opened the door, and Peanut slipped in. Benjy stepped inside as Tippy squealed happily at the sight of Peanut. Lance looked up from his seated position on the floor and frowned.

"We're having a fashion show," he explained. "Don't let the dog knock stuff over."

"Okay," Benjy said. He surveyed the scene Lance had put together. A folded towel formed a runway, and at the end away from Lance stood a dollhouse with four dolls in standing position leaned against it. Each of the dolls wore a brightly colored dress, and they all had shoes on their tiny feet.

Tippy introduced Lance to Peanut and Endora. The cat hopped from Benjy's shoulder onto the bed, where she preened and licked at her shoulders.

"How pretty," Lance said. "I never saw a cat that color before."

Benjy thought about explaining Endora's breed to Lance but thought the conversation might get too complicated. Tippy's next remark put it out of his mind completely.

With her arm around Peanut's neck, Tippy looked up at Benjy and announced in a solemn tone, "My mommy is in heaven."

Oh, crap, I knew I shouldn't have left her alone with this guy. "Really. Who told you that?" Benjy glared at Lance, but the man was oblivious as usual.

"Wance did," Tippy said. "He said my mommy is in heaven, but I can't see her until I go there. That's going to be a wong, wong time, isn't it, Wance?"

"Yes, it is," Lance said as he smiled at the little girl. "You have to stay here with me and be my friend. Your mommy will be fine in heaven. My daddy is there, too, and he'll look after her."

"That's good," Tippy said. "Mommy wikes having a man to wook after her."

Benjy grimaced at that statement. Tippy was way too young to be aware of that kind of thing.

"Yes, I know," Lance said. "I thought I was going to be the man who would look after her, and she was going to look after me, too." He shook his head. "But I think she was going to change her mind about that before she went to heaven."

Tippy looked concerned. "But Mommy wuvved you, she told me she did. I told her I wuv you, too."

"Thank you, sweetie," Lance said. "I love you, too." He cut a sideways glance at Benjy. "I was going to be Tippy's father."

"You can still be my daddy, Wance." Tippy let go of Peanut to lean over and give Lance a kiss on the cheek.

Benjy thought it was about time to change the subject. He felt increasingly uncomfortable. He believed that Lance really did love Tippy. He was like a big kid himself, but with Sondra gone, Lance really had no role in Tippy's life other than as a family friend.

"Tell me about your fashion show," Benjy said.

"Wance can do that," Tippy said. "I have to potty." She walked around Lance and headed for the door.

Benjy followed her into the hallway and watched until she closed the bathroom door behind her. He kept an eye toward the bathroom, but he wanted to question Lance.

"You said you thought Sondra had changed her mind and was interested in another man," he said. "Do you have any idea who it was?"

"No," Lance said. "Sondra wouldn't tell me. I think he was a lot older than her, though." He frowned. "I don't know why she'd want to marry an old guy. We really could have had a lot of fun together."

Benjy kept his eye on the bathroom door. He decided to risk a question. "Aren't you gay?"

Lance didn't appear offended at the question. "What does that have to do with anything? Sondra knew, and it didn't bother her. She told me she didn't like, well, you know, having sex." He blushed.

Benjy couldn't resist rolling his eyes at that, but he was glad Lance couldn't see him doing it. "So you were going to marry her, and the two of you were just going to have fun together?"

"Sondra wanted to get married so she could have her money from her daddy," Lance said. "And she promised to take me to New York so I could be discovered and be a famous model. But I wasn't supposed to tell anybody." He frowned, as if considering that.

The bathroom door opened, and Tippy emerged. She trotted back to Benjy and slipped past him into the room. Benjy sighed and closed the door. He leaned against it for a moment, thinking. He had a lot to tell Miss An'gel and Miss Dickce, but for now he was going watch the big kid give the little kid a fashion show.

~~~

Dickce awoke to the noise of sirens sounding from somewhere close by. She also awoke with a cat curled up on the spare pillow next to her. "Endora, what on earth is going on?" Dickce sat up on the side of the bed and tried to gain her bearings. She had been sound asleep and felt groggy.

The sirens persisted, and now they sounded like they were right outside her window. Slowly she got up from the bed and went to peer out the window overlooking the rear of the house. She blinked in surprise at the sight of an ambulance and a police car pulled up in front of the servants' quarters. Her heart sank. She was afraid Jackson had collapsed, the strain of Mireille's loss too much for him to bear.

Now completely awake, she slipped on her shoes and opened the bedroom door. She cast a glance back at the cat. Endora seemed perfectly content to remain where she was, so Dickce left her in the room. Benjy was already on the stairs, his head and shoulders disappearing as she reached the top of the flight.

She called out to him, and he stopped to look back. Dickce hurried down a few steps until she was two above him. "Do you have any idea what's going on?"

"No, ma'am," he said. "I was on my way to find out."

"What about Tippy?" she asked. "Perhaps I should stay with her and let you go on."

"It's okay," Benjy said. "Lance is with her."

"Lance?" Dickce cast a doubtful glance up the stairs in the direction of Tippy's room.

"She'll be fine with him," Benjy said. "He's really good with her. Come on, let's go find out what the sirens are all about."

Dickce followed him down, but at a slower pace. By the time she reached the foot of the stairs, Benjy was entering the kitchen. Dickce wondered where An'gel was. *Probably smack-dab in the middle of the action.* She hurried to the kitchen.

Dickce was thrilled to see Jackson when she walked out the back door. He stood with Benjy a few feet away. They were watching the scene unfold at the servants' quarters, but from a safe distance. Dickce joined them.

The ambulance and the police car blocked the view of the far end of the building. Dickce thought Estelle's apartment was on that end. Jackson's, she remembered, was the one closest to the house.

"What's going on, Jackson?" Dickce asked.

Jackson turned to her with a frown. "I'm not rightly sure, Miss Dickce. Miss An'gel went over to Estelle's a little while ago, and the next thing I know, sirens are screaming, and they come tearing around the side of the house." He nodded in the direction of the ambulance and the police car.

"Is An'gel still over there?" Dickce wished her sister would turn up.

"I believe so," Jackson said.

"I'm sure she's fine," Benjy said. "Look, here she comes."

An'gel, escorted by Officer Sanford, was indeed walking toward the house. Dickce hurried forward to meet them. She wanted to assure herself that An'gel was all right.

An'gel looked okay, Dickce decided when she was five feet away. But she was holding on to the young policeman's arm like a lifeline.

"Sister, what happened?" Dickce said. "Are you okay?"

"I'm fine," An'gel said. "A bit shaken up, but I'll do." She released her grip on Sanford's arm. "Thank you, young man. I'll go on to the house with my sister. When you need me, you can find me in the kitchen."

"Yes, ma'am." Sanford ducked his head, then turned and walked back to the action.

Dickce took her sister's arm and led her toward the house.

"Tell me what happened," she said. "Is something wrong with Estelle?"

"There sure is," An'gel said grimly. "She's dead."

"Oh dear," Dickce said. "Did she have a heart attack?"

"No," An'gel replied. "She was poisoned, and I believe I saw her killer."

CHAPTER 30

An'gel thanked her sister for the cup of hot tea. After she had a few sips, she said, "I've never seen someone die like that, and I hope I never do again."

"Do you feel up to talking about it?" Dickce asked.

An'gel shuddered. "It's probably better if I do." She looked at her sister across the kitchen table, then at Jackson and Benjy on either side.

"I went there to ask her some questions," An'gel said. "I was determined that she was finally going to talk to me. I wanted to know about the antique wedding gown." She recounted her finding of the scrap that led her to search for the intact gown and its discovery in Mireille's bedroom. "Estelle knew that the gown Sondra destroyed was a fake. I asked her if she put Sondra up to destroying it as a joke, and she said she didn't."

"Did she know who did?" Dickce asked. "That is, if anyone did put the idea in Sondra's head."

"I think she did know," An'gel said. "She told me once before there were things she knew that others weren't aware of, and I got the impression from that conversation that she expected to use that knowledge to her advantage."

"She was nosy," Jackson said. "Always poking her nose into everything. I told her once, she kept doing that, somebody was going to bite her nose off."

"Somebody did, so to speak," An'gel said grimly. "While we were talking, she poured herself some whiskey, several fingers in fact, then she knocked it all back at one go." She paused as the mental image of Estelle's death rictus flashed through her brain. "Then she started shaking and grabbing at her throat like she couldn't breathe. Next thing I knew she was on the floor, dead."

Dickce shuddered. "How awful."

Benjy nodded. "Poor woman. She didn't deserve that."

An'gel told them about the figure she had seen earlier near Estelle's apartment.

"Could you tell who it was?" Benjy asked.

"No," An'gel said. "To be truthful, I'm not completely sure I really saw a person. It was only a fleeting impression, out of the corner of my eye, and by the time I looked, whatever it was had gone."

"You think it was the person who got into Estelle's place and put the poison in her whiskey," Dickce said.

An'gel nodded. "I think it's a distinct possibility. What I'm wondering is, what poison would work that quickly."

"Likely it wasn't poison, Miss An'gel." Jackson frowned.

"Miss Estelle was deathly allergic to peanuts. All somebody had to do was grind up some peanuts real fine like and put 'em in her bottle."

"How awful," Dickce said again.

"Did everyone know about this allergy?" An'gel asked.

Jackson nodded. "Oh, yes. Miss Estelle talked about it to everybody. You know how she was about complaining. Wouldn't ever cook nothing with peanuts, and wouldn't have no peanut butter in the house." He shook his head. "Little Miss Tippy loves peanut butter, and Miss Jacqueline has to sneak it into the house for her."

There was a knock at the back door, and Jackson got up to answer it. He opened the door and stood aside to allow Officers Bugg and Sanford to enter the kitchen.

Bugg looked straight at An'gel. "Ma'am, I need to talk to you about this unfortunate event. You reckon you feel up to telling me about it?"

"Yes, Officer, I do," An'gel said with more conviction than she felt. She knew she had to do this. Best to get it over with. "Would you like to talk here? Or we could go to the parlor?"

"Here'll be just fine, ma'am," Bugg said. "But I'd prefer to talk to you by yourself." He glanced at Jackson, Dickce, and Benjy. They took the hint and excused themselves, though Jackson paused long enough to offer the policemen something to drink. Bugg declined, and Jackson followed the others from the room.

Bugg plopped down across from An'gel in the chair Dickce had vacated. Sanford sat to her left in Jackson's spot. He pulled out his notebook and pen.

"All right, ma'am," Bugg said. "Why were you there in

the deceased's apartment? Was you in the habit of visiting her there?"

"No, I wasn't. I had never been in her apartment before today," An'gel said. "I went there to ask her a few questions about odd things that have been going on in this house."

"Like what, for example?" Bugg put his arms on the table and leaned on them, focused intently on An'gel.

An'gel had to think quickly about what she could tell him without violating Jacqueline's confidence. She didn't want to tell him some things without her goddaughter's permission. As soon as Jacqueline returned from town, she vowed, she would urge her goddaughter to tell everything to the police.

"Ma'am?" Bugg prompted.

"Sorry, just putting my thoughts in order," An'gel said. "The main thing was the incident with the wedding dress that caused my cousin to collapse and have to be rushed to the hospital. I believe I mentioned it when you first came to Willowbank to investigate Sondra's death?"

Bugg looked annoyed. "Yes, ma'am, you did indeed mention it as I recall. The young woman was pitchin' scraps from the wedding dress over the railin'."

"Yes," An'gel replied. "Or so we thought at the time. Mireille collapsed and was rushed to the hospital, where she died." An'gel felt rage all over again at Sondra's nasty trick, and she took a moment to calm herself.

"That Sondra was a hellcat sometimes," Bugg said. "Still, it's hard to believe she'd do something like that to her own grandma. But you said, 'so we thought at the time.' Does that mean it wasn't the real wedding dress she tore up?"

"Yes. Mireille had apparently had a replica of it made

some years ago, and it was the replica Sondra destroyed. In the heat of the moment, though, Mireille and Jacqueline didn't realize that."

"So you went out there to talk to the deceased about this. Why? Did you think she had something to do with it?"

Bugg was more astute than An'gel had earlier thought. "When I told Jacqueline I had found the original dress, we talked about the incident. She swears Sondra wouldn't have done something like that unless someone else put her up to it. I thought Estelle might know something about it."

"Did she?"

"I think she did," An'gel said. "I was trying to get her to tell me what she knew, but she was stubborn. I think she intended to blackmail whoever it was. Then she drank some whiskey and collapsed. She died without ever saying another word to me."

She hesitated for a moment but decided she had better tell the officer about the figure she thought she had seen earlier in the day.

When she'd finished, Bugg stared at her. "You say you don't know who it was, or even if it was a man or a woman. Just an impression."

An'gel nodded. She knew how insubstantial it was.

Bugg was still staring. "Tell me, ma'am. Do you wear glasses? Or contacts?"

Taken slightly aback, An'gel said, "No contacts. I do have glasses I use sometimes for needlework or reading." Then she realized why he was asking about her eyesight. "My distance vision is fine, Officer."

"All right, ma'am." Bugg held up a hand in a placatory

gesture. "Had to check. You're sure you saw *some*thing, right?"

"Yes," An'gel said. She *had* seen something move. She just couldn't swear that it was a person. Given what had happened to Estelle, however, she felt it likely she had seen the murderer leaving after poisoning the whiskey.

"You got all that?" Bugg said to Sanford. The junior officer nodded.

"I reckon we got two murders, then," Bugg said to An'gel. "Coroner's pretty certain now that Sondra was dead before she ever went off that gallery."

"Do you have any idea who's responsible?" An'gel asked, curious whether Bugg would share anything of consequence.

"I got my ideas," he responded lugubriously. "What about you? I checked your bona fides with the police and the sheriff's department over in Athena, ma'am, and they tell me you was involved in several murders a coupla months ago."

An'gel nodded reluctantly. She preferred not to think about those events if at all possible. "Yes, Officer, unfortunately murders were committed in our home."

"That lady deputy in the sheriff's department thinks an awful lot of you and your sister," Bugg said in a tone that to An'gel sounded slightly incredulous. "Told me I should ask you what you think is going on here."

That last sentence sounded like a challenge, An'gel thought. While she appreciated Kanesha Berry's expression of confidence, she did not know Officer Bugg well enough to talk to him as candidly as she had always done with Kanesha. He seemed bright enough, but she didn't want to send him haring off on the wrong tangent by anything she said.

She decided there was one thing she could safely tell him, and let him make of it what he would. "In my opinion, Officer, it's all about money. You figure out who needs money desperately, and you'll find the person who killed Sondra and Estelle."

Bugg looked disappointed, as if he had expected more from her. His words confirmed that. "I ain't dumb, ma'am. I know there's a lot of money in this family. Shoot, Terence Delevan was probably the richest man in this parish. Heck, richest man in several parishes. That means his wife and his daughter both got a lot of money when he died. We know all about that here in St. Ignatiusville. I was hoping you was going to tell me something I didn't know."

An'gel felt justly rebuked, but she wasn't ready to concede. "If you know all that, then you probably also know whose business is on shaky ground and could use an infusion of cash."

Bugg nodded. "Yes, ma'am, indeed I do. Already working on that angle." He stood. "I reckon that's about all I need from you at the moment. If you don't mind, ask Jackson to come in."

An'gel also rose. "Certainly, Officer. I hope I have been of some help." She walked away from the table and out of the kitchen. She found Dickce, Benjy, and Jackson in the front parlor. Jackson was dusting, while Dickce and Benjy sat quietly on the sofa.

"Officer Bugg wants to talk to you now," An'gel informed the butler.

Jackson nodded, dropped his dust cloth on a table, and left the room.

The moment he was out of the room, Benjy said, "I have some things to tell you."

An'gel chose the armchair nearest the sofa. "I'm all ears."

Benjy related the conversation he had overheard while bringing Peanut and Endora back to the house.

An'gel and Dickce looked thoughtfully at each other.

"Sounds to me like Horace and Thurston are in cahoots over something," Dickce said.

"Exactly when was this?" An'gel asked.

Benjy thought for a moment after he glanced at his watch. "At least an hour ago, maybe a little more. Say an hour and a quarter."

"That was around the time that I saw someone ducking around the side of Estelle's apartment," An'gel said.

"So both Horace and Thurston were on the property," Dickce said.

They were startled by a loud noise, the forceful closing of the front door. A moment later, Horace strode into the room.

"Can somebody tell me what in the world is going on out back? Why are the police here?" he demanded.

CHAPTER 31

"Are you just now coming back from town?" An'gel asked in a pleasant tone.

Horace appeared taken aback. Then he laughed heartily. An'gel thought it rang hollow.

"Yeah, I've been in town all morning. Lots to do, like always." Horace laughed again. "You know what it's like for us businessmen." He sobered. "Now tell me, what's going on with the police here?"

"There's been another death," Dickce said.

Horace blanched and suddenly seemed weak at the knees. He stumbled to a chair and dropped into it. "Not Jackie. Please tell me it's not Jackie."

Why would he assume it's his wife?

"No, it's not," An'gel said. "As far as we know, Jacqueline is still in town. I'm afraid Estelle is dead."

Horace looked mighty relieved, An'gel thought. But his expression changed quickly to one of bafflement.

"What happened? She have a heart attack?" Horace asked.

An'gel would have sworn he wasn't faking it. He genuinely did seem puzzled by Estelle's death.

"It wasn't a heart attack," Dickce said. "She was poisoned. An'gel was with her and saw the whole thing."

Horace pulled out a handkerchief and began mopping his sweaty forehead. "Lord, I need a drink." He stumbled to his feet and over to the liquor cabinet. With shaky hands, he pulled out a bottle of brandy and poured himself a healthy shot. He gulped it down and immediately poured another. He brought this one back to the chair with him and sipped at it.

"Sure am sorry you had to see something like that," Horace said as he stared at the diminished contents of his glass. "Why on earth would somebody want to poison Estelle?"

An'gel turned to Benjy. "Why don't you go back upstairs and check on Tippy," she said. "If the police want to talk to you, Dickce can text you."

"That's fine with me," Benjy said as he headed for the door. From behind Horace's back he pointed to the man and then drew a large question mark in the air. An'gel nodded. Benjy turned and left the room.

"About Estelle," An'gel said to Horace. "You've lived with the woman in this house for many years. Why do *you* think someone would want her out of the way?"

Horace shifted uneasily in his chair. "Well, she was

always trying to interfere in stuff that wasn't her business. She wasn't one to hold back on her opinion of anyone or anything, I can tell you that." He shrugged. "Woman like that is bound to rile somebody up."

An'gel decided it was time for the gloves to come off. "Was she blackmailing you, Horace? Did she know something about your money problems that you didn't want Jacqueline or Mireille to know?"

Horace goggled at her and dropped his now-empty glass onto the carpet. He sputtered but no coherent words emerged.

"We know you're having financial problems," Dickce said. "It's obvious to us, and to the police no doubt, that money has to be involved in these murders somehow."

"The question is," An'gel said, "did you kill Sondra so Jacqueline would inherit? I'm sure you think you could get Jacqueline to bail you out. Then there's also what she inherits now from her mother." An'gel could almost see Horace shrinking into his chair.

The two-pronged attack had evidently demoralized the man. He held up both hands, as if in protest.

"Ladies, I swear to you, I would never in my life have hurt Sondra or my mother-in-law. Not for money, not for anything in this world." He took a deep breath. "It's true I'm in a financial bind at the moment, and if I don't get the money I need soon, I'm going to be in the bayou with my head under the water. But no, ma'am, no way, nohow did I kill Sondra or Estelle."

An'gel wanted to believe him, because she didn't want her goddaughter's husband to turn out to be a murderer. But Horace could be lying, even though his words had a ring of truthfulness to them.

Time for another battering ram, An'gel decided.

"You told us a few minutes ago you were just now getting back from town," she said. "We know that's a lie."

Horace goggled at her again.

Before he could respond, Dickce weighed in. "We have it from an unimpeachable source that you were out front within the last ninety minutes or so having a conversation with Mr. Thurston."

Horace picked his glass up from the floor and then got up to refill it. At this rate, An'gel thought, he'd be drunk in no time.

Glass replenished, Horace walked back to his chair. He gulped down about half the brandy before he looked either sister in the eye.

"All right, it's true," he said. "I was here. Briefly. Thurston called and insisted he had to talk to me. I thought he was in his office but he was calling from his car. Said he wanted to meet me here."

"Did he say why he wanted to meet you here? It seems like an odd choice for a meeting." An'gel thought the lawyer's actions were deeply suspicious.

"He said he was bringing some documents out for Jacqueline to sign. He cut me off before I could tell him she was in town," Horace said. "I tried calling him back, but he didn't answer. So I had no choice but to come meet him here."

"Did you enter the house?" Dickce asked.

Horace shook his head. "No, when I got close to the house, I saw Thurston standing down at the edge of the driveway, where the line of live oaks starts. I pulled over there, and we walked around under the trees while we talked." He frowned. "I didn't see anybody else while we were out there."

"Nevertheless, someone did hear a bit of your conversation," An'gel said. "Did you get the impression that Thurston had been here long when you arrived?"

"I really can't say. His car was parked off to the side of the driveway, under that stand of trees at the bottom of the rise. After he called, it took me about fifteen minutes to get here."

"So he could have been here the whole time," Dickce said. "He could have been here already when he called you."

"Guess so." Horace downed the rest of the brandy.

"How long did the two of you talk?" An'gel asked.

"No more than six or seven minutes," Horace said. "Seemed like a waste of time to me, rushing out here for that. He wasn't happy when I told him Jacqueline was in town, but I told him he should have answered when I called him back."

"According to what was overheard," An'gel said, "you and Thurston were discussing money. Money you needed to get you out of the fix you're in. Is Thurston involved in this mess somehow? Or had you merely approached him to bail you out?"

Horace scowled. "A little of both. It was because of him I got involved in the damn thing in the first place. Then I found out he had pulled his money out, and there I am holding the bag. I told him he ought to lend me the money I needed, but he kept saying he didn't have it."

An'gel wasn't particularly interested in the nature of the venture, but she was curious about the sum of money involved. "How much money is involved?"

At first she thought Horace was going to refuse to

answer, but the stern gazes of both sisters evidently convinced him otherwise.

"Ten million," Horace said. He got up and headed back to the liquor cabinet.

An'gel nearly fell out of her chair in surprise. A swift glance at Dickce told her that her sister was equally shocked. The sum was far more than An'gel had anticipated.

"Ten million was your investment in this venture?" she asked. When Horace nodded, she went on. "What about Thurston? Had he put in a similar amount?"

"He told me he put in seven," Horace said.

"I didn't realize Thurston was that wealthy," Dickce said. "Does he come from money?"

Horace shrugged. "Don't think so. He always seems to have plenty of cash. A new car every year, trips to New York and Las Vegas. Has a house in New Orleans and one in Belize, too."

An'gel considered Horace's response to Dickce's question. He had given a believable answer, but An'gel had the feeling he was holding something back.

"Anything more?" she asked.

Horace shook his head and sipped at his brandy.

An'gel changed tack. "Do you know the terms of Mireille's will? And Jacqueline's?"

"Unless either one of them changed them, then yes, I do." Horace's brow wrinkled as he gazed at An'gel. "Why do you ask?"

"Because their wills could have some bearing on the murders," An'gel said.

Horace continued to stare at her, and An'gel could tell

he was thinking hard about her response. Suddenly he stood and set his empty glass on a nearby table.

"You'll have to excuse me, ladies. Got some things I need to take care of." He turned to walk away.

"Horace, you need to tell the police what we've discussed," An'gel said. "If you don't, we certainly will."

Dickce nodded, and Horace stared at them. "All right," he said, then turned on his heel and hurried out.

Dickce looked at An'gel. "Are you thinking what I'm thinking?"

"Probably," An'gel said.

In unison they said, "The lawyer did it."

CHAPTER 32

Benjy had about had his fill of Lance Perigord after fifteen minutes. The dude could yammer on like nobody's business. Between Lance's seemingly nonstop yakking and Tippy's chatter, Benjy was close to a massive headache.

Then, to his surprise, Tippy suddenly ran out of steam and started yawning. Lance convinced her it was nap time, and she climbed into bed. Peanut and Endora sacked out with her, though Peanut kept looking Benjy's way in case Benjy decided to take him outside.

Lance seemed to have talked himself into a nap. He sat on the floor at the foot of the bed, propped against the frame. He dozed right off. Benjy was amazed the guy could sleep like that, but he was thankful for the silence. He did hope, however, that either the police called him downstairs or one of the sisters came to relieve him. He wouldn't mind getting out of the house for a while himself, and Peanut would be ecstatic.

For now, however, he was stuck keeping an eye on Tippy and, by default, Lance. The guy was probably trustworthy enough when it came to Tippy. Benjy had to admit Lance handled the four-year-old well. *Probably because he's like a six-year-old himself.* He willed himself to relax in the rocking chair and chill. One of the sisters would be along soon, and he could have a break.

He was in a doze-like state when he heard footsteps in the hallway approaching Tippy's room. He sat up and rubbed a hand across his eyes. He couldn't believe he'd almost fallen asleep, but the quiet in the room—finally— had made it a bit too easy.

Benjy stood and turned to face the door. He expected to see either An'gel or Dickce, but to his surprise, the visitor was Trey Mims.

Trey stopped right inside the doorway and gazed at the sleeping child. He was looking at her lovingly, Benjy thought. Then Trey's gaze swept the rest of the room, obviously noting Benjy's presence but settling on Lance, who was sound asleep at the foot of the bed.

The moment Trey spotted Lance, he scowled and clenched his fists. Benjy took a step forward, because he thought Trey was about to attack Lance. Another couple of steps, and Benjy had placed himself between the two men. Peanut was now sitting up in the bed, and he emitted a low growl. Tippy didn't stir, nor did Lance. Benjy held up a hand in Peanut's direction, a signal for the dog to be calm. Peanut didn't growl again, but he watched Trey warily.

Trey frowned at the dog, then at Benjy. His hands

relaxed, and he motioned for Benjy to come out into the hallway with him. Trey moved out of the room, and Benjy glanced down at Lance, still completely out of it. Benjy stepped over to the bed to give Peanut a reassuring pat on the head, and the dog settled down.

Benjy pulled the door about two-thirds closed before he faced Trey. "What can I do for you?" he asked.

"Where's Jacqueline?" Trey demanded. "Why isn't *she* looking after Tippy?"

"She had things she had to attend to in town," Benjy said in a calm tone. He added deliberately, "Arrangements for two funerals, I guess."

Trey looked slightly abashed. "Yeah, I guess that makes sense. When did Lance turn up?"

"Around breakfast time," Benjy said. "He's been here ever since, mostly playing with Tippy."

Trey scowled. "I don't like him being around her so much. He's got about as much brainpower as one of her dolls."

"Yeah, the dude isn't too smart," Benjy said. "But he really seems to love her, and he's good with her, too. He's kept her entertained."

"I don't care, I still don't like it," Trey said. "I told Sondra I didn't want him around her all the time, but Sondra never paid any attention to what I wanted."

"Why is it any of your business what Sondra did with her daughter?" Benjy was genuinely puzzled.

Trey glared at him. "Because I'm Tippy's father, that's why."

"Oh." Benjy felt like an idiot. He wondered briefly if the sisters knew this and had forgotten to tell him. "I didn't know that."

"Nobody outside the family does," Trey said bitterly. "Sondra's grandmother was too embarrassed because she said everyone would think it was incest." He snorted in derision. "Sondra and I weren't related, except that my father married her mother. The whole thing was ridiculous."

"Why didn't you get married?" Benjy asked.

"The old lady wasn't happy when my dad married Jacqueline. I guess she thought the Mims family wasn't as high-and-mighty as the Champlains or the Delevans. Then she had a gigantic fit and threatened to throw everybody out of the house when I wanted to marry Sondra. I didn't care if she did, frankly, but my dad is so in love with Jacqueline, he won't do anything to upset her. Jacqueline kept thinking she could talk the old woman around, but it didn't happen."

Benjy felt sorry for Trey. He really did get a raw deal, and Benjy couldn't blame him for the obvious resentment he felt for Mireille Champlain. She had seemed like a nice old lady, but then again, so had his stepfather's mother, and she turned out to be a nightmare.

"Sondra seemed like she did whatever she wanted, no matter what anybody else thought," Benjy said. "I'm surprised you didn't elope."

"I wanted to, but Sondra was too young."

"How young?" Benjy asked, surprised.

"She was only seventeen," Trey said. "By the terms of her father's will, if she married before she was twenty, she forfeited her money, and it would all go to her mother." He shook his head. "I couldn't have cared less. I was already working for my dad and making a decent living. I could have taken care of her and Tippy, but that wasn't enough for Sondra. She wanted that money. She didn't mind getting pregnant and having my baby, but she wasn't going to marry me and give up being rich."

No wonder the guy was in such a bad mood all the time. Benjy didn't think Sondra sounded like she was worth all the drama and heartache she'd put Trey through, but it wasn't his life, his choice.

"I'm sorry," he said. "You deserved better, I'm sure."

Trey looked away, as if embarrassed by Benjy's sympathy. "She wouldn't marry me, and then she taunted me by telling me she was going to marry that idiot in there, just so she could get her hands on her father's money." He made a sound of disgust.

"He doesn't seem like such a bad guy," Benjy said. He was surprised to find himself defending Lance. "I mean, he's not too bright, but I guess he'd do whatever Sondra told him without arguing about it. Maybe she wanted a husband she could control."

"Maybe," Trey said. "But don't let Lance fool you into thinking he's too easygoing. He has a temper. His mama has spoiled him about as much as Jacqueline and the old lady spoiled Sondra. He can get nasty when he doesn't get what he wants."

Benjy found that a little hard to believe. Lance so far had shown no evidence of a temper like Trey claimed he had.

Trey evidently realized Benjy was skeptical. He pushed the dark, thick hair off his forehead with his right hand. "Look at the scar there, just below the hairline. See it?"

Benjy took a step closer to peer where Trey indicated.

Sure enough, there was a scar about two inches long, parallel to the hairline. He stepped back.

"Lance did that?" he asked.

Trey nodded. "He sure did. I was maybe seven, and so he and Sondra would have been about five. We were playing, and he was losing like he always did, unless we let him win. He got mad and picked up some scissors and came at me with them. Thought he was going to poke my eyes out, but Sondra jumped on his back. He still managed to cut me pretty good. My dad always made me wear my hair really short when I was a kid, and I swear I thought he'd scalped me. I passed out from all the blood loss." He looked slightly green around the gills, Benjy thought, as if the memory of the blood made him queasy.

"He really could have done some damage," Benjy said. "You were lucky Sondra got him off you before he could do anything worse."

"The weird thing—Sondra told me about it later, when I came out of the faint—Lance was calm two minutes after, like nothing had happened. Sondra said he acted like he couldn't remember doing it." Trey shook his head. "I think he got brain damage when he was little or something."

"Did he ever do anything like that again? Turn violent, I mean, and then forget what he'd done?" Benjy had begun to wonder whether Lance had killed Sondra in a sudden fit of rage and then had forgotten.

"A couple of times, when he was still a kid," Trey said. "I've never heard about him doing it after that. Of course, his mama would do anything to cover up something like that." His eyes narrowed. "Are you thinking he killed Sondra and doesn't remember?"

Benjy shrugged uneasily. "After what you just told me, don't you think it's possible? He told me earlier that Sondra had decided not to marry him because she was interested in some older guy."

Trey's nostrils flared, and Benjy could see the anger and alarm building in the guy. Trey pushed past him and stormed into the bedroom. Benjy was right on his heels, afraid that Trey meant to attack Lance.

To his surprise, Trey merely shook Lance a little to wake him up. Lance looked up, blinking and yawning. Trey laid a finger across his lips to indicate Lance should be quiet. Then he motioned for Lance to get up and follow him out of the room.

Lance got to his feet, obviously puzzled. He glanced at Tippy, still sleeping, then walked out of the room ahead of Benjy.

Benjy gave Peanut another quick pat to indicate everything was okay—he hoped—and glanced down at Endora. The cat yawned and stretched, and then curled up again. Benjy hurried out and pulled the door shut.

Trey had his hands on Lance's shoulders, his eyes boring into Lance's. "I don't believe you."

"I don't know why," Lance said. "Sondra said she told you, too."

"Told you what?" Benjy asked.

Trey didn't take his eyes off Lance, but he answered Benjy's question. "Told me that she decided at the last minute to elope with this other guy. But I'll swear it on a stack of Bibles. Sondra did not tell me anything about eloping, not with you, not with anybody." He gave Lance a shake, and Benjy stepped forward, ready to intervene.

He wasn't anxious to get hit, because Trey was pretty muscular, but he knew how to defend himself.

Trey released Lance, who stumbled back.

"Looks like she didn't want to marry either of us," Trey said.

"No, I guess not," Lance said.

"Did you get angry with her when she told you?" Trey asked. "Remember how you used to get angry when you didn't get what you wanted?"

Lance frowned. "I guess so. I hit you one time, didn't I?"

"Yes, you did," Trey said. "I can show you the scar to prove it."

"No, thank you," Lance said. "I don't like scars. They're ugly."

"Yeah, they are," Trey said. "Tell me, Lance. How angry were you when Sondra told you she was going to marry somebody else?"

"I don't remember." Lance sounded sulky.

"Are you sure?" Trey said. "Did you hit Sondra, like you hit me when we were kids? Did you hit her over the head with something?"

CHAPTER 33

Jackson came into the room seconds after the sisters proclaimed Richmond Thurston's guilt in unison. An'gel was startled by his appearance, and she hoped that he hadn't heard her and Dickce just then. They didn't think they were ready to share their conclusions with anyone else.

The butler's mien gave no indication he had heard them name the lawyer. "Miss Dickce, the policemen would like to talk to you now."

Dickce rose. "Thank you, Jackson." She waited till he nodded and retreated from the room before she spoke to An'gel. "Should I tell the policeman what we discussed with Horace?"

"No," An'gel said. "Horace needs to be the one to talk to the police. If we find out he hasn't, we will certainly inform Bugg."

"What about our suspicions of the lawyer?"

"Better not talk about that either. We don't really have proof, only speculation. When I talked to Bugg, he said he was investigating financial angles. We have to hope that if Thurston has been dipping his hand into places he shouldn't, the police will discover it. In the meantime, the minute I can get Jacqueline alone, I'm going to talk to her about Thurston."

"Good idea," Dickce said. "I'd better get to the kitchen." She hurried out.

An'gel felt suddenly restless. She had an urge to get out of the house. Perhaps a short walk up and down the driveway would help. She went to the front door and out onto the verandah. The day was still cool, a bit of a breeze, with the sun bright and warming. She stood on the verandah and looked out over the grounds in front of the house.

The live oaks, ten of them on either side of the driveway and more out on the grounds nearby, towered over everything around them. Majestic, old, impressive. An'gel marveled to think that these trees likely had been there when the first Champlain decided to build his house on this spot in the late eighteenth century. They had trees nearly as old on the grounds of Riverhill, and An'gel loved every one of them.

She could understand Mireille's feelings about her home. The trees embodied so much, had witnessed so much, of the family's history. One didn't lightly give up the land or a house like Willowbank. An'gel knew she and Dickce would go to almost any lengths to preserve Riverhill, and she knew without a doubt that Mireille felt the same way about Willowbank.

What about Jacqueline, though, Dickce wondered. Did she have the same reverence for the past? She was pretty sure Sondra hadn't cared much at all, but Jacqueline might. Especially now that she had a grandchild to look after. Surely this was all worth preserving for Tippy? Without Mireille, however, Jacqueline might be disheartened and ready to let the past recede, step away from it, and focus only on the future.

An'gel could understand that, in a way, but she knew roots were important. Roots gave you a foundation, something solid on which to build a life, a future. She hoped that Tippy would have the chance to know and feel proud of her roots, not have them taken away before she was old enough to appreciate them.

What has got you in such a strange mood?

Death, An'gel decided. Death had put her in this mood. Two murders and a death provoked by a vicious prank. Three lives taken away, and others damaged by the losses and the wickedness behind them.

The malice behind the events of the past two days worried An'gel. How could it be stopped when you weren't certain who was responsible? She and Dickce had fixed on the lawyer, Thurston, as the culprit, but they had no proof.

The police might find the necessary evidence, but how long might it be before they did? An'gel prayed they found it soon, because she feared the malevolent will behind two murders might not balk at another. She worried that Jacqueline or Tippy could become a target. Maybe both of them were targets already. What exactly was the killer after?

If Horace was the killer, the answer was obvious. He wanted money. Now that Jacqueline had inherited from both her daughter and her mother, she was a very wealthy woman. An'gel couldn't shake off the notion that Horace was ruthless enough to kill in order to get his hands on the money.

But there was the lawyer. Lawyers who helped themselves to their clients' money were not a rare breed, An'gel knew. Many lawyers had absconded with their clients' fortunes in some way or another. Horace said Thurston had a flashy lifestyle, with new cars, trips to New York and Las Vegas, and multiple homes. Was the source of his wealth Sondra's inheritance from her father?

If such was the case, how did he benefit from Sondra's death? The money reverted to Jacqueline. How did that help the lawyer?

It could delay, at least for a while, discovery of his embezzlement, An'gel decided. He also might think he could access the money through Horace. If he had sufficient hold on Horace, he might think he could continue to bleed the estate dry by forcing Horace to beg Jacqueline for more and more money to bail him out.

Thurston wasn't the only trustee of Sondra's trust, An'gel recalled. There was a banker, a man that Jacqueline referred to as a *fussy pants* or something similar. An elderly man who kept a tight rein on the money and wouldn't let her borrow against her own income. An'gel wished she knew his name. She would like to talk to him.

Well, why shouldn't she talk to him? She ought to be able to find out easily enough his name and his address. She glanced at her watch. It was only a few minutes past four. More than time enough to go into town and talk to the banker.

Jackson might know, she decided. She went back into the house to track down the butler and ask him. She found him in the kitchen. Evidently the police had finished using it for questioning witnesses. Jackson stood forlornly at the sink, staring out into the yard behind the house.

"Hello, Jackson," An'gel said. The butler started, then turned to face her.

"Something I can do for you, Miss An'gel?" he asked.

"Yes, there is," she replied. "Do you happen to know the name of the banker who is one of the trustees for Jacqueline and Sondra?"

"Yes'm, that'd be Mr. Farley Montgomery at the bank in St. Ignatiusville," Jackson replied. "You need to talk to him about something?"

"Actually I do," An'gel said. "Do you have any idea what kind of hours he keeps? I'd like to see him this afternoon, if at all possible."

Jackson smiled. "He'll be at the bank till at least six o'clock, Miss An'gel. He's been keeping the same hours ever since he started there fifty-three years ago. Hasn't ever missed a day that I recall hearing of."

"That's impressive," An'gel said. "He sounds like a dedicated man."

"He sure is that," Jackson said. "You know where the bank is?"

"No, I don't, so I'd appreciate directions."

Jackson explained that the bank was on a side street off the highway that ran through St. Ignatiusville. "You can't miss it. It's going to be the second street to your left, after you pass the light in front of the big Baptist church."

An'gel nodded. She remembered the church. "Thanks, Jackson. Now I just need to find my purse and keys and I'll be on my way."

"They're in your room, Miss An'gel," Jackson said. "I found your purse in the dining room earlier, and I put it in your room."

An'gel thanked him again and vowed to herself to do a better job of keeping track of her purse. "When you see my sister, please let her know I'm running an errand in town. I should be back by six at the latest."

Jackson said he would inform Dickce, and An'gel hurried out of the kitchen to retrieve her purse. As she reached the second floor, she spared a thought for Benjy upstairs, still watching over Tippy. Perhaps Dickce would go and relieve him. Right now, she was determined to get to the bank and get in somehow to talk to Farley Montgomery.

A few minutes later she was on her way to St. Ignatius-ville. She checked the brakes before she left the property, the thought having occurred to her before she had gone five feet. The killer had no reason to tamper with her brakes, she thought, but she didn't want to take any unnecessary chances.

She drove more slowly than usual, just in case. The brakes seemed fine, however, and within minutes she was in town. She watched for the church and, when she spotted it, concentrated on a left turn on the second street past it.

She had to wait for more than a minute before she could turn left because there was a steady stream of traffic. Finally she saw an opening and took it. She hit the gas, and the Lexus jumped through the intersection.

The bank sat on a corner a block from the highway. An'gel found a slot right in front of the doors and parked.

Inside the building she surveyed the scene for a moment before deciding whom to approach. Her gaze settled on a young woman at a nearby desk who didn't appear to be busy at the moment. An'gel walked over to her and greeted her. "I'd like to speak to Mr. Montgomery, please."

The young woman looked up at her. "Do you have an appointment? He's pretty busy this afternoon."

"I'm afraid I don't." An'gel gave her a rueful smile. "It is urgent that I talk with him. If you'll tell him I'm here on behalf of Mireille Champlain, I'm sure he'll see me."

The Champlain name was evidently the magic word, because the girl immediately picked up the phone and punched in a number. After a brief conversation, the girl hung up the phone. She stood. "If you'll come with me, ma'am, I'll show you to Mr. Montgomery's office."

An'gel nodded and followed the girl to a discreet door in the corner. Moments later, down a short hallway, the girl ushered her into an office with floor-to-ceiling windows at the back and a view of a park. In front of the window, at a large desk, sat the thinnest man An'gel had ever seen.

He rose and dismissed the girl. After she had closed the door behind her, he spoke to An'gel. "Good afternoon, madam. I am Farley Montgomery. Whom do I have the pleasure of addressing?"

An'gel was so fascinated by studying the man's appearance that she failed to respond immediately. Then she realized he was waiting, and she introduced herself. "I am An'gel Ducote. I am Mireille Champlain's cousin, and I have come to talk to you about matters affecting my cousin and her family."

The banker's face did not betray any hint of emotion at her announcement. He waved a hand with long, exceedingly thin fingers, and bade her be seated. He waited until she had done so before he resumed his own seat.

"You must understand, Miss Ducote, that I am not at liberty to discuss details of my client's affairs without her permission," Montgomery said in a sententious manner.

"Yes, I understand that, and under normal circumstances I would not have sought you out. Because of the events of the past two days, however, I felt I had to consult you."

"I presume you are referring to the sad demise of Mrs. Champlain's granddaughter."

"Yes, I am," An'gel said. She thought it odd that the banker hadn't mentioned Mireille's death. Surely Jacqueline would have informed him? "There is also the matter of my cousin's death as well. Surely you are aware that Mireille passed away as well?"

"Yes, of course," Montgomery said hastily. "Yes, Jacqueline did call to tell me."

An'gel regarded him in silence for a moment. Something about his response struck her as odd, but she couldn't figure out why. She'd think about it later. She decided to get straight to the point.

"I need to ask you some questions about the trust funds you help administer for both Sondra and her mother. I know you will think this is none of my business, but I have to tell you frankly that I believe Sondra's murder is connected directly to her inheritance. Someone is anxious to get his hands on that money."

An'gel knew she was taking a risk in confronting the banker like this. Despite what Jacqueline had said about him, there was a strong chance he was in cahoots with his fellow trustee, Thurston. They might be embezzling together, and here she was, letting him know she suspected what was going on.

But, she thought, sometimes you had to rattle the cage to make things happen. She waited for the banker's response to her rattling.

Montgomery maintained his calm, reserved manner. He didn't appear to be fazed in the least by her statements.

"While I cannot discuss the details with you, Miss Ducote," he said in his dry, precise manner, "I can assure you that there has been no malfeasance with the trust funds under my purview. By the terms of the trust, both my fellow trustee and I have to agree on any disbursement of funds. And as those funds are deposited in this bank, and as my signature is required before they can be released in any way, I can assure you the trust has not been violated."

An'gel took a moment to absorb the meaning of the banker's stilted language, and then she was baffled. Montgomery sounded convincing. But if there had been no embezzlement from Sondra's inheritance, what was the motive for her murder?

CHAPTER 34

"Ordinarily, you understand," Montgomery continued, "I would not tell you as much as I have. But as you said, the circumstances are indeed unusual because of the sad loss. Losses," he added quickly.

An'gel was too distracted by her own thoughts to pay much attention to the banker. Had she and Dickce been so obsessed with the money angle that they were overlooking a more obvious answer? Was Sondra's death a crime of passion instead?

Trey had a violent temper. An'gel had seen evidence of that. He hadn't wanted Sondra to marry Lance Perigord. Had he struck out at her during an argument and killed her by accident? Or even deliberately? She would have to go back to Dickce and share the banker's words with her.

"Miss Ducote, is there anything else I can assist you with?" Montgomery said.

An'gel surfaced from her thoughts to find the banker observing her with a puzzled expression. "I do beg your pardon, Mr. Montgomery," she said. "I thank you for your time and for answering my questions."

The banker rose and inclined his head. "I'm pleased to have been of assistance. I regret only that I could not assist you more."

An'gel was about to bid him good-bye, but another question occurred to her, and she was sure he would know the answer.

"I do have one more thing to ask," she said. "Jacqueline has been busy in town most of the day, and I haven't wanted to disturb her. Could you tell me the funeral home that will be handling the funerals?"

"I believe Emile Devereux and Sons are in charge of the arrangements," Montgomery said.

"And where might I find them?" An'gel asked.

"Another two blocks down this same street," Montgomery said. "Might I inquire whether you are intending to go there this afternoon?"

"I thought I might," An'gel said. She actually hadn't intended to; she had simply wanted the information in order to arrange for flowers. Something in the banker's manner, however, piqued her curiosity. "Thank you again, Mr. Montgomery. You've been most helpful."

"Again, you are indeed welcome." The banker inclined his head once more.

An'gel headed for the door. She opened it and stepped through, pulling the door almost shut behind her. She peeped through the crack to see whether the banker was in her line of sight.

He was not, but his arm reaching for the phone was.

"May I help you?"

The voice at her back startled An'gel, and she turned to see the young woman who had helped her earlier standing there with an annoyed expression.

"No, thank you," An'gel said as she pulled the door gently closed. "I'll see myself out." She strode down the short hallway, head held high, as if she hadn't been trying to eavesdrop on the president of the bank. And if her cheeks were slightly red, well, one might suppose it was because she was walking rather fast.

In the car, she glanced in the mirror. Her color was back to normal. She felt foolish. She shouldn't have tried to eavesdrop, but she had been curious to see what the banker did after she was out of the room. There was something odd going on, but she had no idea what.

Perhaps the banker *was* in cahoots with Thurston and had lied to her about the state of Sondra's inheritance. He didn't seem the type to embezzle, though. He emitted an air of rectitude like the sun in the sky.

She headed down the street, looking for the funeral home. She found it two blocks down on the other side of the street. Jacqueline's car occupied one of the parking spaces, and An'gel pulled in beside it. The building took up at least a third of a block.

Emile Devereux and Sons, Mortuary Services, occupied a house that An'gel decided must date from the late nineteenth century. She mounted the steps to the porch and opened the door. When she stepped inside, she found herself standing in a spacious and impressive foyer. An ornately carved wooden staircase mounted to the second floor about a dozen feet or so in front of her. There was a small reception desk to her right. Beyond that, a parlor. There was another like it to her left.

A heavy floral scent filled the air, but there was an undertone of another scent, a chemical one. An'gel recognized the faint whiff of embalming fluid. She walked over to the parlor on the left side and found it empty. She turned back and went to the right-hand one. Empty also. There was a large sign with removable letters near the stairs, but it was blank except for the name of the funeral home.

A voice coming from behind her startled An'gel.

"How may I assist you, madam?"

An'gel turned to see a handsome young man, black hair slicked back, dark suit, dark shoes, and an unctuous smile, regarding her.

"Good afternoon," An'gel said. "I am looking for my goddaughter, Jacqueline Mims. I need to talk to her."

The young man shook his head. "I'm sorry, madam, but she is not here."

An'gel responded tartly, "I parked beside her car just moments ago. Did she abandon her car here for some reason?"

The young man, whom An'gel assumed was one of the sons of Devereux and Sons, didn't bat an eyelid. "Ah, my mistake, dear lady. Mrs. Mims must still be here." He gestured with his right hand and arm. "If you will wait in here, I will locate her and tell her you wish to see her."

"Thank you," An'gel said. She walked into the right-hand parlor and seated herself on a Victorian-looking divan. "Tell her Miss An'gel Ducote would like to speak to her."

The young man bowed. "Certainly, madam." He disappeared, and An'gel thought she heard him on the stairs. From where she was sitting, she could not see into the foyer.

She supposed Jacqueline was upstairs in an office or a showroom, making decisions about the two burials. She didn't really want to intrude on her goddaughter at this time, but An'gel wanted to see the two murder cases brought to a swift conclusion. She needed to ask Jacqueline a few questions. There were missing pieces, and she hoped her goddaughter could help her fill them in.

"*Tante* An'gel, why did you come all the way into town?" Jacqueline was bearing down on her. "I was getting ready to leave and would have been home soon." She seated herself near An'gel on the divan.

"I was restless, feeling cooped up," An'gel said, "and I decided to get out and come to town. Have you heard the latest news?"

Jacqueline shook her head. "No, I haven't talked to anyone except Mr. Devereux and his sons. I think I left my cell phone in the car. Why? What has happened?"

Bugg might be annoyed with her for telling Jacqueline about Estelle's murder, but he would just have to be annoyed, An'gel decided.

"Estelle is dead," she said. "I was with her when it happened."

"Her heart, I'll bet," Jacqueline said, looking stricken. "She was devoted to *Maman* and all this has been too big a strain for her." She glanced up, as if to heaven, and sighed heavily.

"No, it wasn't her heart," An'gel said. "She was poisoned."

Jacqueline shot up from the divan. "Poisoned? Oh, dear lord." She sank back down. "That's horrendous. Why would someone murder her?"

"Because she knew something that Sondra's murderer didn't want her to tell anyone else." An'gel leaned toward Jacqueline. "Estelle told me at least twice that she knew things, and she said it in a way that led me to believe she was planning to blackmail someone. For all I know, she tried, and the murderer poisoned her."

She went on to explain the figure she thought she had seen, and she repeated what Jackson had told her about Estelle's allergy to peanuts.

Jacqueline nodded. "Yes, she was deathly afraid of peanuts in any form." She covered her face with her hands and said something, but it was too muffled for An'gel to understand.

"What did you say?" she demanded.

Jacqueline dropped her hands and clasped them together in her lap. Her expression one of anguish, she stared at An'gel. "I said what an awful mess this is. What a nightmare." Tears rolled down her face.

An'gel reached over and squeezed Jacqueline's hands. "Yes, dear, I know. That's why we need to do whatever we can to put an end to this. There is something evil at work, and it has to be stopped."

"Yes, you're right," Jacqueline said. "But how? I'm terrified of what might happen next. Is someone staying with Tippy? Maybe I need to get home and look after her myself." She half rose from the divan but then dropped down again.

"Tippy is safe," An'gel said. "Either Dickce or Benjy will be with her at all times, and they won't let her out of their sight. They will protect her. There's also Peanut. He has apparently taken a shine to Tippy, and you can bet he won't let anybody hurt her if he's anywhere nearby."

"Thank you," Jacqueline said. "If something happens to her, I don't know what I'd do."

"She's going to be fine," An'gel said firmly. "We are going to figure out how to put an end to this, and you and she will both be safe."

Jacqueline nodded. "What can we do?"

"The first thing we have to do is establish the motive for Sondra's death," An'gel said. "Once we know that, everything else should fall into place."

Her goddaughter stared expectantly at her, so An'gel continued. "In my mind, there are two possible motives. One is passion, the other is greed. Until a little while ago, I was convinced, as was Dickce, by the way, that greed was at the root of this. We were certain that someone was in desperate need of money and killed Sondra because he wanted access to her inheritance."

"You mean Horace, don't you?" Jacqueline said sadly.

"Possibly," An'gel said. "He is in deep trouble financially, probably far deeper than he's told you. But he's not the only one we considered. Dickce and I are highly suspicious of your lawyer. I even went to the bank just now to talk to Mr. Montgomery because he is the other trustee." She sighed. "But he assured me there was no way Thurston has embezzled any of Sondra's money. If he's telling the truth, then I think we have to look at passion as the motive."

"If Farley Montgomery says there's no way the money can be embezzled, then you can believe him."

For a moment An'gel thought she was having an

auditory hallucination. She was looking at Jacqueline, but it was Mireille's voice she heard. Jacqueline was staring past An'gel and not talking, however.

An'gel turned in the direction Jacqueline was staring, and she almost fainted.

Mireille Champlain stood in the doorway looking at her, every bit as alive as An'gel was.

CHAPTER 35

"I'm sorry, *Tante* An'gel," Jacqueline said, sounding stricken. "I wanted to tell you, but *Maman* insisted that you had to be kept in the dark, along with *Tante* Dickce."

"Yes, I did," Mireille said as she advanced into the room. She sat between An'gel and Jacqueline on the divan.

An'gel's heart was beating so hard she thought she might pass out. She did her best to slow her breathing and the beat of her heart while she stared at her cousin. Mireille looked perfectly fine, as if she hadn't had any kind of heart attack at all.

"I, too, am sorry, An'gel," Mireille said as she took one of An'gel's hands and rubbed it between both of hers. "I hated to put you and Dickce through all this, but I couldn't take the chance that one of you, without meaning to, might give the whole thing away."

An'gel wanted to be angry with Mireille, but she sensed

that her cousin was frightened. "I'll get over it. I'm too happy and relieved to be upset for long," An'gel said. "May I tell Dickce?"

Mireille sighed. "I'd rather you didn't, but I know how close the two of you are. You might as well. I'm hoping this will all be over soon, anyway, if we can simply figure out a way to make it happen."

"If you'll tell me why you decided to carry out this elaborate charade, perhaps I can help. I want to get this over with, too, before anyone else is hurt. Frankly, I'm concerned about Jacqueline and Tippy's safety," An'gel said.

"I'm worried, too," Mireille replied. "I've taken steps to close the one loophole that leaves them vulnerable, but we have no proof as to what's really going on or exactly who is responsible."

"We'll figure it out together," An'gel said. She was feeling almost back to normal again and ready to tackle the problem. "First, though, I'm afraid I have bad news for you."

Mireille gasped and squeezed her hand hard, and An'gel hastily pulled her hand free. "Sorry," Mireille said. "Involuntary reaction. What is it?"

"Estelle died earlier today," An'gel said. "She was poisoned."

Mireille closed her eyes, crossed herself, and uttered a quiet prayer. Her eyes fluttered open when she finished, and An'gel saw that they were damp. Mireille brushed the tears away with a handkerchief she pulled from her sleeve.

"Poor Estelle," she said. "She was so unhappy. I tried my best to help her, but it was never enough."

"You did more than enough for her, *Maman*," Jacqueline said hotly. "She was sour and mean-spirited."

"Yes, you're right," Mireille said. "But she was my friend." She looked at An'gel. "Why do you think she was killed?"

"I think she was trying to blackmail someone," An'gel said bluntly. "Now tell me, did Estelle know about this charade of yours?"

Mireille shook her head. "Goodness, no. Estelle was not in the least discreet. I could never trust her with anything like this. The whole thing would have fallen apart immediately."

"She told me she knew the moment you died," An'gel said. "Frankly, it was eerie. She seemed so convinced."

"She fancied herself as a psychic," Jacqueline said scornfully. "She was no more psychic than I am. Which is not at all."

"Estelle was always trying to make herself seem special," Mireille said. "She could never let go of the bitterness that stemmed from her poverty-stricken childhood."

"That truly is sad," An'gel said. Estelle had evidently been trapped by her own inability to let go of her unfortunate past, and An'gel felt a surge of pity for her. Time to focus on the present, however. She had more questions for her resurrected cousin and her goddaughter.

"I imagine Jacqueline has already told you this," An'gel said, "but I discovered that your grandmother's wedding dress was intact and in the bottom drawer of your chifforobe. I began to wonder about that whole incident, Sondra's tantrum and tearing up the dress. Jacqueline said someone must have put Sondra up to it."

Mireille sighed. "I put her up to it. Jacqueline told you about the destruction of possessions that had great sentimental value to me. That all upset me, and I knew that the person who did those things meant me harm. They were meant to intimidate me as well, because I refused to give Horace money to pay off bad debts."

An'gel wanted to pursue that point, but first she wanted to hear more of an explanation about Sondra's role in Mireille's plan. "How did you talk Sondra into going along with your plan?"

"She wanted to be an actress," Jacqueline said. "Going to New York after she married was mainly for her benefit, not Lance's. With her inheritance to back her up, she was convinced she would soon be on the stage in New York. She thought she could finance the plays herself."

"Good heavens," An'gel said faintly.

"I know," Jacqueline said. "It was a crazy plan, but I couldn't talk Sondra out of it or get her to understand that she would just be throwing her money away. She could act a little, but not enough to carry a Broadway show."

"I think she might have surprised all of us," Mireille said. "There was more to her than people credited her with, but her great failing was her inability to step into anyone's shoes other than her own." She shook her head. "I told her I wanted to stage a dramatic scene for you and Dickce. Estelle was not part of the plan, however."

"So Estelle told that awful story about the dead bride without anyone prompting her?" An'gel asked.

"Yes," Jacqueline said. "I was furious with her myself, and she made Sondra go ballistic. It helped add to the drama for *Maman*'s plan, but it was unexpected."

"It worked well, because Sondra really was livid with me for not firing Estelle," Mireille said. "She wasn't acting when she ripped apart the replica and threw the pieces over the railing. We had already planned that. Estelle unknowingly increased the theatrical factor."

"If she had any acting talent," An'gel said wrily, "she got it from you." She pointed to Mireille. "You certainly convinced Dickce and me that you were having a heart attack." Then she pointed at Jacqueline. "You were convincing, too."

Jacqueline had the grace to look abashed. "I know, and I can't tell you how sorry I am."

"It was drastic," Mireille said, slightly defensively, "but I had to get out of that house, and I had to convince my persecutor that I was beyond his reach. I wanted him to think he succeeded in bringing about my death."

"*Maman* hoped it would end there," Jacqueline said. "We thought by faking her death we could buy a little time to find the evidence to put a stop to all this. *Maman* didn't want to go to the police. She wanted to handle everything this way."

"And buy time for me to make a new will," Mireille said with a small touch of smugness.

"We didn't think he would target Sondra," Jacqueline said.

Mireille grasped her daughter's hand and held it tightly. An'gel felt sorry for them both.

"I'm assuming Sondra knew you were faking the heart attack?" she asked.

"Yes," Mireille said. "She knew, but she didn't know the real reason, of course."

An'gel couldn't keep a note of exasperation from her voice when she asked her next questions. "Weren't you afraid she would slip and give the whole thing away? To her killer, for example?"

"I told her that if she didn't sustain the charade," Mireille said, "it would show that she wasn't a good enough actress. She had too much pride to give anything away."

An'gel was surprised that her cousin had been willing to manipulate her own grandchild to such an extent. Couldn't she have found another way to protect herself and identify her persecutor?

An'gel decided there was no point in telling Mireille and Jacqueline that now. Instead she asked another question.

"Why were you willing to let Sondra marry Lance and go off to New York? Surely you realize how unsuitable he is."

Mireille and Jacqueline exchanged glances, then Mireille turned back to An'gel. "Yes, we're aware of Lance's unsuitability. And his proclivities. We aren't blind."

"But Sondra was bound and determined to get married and get away from St. Ignatiusville," Jacqueline said. "And if nothing else, Lance comes from a good family."

"Yes," Mireille said. "And I certainly didn't want to see her marry Trey Mims." She sniffed. "One Mims in the family is already one too many."

Jacqueline glowered at her mother but didn't say anything.

Mireille really could be a snob, An'gel reflected. Perhaps if she had let things alone, let Trey and Sondra get married, things would have turned out far differently. She doubted, however, Mireille would agree with her.

A sudden trill emanating from her handbag startled An'gel. "Excuse me," she said to the two women. "I'd better at least check to see who it is." She pulled the phone from the bag and glanced at the display. Benjy was calling. "I should take this," she said. "It could be important."

Mireille and Jacqueline nodded, and An'gel answered the call. "Hello, Benjy, is everything all right?" She listened for a moment. "I see. Yes, do tell me." She listened for a couple of minutes this time. Finally she said, "Thank you. I'm glad you called. I'll be back at Willowbank in half an hour probably." She ended the call and dropped the phone back in her handbag.

"What was all that about?" Jacqueline asked. "Tippy is okay, isn't she?"

"Yes, she's fine," An'gel said. "Dickce is with her now. Benjy was with her most of the afternoon, along with Lance, and then Trey. Dickce sent Lance and Trey about their business, though."

"Good," Mireille said. "That was a long conversation, just to tell you that much."

"Indeed," An'gel replied. "Benjy had more to tell me. He had a chat with Trey and found out two very interesting things. One is that Lance evidently has a violent temper when he's thwarted, though he seems not to remember the incidents after he has struck out at someone."

"Yes, that's true." Jacqueline frowned. "But I thought he'd grown out of it. The last time I remember him doing something like that was when he attacked another child at school when he was ten years old."

"I'm not sure it's something one grows out of," An'gel said. "That ties in with the second thing Benjy discovered. Trey told him he had argued with Sondra on the night she died about marrying Lance. He was determined to stop her, but she told him she wasn't going to marry Lance after all. Instead, she was going to elope with another man. An older man. Benjy thinks it's possible that when Sondra told

Lance, he might have become enraged and struck out at her. The coroner is sure she was dead before her body was thrown off the gallery to the ground below."

An'gel knew that last bit was rather brutal, but this was no time to be mincing words.

"Do you think Lance could have killed Sondra?" she asked. "And do you think he was behind those vicious attacks on you, Mireille?"

Mireille stared at her. "I suppose he could have killed Sondra in a fit. But he simply doesn't have the cunning to have carried out that nasty campaign. Nor did he have the reason."

"What *is* the reason?" An'gel asked.

"To intimidate me into signing over most of my income and capital to Horace," Mireille said.

"So Horace is behind it?" An'gel said.

"No, I think he's an unwilling party to it, however." Mireille grimaced. "The person behind it is my lawyer, Richmond Thurston."

"He can't get at the money Terence left me and Sondra," Jacqueline said, "unless he murders poor Mr. Montgomery. But he can get at *Maman* through Horace and then through me. He drew up *Maman*'s will, and he knows everything comes to me."

"And with Mireille out of the way, he can extort the money from Horace because you would do anything to help your husband," An'gel said.

"Yes," Mireille said. "But what he doesn't know is that I have now changed my will and hired a new lawyer. There's no way he can get the money now."

"Do you think he killed Sondra?" An'gel asked. "Is he the older man she was going to elope with, do you think?"

"Yes," Mireille and Jacqueline said in unison.

Mireille went on, "Rich Thurston can be a very charming man, and I think he was using Sondra as his backup plan. He's desperate for money all of a sudden."

"Then why would he have killed Sondra?" An'gel asked. "Once they were married, he'd have had access to her money, and Mr. Montgomery would no longer be able to stop him."

"I don't know," Mireille said. She got up from the divan and began to pace back and forth. "This thing has got to end. Maybe I should just go and confront Rich Thurston right now."

"No," An'gel said. "I wouldn't do that." She had the beginnings of an idea. "I think it would take more than that to put an end to his nasty schemes." She thought for a moment. *Yes, it just might work.* "Okay, here's what I think we should do." She motioned for Mireille to resume her seat, and then she outlined her plan.

CHAPTER 36

An'gel pulled the Lexus into the parking lot behind Emile Devereux and Sons and switched off the ignition. "Remember now, we must be extremely careful not to give anything away."

"You've said that at least seven times in the last fifteen minutes," Dickce said. "My nerves are every bit as strong as yours, Sister. I won't be the one to spill the beans."

"All right," An'gel said. "No more admonitions, I promise."

"I never knew that Emile Devereux was Mireille's first beau," Dickce said as she stared at the sign at the back of the building.

"I didn't either, but it explains why she took refuge in the funeral home," An'gel said. "Even though he married another woman, he still loved her, and she trusted her safety to him and his grandson."

"Romantic, in a way," Dickce said as she opened the door.

An'gel forbore to comment as she opened her own door and stepped out of the car. She checked her watch. Six forty-five. Right on schedule. "Come on," she said and started briskly up the sidewalk and around to the front door.

"Good evening, ladies," Emile's grandson said as he opened the door for them. He ushered them into the parlor on the left side. "If you don't mind waiting here, we'll be opening the doors for the viewing at seven." He winked.

An'gel suppressed a smile. Earlier when she had explained her plan to him and his grandfather, he had agreed to play his part enthusiastically. An'gel suspected that he was happy to do something that fell outside the usual pattern of the mortuary business.

He leaned close to An'gel and whispered, "The policemen are already in place in there." An'gel nodded, and he went back to wait by the door.

She and Dickce walked into the parlor and chose two chairs to the back of the room. They wanted to be sure the chairs closest to the door were free for others.

The waiting was going to be the most difficult part, An'gel knew. She probably should have planned their arrival for a few minutes later, but she wanted to be there with Dickce before any of the others turned up.

Farley Montgomery was the next to arrive, and An'gel introduced him to her sister.

He bowed over Dickce's hand and murmured, "Such a grievous occasion on which to meet, Miss Ducote."

"Yes, it is," Dickce said sadly.

The banker nodded and moved away to sit on a sofa at the side of the room. He crossed his bony left leg over the right, folded his hands, and rested them atop the knee.

An'gel and Dickce exchanged a quick glance. "See, what did I tell you?" An'gel whispered. Dickce raised her eyebrows in response.

The door opened, and Horace and Jacqueline walked in, accompanied by Trey. Jacqueline's eyes were red, An'gel noted when they drew close, and she held a handkerchief to her nose.

Horace nodded to acknowledge them. Trey did the same before he sat a couple of chairs down from An'gel. Jacqueline maneuvered Horace to a chair in the front row and, when they were seated, leaned her head against her husband's shoulder.

An'gel noted her goddaughter's behavior and approved. Jacqueline was striking the right note for the occasion.

Next came Benjy, with Lance in tow. Lance appeared confused, but Benjy had a firm grip on his arm and steered him into a seat near Jacqueline. Benjy sat next to him. A close friend of Jacqueline's was staying with Tippy, Peanut, and Endora at Willowbank.

Right on the dot of seven, Richmond Thurston walked into the funeral home. An'gel eyed him critically. He was properly dressed in a dark suit with a white shirt and a dark tie. His expression was appropriate, a polite mixture of seriousness and sadness. He advanced into the room, moving straight toward Jacqueline. He put his hands on her shoulders and leaned in to kiss her cheek. "Such a sad occasion," he said as he drew back. "I'm so sorry for your loss." He nodded at Horace to include him.

"Thank you, Rich," Jacqueline said with a little sob in her voice. "It would mean so much to *Maman* to know that you're here."

An'gel had the sudden urge to giggle but managed to suppress it. Dickce was the giggler in the family. She cut a swift look at her sister, but Dickce's composure remained unruffled.

Emile Devereux, a tall, stately man soberly dressed as befit his profession, walked into the room. He surveyed the group for a moment before he spoke.

"Good evening, ladies and gentlemen. I apologize for the delay in the viewing, but Mireille Champlain was a very dear friend, and I wanted to take the utmost care to ensure that everything was done properly, as befits such a wonderful woman." He turned and gestured toward the doors across the hall, and his grandson stepped forward to open them.

Richmond Thurston stood aside to let Horace and Jacqueline precede him, but he was close behind them. Lance appeared reluctant. Benjy propelled him gently, but firmly, toward the room. Trey trailed behind An'gel and Dickce with the banker, Farley Montgomery. Jackson had remained at Willowbank, where An'gel had encouraged him to stay for fear that the jolt of seeing Mireille still alive might be too much for him.

An'gel was pleased to note the dim lighting in the room. She shivered when she glanced toward the casket. She admired her cousin for having the fortitude to play the most important part in the final act of the charade. An'gel was simply glad she wasn't the one in the casket.

"I'd like to go alone, if you don't mind," Jacqueline said to Horace in a clear voice that all could hear.

"Of course, my dear, if you're sure," Horace said. He stepped back to stand beside the lawyer. Jacqueline nodded and approached the casket.

She stood there for perhaps a minute, her back to everyone else in the room. She appeared to be praying. An'gel, from her vantage point slightly to one side, saw her goddaughter make the sign of the cross as she bowed her head.

An'gel heard a faint rustle behind her, and she glanced toward the doors into the foyer. Bugg and Sanford stood there. No one else seemed to have noticed their presence, and that was good.

Jacqueline stepped back from the casket after crossing herself again, and when she turned, An'gel saw tears streaming down her face. She dabbed at them with her handkerchief. When Horace reached out to her, she shook her head and motioned for him to take her place at the casket.

Horace looked a bit queasy, An'gel thought. A sign of guilt, perhaps? He stepped forward and stared down at his mother-in-law.

"She looks so life-like," Horace said, loud enough for everyone to hear. He sounded surprised. He gazed at Mireille a moment longer, and then he turned to join his wife.

Richmond Thurston glanced solemnly at Jacqueline. He said again, "I'm so sorry for your loss." Then after a short pause he added, "She was such a wonderful woman." He sighed and then walked up to the casket.

He stared down at Mireille as Horace and Jacqueline had done.

An'gel held her breath. Any moment now.

Suddenly Mireille sat up and yelled, "Thief! Murderer!" She pointed right at Thurston.

Thurston screamed and stumbled backward into Horace. Horace pushed the lawyer away. "It was all his idea!"

Horace yelled, the shock apparent on his face. "I didn't want to, but he blackmailed me."

"Shut up, you fool!" Thurston was breathing heavily as he continued to stare at Mireille sitting in the casket. Her finger still pointed at him.

"Thief! Murderer!" she yelled again.

"He killed Estelle," Horace said, wringing his hands. "Oh, lord, it wasn't me, you have to believe me."

Thurston drew back his right arm and launched a vicious punch toward Horace's face. At the last moment, Horace managed to duck, and the lawyer's fist missed him.

Bugg stepped forward, along with Sanford, and grabbed hold of Thurston. "Richmond Thurston," he intoned solemnly, "I'm placing you under arrest for the murders of Sondra Delevan and Estelle Winwood."

Thurston struggled to break loose, but to no avail. "I didn't kill Sondra, I swear to God. I was going to marry her, you idiot!"

Bugg paid no attention. Sanford managed to get the cuffs on the lawyer, and the policemen escorted him out.

"Will someone help me out of this thing?" Mireille demanded. "I want to get out now."

Emile Devereux and his grandson hurried to assist her out of the casket.

Jacqueline, in the meanwhile, was berating her husband for his part in Thurston's plan. "How could you, Horace? I trusted you, and this is how you repay me? How you repay *Maman*?"

Whatever response Horace was about to make was drowned out by a loud yell.

"Stop him."

An'gel turned in time to see Benjy and Trey lunging after Lance. They each managed to grab an arm before he got out the front door in the wake of the police. They dragged him back in the room, yelling, kicking, and trying to bite his captors.

Mireille walked up to him and screamed his name. The moment he focused on her, she drew back her hand and slapped him so hard his neck snapped back, and he fainted. Mireille stepped aside, holding her hand gingerly.

"That felt good," she said.

"Why did you do that?" Jacqueline asked.

"To stop him from trying to get away," Mireille said. "Also because he killed Sondra. I believed Thurston when he said he didn't kill her."

"But he did kill Estelle," An'gel said. "I'm sure Bugg will find some kind of evidence that she was trying to blackmail him."

"I'm sure he will, too," Mireille said. "I imagine Estelle figured out he was the one behind the destruction of my treasures and then thought she could extort money from him. I don't know if I could ever have forgiven her for that kind of betrayal."

CHAPTER 37

An'gel looked at her sister. "What did you say?"

Dickce grinned. "I *said*, I am *so* happy to be home, I could run through the house naked and screaming."

"Sister," An'gel hissed. "Have you lost your mind? You shouldn't say things like that where Benjy can hear you."

"Oh, pish tosh, An'gel." Dickce waved a hand in a negligently dismissive gesture. "He was probably halfway to the kitchen with Peanut and Endora by the time that came out of my mouth."

An'gel knew when to give in, and besides, right now she was too frazzled to argue anymore. The drive back from St. Ignatiusville had tired them all out, especially after the events of the past few days. Peanut and Endora had been fractious in the car, requiring Benjy to devote attention to them every few minutes. The fact that Dickce, who had insisted on driving them home so Benjy could see to the animals, looked at speed limits as suggestions to be regarded at whim had done little to soothe An'gel's frayed nerves. An'gel was seriously considering asking Clementine to serve Bloody Marys at lunch, which should be on the table in about twenty minutes.

Her mind kept returning to the confrontation in the funeral home two days before like a movie reel that wouldn't stop. She would never forget the sight of her cousin popping up in the casket to accuse Richmond Thurston. She could laugh now, but at the time she was too nervous to see the humorous side of it.

She grinned. The lawyer had screamed like a toddler who had been frightened out of his wits. She also wondered if he'd had any other involuntary reactions but reprimanded herself for the unladylike thought. The main thing was, the thieving, murdering rat was in custody. She expressed that thought aloud to Dickce.

"Yes, thank goodness, he is." Dickce sighed. "I'm only sorry that he wasn't responsible for Sondra's death as well as Estelle's."

"Why on earth would you say that?" An'gel demanded.

"Oh, I don't know," Dickce said. She slipped her shoes off and swung her feet onto the sofa. "Ah, that's better. My legs are tired from driving for nearly six hours."

From speeding, you mean, An'gel wanted to say. "I offered to take a turn, and so did Benjy," she reminded her sister.

"Yes, and we'd still be on the road as slow as the two of you drive," Dickce retorted.

An'gel didn't rise to the bait. Instead, she said, "Back to what you were saying about the lawyer and wishing he had done both murders. Again I ask you, why?"

"I feel sorry for Lance, I suppose." Dickce wiggled her toes. "The poor boy has such a limited intellect, do you think the judge will go easy on him?"

"I haven't the faintest idea," An'gel said. She also felt sorry for Lance, but she thought his general stupidity wasn't an excuse. She expressed this thought to her sister.

Dickce snickered. "I guess you have a point. I mean, how many killers are actually dumb enough to drive around with the murder weapon in the trunk of their cars?"

The news yesterday that the police had found a missing andiron from the fireplace in Sondra's bedroom in the trunk of Lance's car had shocked everyone. The blood and bits of other matter clinging to it, along with Lance's fingerprints all over it, were enough to keep him in custody as well until he could be arraigned along with Richmond Thurston.

"Probably more than you realize," An'gel said. "Dumb as the poor boy is, at least he didn't try to harm Tippy, though he must have known she overheard his argument with Sondra."

Benjy came back from the kitchen, followed closely by Peanut and Endora. He bore a tray with a pitcher of lemonade, three tall glasses with ice, and two small bowls of fresh boiled chicken. He set the tray down, poured lemonade for the sisters, and then put the two bowls down for the animals. An'gel was relieved that he chose a spot not covered by the antique Aubusson carpet. The hardwood would be much easier to clean. Then Benjy poured a glass for himself and took a chair near the sofa.

Benjy raised his glass. "I propose a toast to a safe return home."

"Hear, hear," An'gel said, and Dickce nodded. They both raised their glasses, then all three took hearty sips.

The cool liquid felt wonderful going down, and An'gel relaxed even further.

"What were you discussing?" Benjy asked. "I thought I caught Lance's name when I was coming down the hall."

"We were talking about him and how I felt sorry for him," Dickce said. "An'gel, perhaps not so much."

"He is kind of sad and pitiful," Benjy said. "Poor guy is the dumbest person I've ever met. Too bad he has such a violent temper."

"The ironic thing is that Sondra and Lance were so much alike," An'gel said.

"What do you mean?" Dickce said. "Sondra was much smarter than Lance."

"Yes, she was," An'gel said, "but I wasn't talking about intellect. I've been thinking about it. They were both beautiful, terribly spoiled, and intent on getting what they wanted, no matter how unrealistic their choices might be. Then Lance ended up killing Sondra because she was taking away perhaps his only chance to achieve his dream."

"If she hadn't been so selfish, she might have saved herself, you mean," Dickce said.

An'gel shrugged. "Perhaps."

"That was the lawyer's fault, though, wasn't it?" Benjy asked. "I guess he convinced her somehow he was in love with her and she should elope with him."

"That sounds reasonable," Dickce said. "We won't ever know for sure, though, unless he decides to confess. I sure would love to know why he thought he had to kill Estelle."

"I figure she must have seen him around the house, without him realizing it, when he was vandalizing Miss Mireille's treasures," Benjy said. "She seemed to kind of pop up out of nowhere when you weren't expecting her." He frowned. "She spooked me a couple of times that way."

"You're probably right," Dickce said. "She did something similar to me. All the same, though, I know Mireille will miss her in an odd way."

"I'm truly sorry for Mireille and Jacqueline for their losses, and little Tippy as well," An'gel said. "Though a part of me can't help but think she'll be better off in the long run without a mother like Sondra."

"I don't know," Dickce said. "Jacqueline and Mireille will be raising her, and they didn't do such a great job with Sondra."

"Surely they've learned from their mistakes by now." An'gel grimaced. "Though if Jacqueline is truly serious about taking Horace back after all this mess, she may not have learned anything after all."

"I think Mireille will talk her out of it," Dickce said. "She'll never forgive Horace for what he did, and I can't say that I blame her."

"Well, we're out of it, thank heavens," An'gel said. "I am not planning on a return to St. Ignatiusville for a long, long time."

Benjy grinned. "That's fine with me." He shifted in his chair, and An'gel heard a crinkling sound. "Oops, I almost forgot." He stood and extracted a folded piece of paper from his back pocket. He handed it to An'gel and then resumed his seat. "Clementine asked me to give this to you. This lady has been calling the house every day since we've been gone. Clementine says she's having a hissy fit to talk to you."

An'gel opened the note and immediately wished she hadn't. She knew why the caller was so insistent. It was almost time to start planning the Athena Garden Club's spring show, and the caller was obsessive about each tiny detail.

She told Dickce who it was. Dickce grimaced. "You're not going to call her back now, are you?"

An'gel shook her head as she folded the note and dropped it on the table next to her.

"No, she can wait another day. Tomorrow will be better. It always is."

New York Times *bestselling author Miranda James
returns to Athena, Mississippi, with an all-new mystery
featuring Miss An'gel and Miss Dickce Ducote, two
snoopy sisters who are always ready to lend a helping
hand. But when a stressed socialite brings murder
right to their doorstep, even they have trouble
maintaining their Southern hospitality...*

BLESS HER DEAD LITTLE HEART

A Southern Ladies Mystery

"[A] classic and classy whodunit, but also a romp filled
with Southern charm, Southern eccentrics, and,
of course, the antics of the engaging Diesel."
—*Richmond Times-Dispatch*

"*Bless Her Dead Little Heart* kicks off a charming
series with humor and heart."
—*Lesa's Book Critiques*

catinthestacks.com
penguin.com

FROM *NEW YORK TIMES* BESTSELLING AUTHOR
Miranda James

- The Cat in the Stacks Mysteries -

MURDER PAST DUE
CLASSIFIED AS MURDER
FILE M FOR MURDER
OUT OF CIRCULATION
THE SILENCE OF THE LIBRARY
ARSENIC AND OLD BOOKS

Praise for the Cat in the Stacks Mysteries

"Courtly librarian Charlie Harris and his Maine coon cat, Diesel, are an endearing detective duo. Warm, charming, and Southern as the tastiest grits."

—Carolyn Hart, author of the Bailey Ruth Mysteries

facebook.com/TheCrimeSceneBooks
penguin.com